Gabriel

Father's Loneliness

VOLUME II

VICTORIA DUTU

authorHOUSE®

AuthorHouse™
1663 Liberty Drive
Bloomington, IN 47403
www.authorhouse.com
Phone: 1 (800) 839-8640

Published by AuthorHouse 12/29/2017

ISBN: 978-1-5462-2305-4 (sc)
ISBN: 978-1-5462-2304-7 (e)

Motto: The prayer is mind-washing with the light of God ... but I must ascend into my inner beauty, there I find my strength, in the prayer that becomes creative ...

Chapter 1

I do not know whether fear continued to be a state that she could not evade from, but she was trying each time to control herself with a persistence that made her marvel. She decided to let no one intimidate her and she felt that she could become a strong person that way. She would not allow others to bring her to her knees. It was not always the case. Words were so important and she could not ignore them. She would go to work, but her life was a turmoil. She used to be at hospital caring for the child at night and, during the day, she was going to work, where she had to be efficient and that was no joke.

It is true that she had great help from her mother, who was essential to her, often wondering how come she had such strength. It was amazing. She would see herself in about twenty years and said to herself:

-Will I be the same for Gabi, just as strong?

She has never felt this help coming from her mother and God, so alive, so real, as now, everything she was getting was totally and completely different. It seemed that this entire ordeal was for her to become aware of this spiritual energy, to realize this unbreakable bond that exists within her soul with all that surrounds her. She lived with such intensity that moments seemed longer, they grew more powerful, stronger. The moment was like a stone that she had to try, to see, to assess its firmness or how hard it could get in time. The words now had consistency, she was experiencing another existence of mind.

"Could this suffering show me that, teach me that, how real is this moment I have now and here?"

Her life seemed to unfold in slow motion. Sitting on a hospital bed and watching her child, having sleepless nights, severe insomnia she could not escape from, she would often wonder about the meaning world's woes, the meaning of misery, the meaning of life. When life was so hard on her, she felt like mourning even more for those who do harm.

"Yes, there are sick people, just as this sick child. Those who deliberately do harm are soul-sick. There is a spiritual disease and there are no doctors and hospitals for that because everyone shifts for himself. How can you live the whole life in such a deception and do only whatever seems to you that is good? And never doubt that you could be wrong."

She felt so sad for Mihai, he would never come see the child. She was so sorry for his sickness, because she saw Mihai as a sick man, a sick-soul, seemingly sicker than this child of hers who belonged to her and her alone.

"Oh, Lord, you have given me such a challenge, but thinking of all these, I feel that something is happening to me amid this difficulty. I not only live, but also discover meanings that I wasn't able to grasp in the past. Perhaps I would have overlooked them and would have never understood them, but, thus, I do get their purport. Poor, Mihai, he is a traitor, but, at the same time, he understands nothing and refuses to think. I asked him many times why did he behave that way, but the answer has always been the same: silence. He would not give me an answer because he refuses to speak out. Why this refusal to think. And take the attitude that matters? Oh, yes, thinking is such a great act, so difficult, thinking only for yourself is a truly courageous act, which is not rewarded with money, but with human dignity. But turning the thought into reality is even harder. That is to turn a bad thought into a good one and not just any thought.

So, thoughts keep coming, but our reason is strong and you need to make a selection. These thoughts must be directed towards the good, strong part of life, not to the day-to-day hatred which leads through indifference to self-destruction and death, you must defeat death and suffering, you have to fight against despair, you must not remain so, God wants us to be victorious and powerful, not cowards and traitors, and all these things, these facts are not in this weak world, but in a secure one which is here in my heart, in my soul, which hurts so bad, this is the hardest and the harshest reality."

Maria had moments when she hated Mihai, she hated him terribly. She could not explain this hatred. She panicked when she discovered in herself states she couldn't have imagined in the past that she could experience, saying to herself: "Our inner state is often quite different from what we are in the outer reality. Are we really are so split inside and have moments when we fall apart." When she had no more tears to cry, she did not want to see him at all, not even in her mind. Why, because what he was doing to her was subhuman. This abandonment, this betrayal was not only incomprehensible, but also unacceptable. There were many times when she would not understand the situation, but she accepted it as it was, without further investigation, but her husband's attitude was driving her mad, she could not believe that he was capable of so much indifference. She could not accept that he could act so. To no longer see his child, to refuse him, just because he had this medical problem, this pain, this disaster. She would have wanted this to be just a fantasy and she was hoping that he would change suddenly. She was anxiously waiting for that moment, that miracle when he would suddenly become the person she wanted. She was so wrong.

She came with all sorts of excuses and avoided the ugly truth oscillating between acceptance and denial with a pain that she could no longer endure. The suffering was too excruciating to stand. She was abandoned by the man she had lived for and whom she loved so much, she had given him everything, her life, her soul, her child, he had become everything to her, maybe even more important than God. When she got to this comparison she suddenly stopped the hatred she was feeling for him, murmuring:

"Yes, yes, I think this is the mistake I've made, I loved him more than I loved Him, God. No man deserves to be loved more than God. I reckon this is my biggest mistake. I gave everything, I gave him everything and I have never kept anything for me. It is as if I had not lived for me, it is as if he lived so I could live. I feel the same now for this child, living my life through him. I feel that my life and my thought make sense only for this child to live. Gabriel's life becomes more important than my life. Anyway, I will work and make everything more valuable than before, so that Gabitu be well, happy. I believe that, eventually, the child will be fine, it is impossible, Lord, so many surgeries, I feel I can't take it anymore. An operation is barely healed and the next one begins. Is this child of mine only an experiment? What if he is a successful experiment in the end?"

Her pain as a mother would often grow hard and deep, she felt she could not resist living another hour, another day, she felt as if a sword was cutting her heart slowly off and she could not breathe anymore and, in this state of suffocation, her soul could barely breathe and she could see the outside world living, moving and existing, but it was all useless to her.

Chapter 2

Maria faces a dreadful situation.

We often wonder what did Christ the Savior mean when he said those words in Lord's prayer: "and lead us not into temptation and deliver us from evil". That God would not take us into temptation. Let us pray for that.

Well, this is what Maria was doing, she was taken into temptation, she somehow lived this state of prayer, even when we are really led into temptation, as was Christ the Savior. He was so tempted, but he was almighty and did everything according to the will of the Father. He let himself in God's hands. That is what we do in moments of despair, that is what Maria is trying to do, to let God care for her so she would no longer suffer.

She married Mihai after college graduation, they climbed the social ladder very fast, moved to Bucharest where they got important positions in large companies, as they were particularly clever and, when Mihai had anything in mind, he would never give up until the target was met. Maria, as she was so fair and smart, was quickly promoted in the company up to the second highest position after managers. She used to control everything and earned much money without even thinking about the future. She was respected and appreciated because she was a competent and professional in every sense of the word. Maria is and will remain the right person for these times, where everything is in an alarming speed and, if you want keep up with the others, you have no choice but run at the same pace because you fall behind otherwise.

The urge to earn much money enthralls us all. She would remain at the company until late at night and, when she was too exhausted, she would take her work home and work on weekends, just to finish everything well and deliver the documents on time. The company was thriving because she was running everything there. Likewise, Mihai, wherever he was, would do his best for everything to go well and be profitable. His travels abroad were quite frequent as he worked in a multinational, which had a subsidiary here, in Romania, and he had to go to Germany on monthly basis to deliver the reports. He was a powerful man because he knew English perfectly and was able to tackle any situation. So, the money issue was inexistent to them. When you earn so much money per month, it is normal to want a different standard of living. You don't find it satisfactory to live in a three-room apartment anymore, you want something bigger, the needs grow as well as the demands, in relation to the money you earn. Mihai really wanted his own villa, like in American movies and in the latest fashion magazines, as the rich have in the West.

As always, the West remains the last and greatest fascination of our man, because he has nothing else to relate to, other than what he sees and feels that it is there and should be here, too. This is the obsession of every provincial. Even though he cannot live in downtown, at least he would lead a life similar as in downtown, with any effort, any sacrifice. It doesn't matter that his work is so frustrating and difficult, that it eats him up inside. Never mind that he has no time for himself. This megalomaniac chase after money is important, so he can pay the bills for everything he builds and all these are constantly growing.

He must work more, to pay them as he wants that house he had dreamed for so long. He wants that big house where he will live just with his wife and child, he wants the desired things to have in the future, the rest is not important.

All that matters is this work that tires him and brings him to his knees again and again to get him somewhere, up there, where one day, in the future, he will be relaxed and pleased, that is happy, but he would not realize that this happiness thrown somewhere very far in the future is a deceptive happiness, like a Fata Morgana that appears on the horizon. He only has one life and he wants to live it as he pleases, so there can be no contradiction in anything he does, as it all depends on him alone and that's the only way. He felt powerful and strong because, thus, he could control the world or part of it.

When he was the most important person in the company, he could not feel but someone, proud and conceited, ready anytime to look down on another. He was running destinies and his subordinates and, why not, maybe even the others, depended on him. Even his bosses agreed with him, at one point, he had more information than them because he had tackled the issue which had been assigned to him.

So, Mihai wondered at one point when he was home watching TV:

"Wait a second, I know so many things, I am more powerful, why not have my own company. I've learned to manage, I know all sorts of trickeries, scams, so called financial engineering, collaborations. If I'm really the most powerful here and I have so much knowledge and I know everything, why not leave, why not pull a hoax on them, I've made millions of dollars for them, they wouldn't have managed without me, why work for them and not work for me. Why not make the best of it for me, especially since those from overseas know me better than they know them. It's true I signed a non-compete agreement for a five-year period, I will stay here five years, but I will leave in the same year when the contract expires. I'll have everything ready for me. Until then, I must go for customers and, why not, make my own company linked to this company or another one from overseas, where I can work by myself on sales, even take their customers with me when I leave. I'll find the way when I go to Germany and then to France, then Switzerland."

Mihai used to dream about that day and night, what to do to become the most notorious and the richest person, or among the richest people in Romania, just like billionaires in America. Why not be very rich people in Romania just like in the West. Wherever he went, wherever he got, he wanted to become someone, an important man among the great ones, even if he was a provincial. When he was watching television in the evening, with a glass of wine in hand, because that was the only way for him to calm down, with alcohol, he would not understand those people, from TV how come they talk so much about corruption, and, mainly, about Westerners' desire to eradicate corruption from us:

"What nonsense, they, the Westerners have the biggest corruption, where did our people learn all the crap and stupid things from, wasn't it from them, haven't they come up with the biggest doggone manipulation techniques. Who is honest in the West, simple people who have no choice because they lose everything otherwise, they lose jobs, they lose fortunes accumulated by entire families, with many years of work and sacrifices, they lose social status. The big ones, they do all the games. Same here, who are the honest ones, the flunkies from my company, who are fired unless they do their job properly, in fact, I'm the one who fires them. What, am I honest, I should be so stupid, I need to follow my interest, it's like in college when I had to pass all sorts of exams that I did not want to learn for and had to make it somehow, to copy. It's amazing how I continue to have this structure." Then, he spoke up:

-Maria, bring me that food, when is it ready?

-Now, I am taking it out of the oven.

-I'm starving. Plus, the alcohol makes me hungry, badly.

-Hold on, hold on, have some patience, I'm coming.

Maria came into the living room where he was lounging in the armchair watching TV with glass in his hand, she caressed his head, kissed him on his hair and said to him while giving him a kiss:

-Relax, I'm coming in a second.

-I'm hungry, starving actually.

-I think you also have a different kind of hunger, hunger to get rid of the fatigue you have in you, was it hard at work today? Who else have you fired?

-Well, I haven't fired anyone, because everyone behaved properly, but, still, I did something a few days ago.

-What?

-We have a colleague, Cristina, who's quite indecent at work!!!…

-Oh, how come?

-She comes with short skirt and some panties, you wouldn't believe it, and we are all staring at her instead of paying attention, she instantly catches the eye.

-So, what did you do?

-I went to my boss and said: 'You know, I love my wife, I have nothing against it, but when Cristina comes in I feel stressed because she dresses like she does and I'm man, I cannot control myself?"

-Did you do that?

-Ha, ha, if I tell you, Cristina doesn't know who started the whole story about her clothes.

-And what happened?

-She came with a pair of jeans the following day, you can imagine.

-And is she still coming dressed like that?

-She's not, as boss would see her, but if she knew who put the spotlight on her!!! I guess she wouldn't speak to me anymore.

-So, then, you're fooling around.

-Well, not at all.

-You are an important person so nobody messes with you, look, I brought you food, here it is, on the platter.

-See that you haven't brought napkin.

-I'll get you a napkin in a second.

While Maria went into the kitchen to fetch him the white napkin, Mihai's favorite, he smeared the sauce on his fingers and cried:

-I'm all dirty, won't you come clean me?

-Yes, yes dear, yes, aren't you my only baby, the best and most troublesome, especially if you get so intimidated at work by female colleagues who dressed up so provocatively.

-Well, all this century is provocative.

-Give me an example of a historical time which had nothing provocative.

-Oops, my sweetheart goes into metaphysics.

-What, don't your like metaphysics?

-I sure do, but metaphysics mixed with vodka is the best.

In the morning, they both would jump into separate cars and drive off to work because they had to be there first, otherwise things didn't go well. And so, they were living quite normal lives, without too much stress, they were both extremely free, without being able to do anything more, they thought they were invincible and that nobody and nothing in this world would break them apart. Mihai would fall asleep thinking about what he had to do to have his mansion and his money, his business and his moments of relaxation, he had only these dreams, other than that, he had much sleep and cattle work on other people's land. He would sleep all weekend, when they were not working, he slept in one room and she in another. The fatigue accumulated throughout the week did not let room for anything else. Besides, there was one more thing, they were fed up with restaurants, receptions because they had plenty of these.

When he went abroad, he had everything provided for there, whereas she had all sorts of parties on various occasions at her work, they would go to restaurants with various clients, so she and he were fed up with such a vibrant life. They really wanted something, and that something was to stay at home quietly and sleep together, or in separate rooms. They wanted to be physically together and to stay peacefully, that was their greatest wish, to be together at peace.

Maria was a very calm girl, she was not quarrelsome and she was quite mild inside, all she wanted was that calmness for the two of them and nothing more, as if it was them against the world.

They are the ones who broke through, the ones who pulled it through. They took a loan and bought the house, they paid the loan off in only three years, because they had money. They also took loans to buy the cars, she changed the Romanian car and bought Minimoris for her and a Toyota for him. They were happy, all they had to do was to finish the house and everything was ready for the baby they wanted to come.

-When I finish things at the villa, I'll have my own company, my loyalty agreement will expire and I'll start the action. I've already found some clients whom I'll charge lower commission fees.

-You mean you'll steal their customers, from those you work for.

-I'm not stealing, it's customary, I somehow made a suggestion and they continued to encourage me to also work for them. Because they've had enough, they want someone who will exclusively handle their sales. In a way, I'll have my own company, a small company, to handle distribution and sales, I will have to struggle for Romanian clients and mediate with those from abroad. But I'll do this exclusively and I will work only for their companies. They said the current company has too many things to do, they are late with some projects, they weren't too pleased with the services rendered, so they want someone reliable:

-And you're the one reliable.

-So it seems.

-You don't say.

-And if you will want to expand, what will you do?

-Well, as if they know all that I do, look, I will open one more branch in your name and, then, they won't be able to control everything. But I will explain to them that, in case I want to expand sometime in the future, we should not sign any loyalty agreement, or at least, just for a short period, to see how it's done.

-Well, then, you will soon be my new boss.

-I am your boss.

-Really?

-Since when are you my boss?

-Since always.

-I'll stay quietly at my company and, if you wish, I'll provide you with all my experience of boss and subordinate, my boss, and Maria laughed with glee, then she added:

-I think we should go to sleep earlier, because we'll have a long day tomorrow.

-Yes, and a hard time, my boss is coming from Switzerland, I'll see how I'll pull it through because there are some clients who have not made their payments. I'll see how we will stress them out so they pay their fees to us. And the boss is not too happy when I cannot handle things, especially when it comes to money.

-Yes, everything but the money.

-Yeah, what's with those bosses, only women in charge lately, fewer men, but men hold financial control.

-We are moving more and more towards an era of women.

-We already are in the era of women, I reckon.

-We'll see about that, good night, said Maria and went to bed.

-We'll talk tomorrow night.

Mihai was already tired and dizzy, he ate quite a good meal and, since he was full, he went to bed to sleep, he listened the TV for a while then he fell asleep without thinking to anything else.

Yet, Maria could not sleep. She was dreaming, meditating on what she had to do the following day. The boss had told her to fire a girl who was not competent, she was not too good, she made huge mistakes, she took a long time to learn, she couldn't adapt. She had to be constantly controlled, corrected by somebody and that couldn't last too long. Since the girl had made no progress and had had no results in three months, she couldn't help her. The trial period when she should have adapted and made no more mistakes had long passed, there was nothing to do but to fire her. And Maria had to give the verdict on her layoff and she resented it, especially since the girl had some problems at home. Sick mother and she had to earn money somehow, so she can help the others, plus their father did not make much money, it was hard for them. Maria kept thinking how to reprieve that girl and not fire her, she would stay with her overtime to teach her what to do, but the girl was not skilled and she couldn't find a job elsewhere.

She kept praying to God asking what to do, because, in a way, she felt guilty for what she was about to do, but had no choice. She had to brace up and dismiss her, otherwise the boss would come and make a scandal before kicking her out, it would be even worse. She kept thinking how to tell her and how to encourage her, to tell her not to give in and go elsewhere to look for a job, because it's not a tragedy that she hasn't made it here as this is a tough company, but she may find something easier some place else and she'll be fine, to go with God. To keep trying because she could find good job, all she had to do was to look for it. She kept praying until she fell asleep.

She woke up the next day, went to work, but the thing had already been done. The boss had come and had found that girl there and had kicked her out immediately telling her that she should no longer come to work as she had done enough damage, had made too many mistakes which must be controlled and checked by another person over and over again, that she was incompetent and should look for a job elsewhere. The girl left in tears. Maria met with her at the door, she tried to encourage her by no one listened because the girl ran off, she didn't want to see anyone. Maria said a prayer in mind for that girl and couldn't say anything more as she heard her boss screaming at her:

-I told you to fire her, it's been some time since I told you that, I said that if I come and see her here, I don't know what happens!

-...

Maria didn't say a word, she sat down at her desk and the boss went into the office slamming the door.

Maria said to herself, "These are techniques of manipulation and intimidation, they are copied from the West, unless they lack common sense and disrespect for others. How can this woman be like that? If I ever become a boss and coordinate some employees, will I act the same? The truth is that this girl did many stupid things since she has been here and I protected her, I can't help her now, she should have pulled herself together. I often think that as a boss you need to have something much more than others, you need a force of persuasion, you need this diabolical power to subjugate others. I think it's not good to be like this woman, plus she is never calm and treats everyone the same. Hadn't she been some kind of viper and had she spoken more diplomatic, would she have had more to gain. But what does she gain from this girl, because everything was against her here. In a way, I'm just as guilty because I had to get over with that person, as she has made quite some blunders which could have resulted in some heavy fines in case those from the financial administration would have come in inspection. Who would have been responsible, me, because I was the one to sign."

Maria was a kind of receptacle, she was memorizing everything that happened in the company and meditated, she was having in her great mind and small body all sorts of thoughts and ideas that she would share to nobody, not even to Mihai. She had a different kind of relationship with him, when they met in the evening, as they had not been together during the day, she wanted to relax and not think about anything. She turned off her cell phone so nobody would call her and live quietly, to live that peace that she didn't have throughout the day, she wanted to be only with her husband to get well, her husband was her medicine.

When they were at work, their moods changed completely. Such a tiring day, when you sit at the computer for so many hours, exhausts you, makes you feel like you're draining out and you want to sip from a water that is not of this world and you seem to live in another time. She felt she couldn't do anything and it all went down to just a phone call, her communication with him boiled down to what she could say by phone, just a few thoughts and that was all or, some other times, not even that, because they couldn't speak on the phone, it was quite uncomfortable for both of them.

The work brought her the daily stress or the daily share of stress, which she was supposed to relieve at night, that was actually the heaviest burden, to relieve the stress, everything you have experienced during the day. Because everything you live happens so fast that you no longer know where you are or who you are, maybe you're just that strange thing connected to a device and nothing more. That was how Maria felt so often, she would see the world that way, as people connected to devices who subsequently leave wherever their legs carry them.

She kept repeating on her imagination display, when she was eating or when she had five-minute break, until a late fax arrived or the computer was processing, to deliver a series of data. Flashes came to her mind, images from childhood, botanical garden, roses or the patch of sky she had admired in the car's mirror on that evening, actually on the evening before. As if she wanted to cling to him, yes, just a piece of sky, then she also saw the sunset in the mirror. She had this blessing to see a sunset in the left mirror. It was about seven o'clock in the evening, traffic jam and cars were rolling bumper to bumper and a biker passed her and slightly moved the mirror and tilted it, and she could see in the flipped mirror more of the sky and a gorgeous sunset. This image came to her mind now when she was in the office waiting for a fax that wouldn't come and she needed badly. The fax had come for some time and Maria kept thinking about that image that she couldn't let go. As if the entire computer screen displayed that sky from memory's mirror and she was carrying that patch of sky inside her impound and hosted, in a surrounding world which ties us down, that we want to get rid of and we don't know to do it.

How were the people in the past? Were they confined in the field that they had to work every day, because otherwise they could no longer live and would have died of hunger. I think that those images are on repeat somehow. They used to stay head-down and that was the reason why they couldn't see the sky and we stay at the computer or lie down too long to be able to see the patch of sky or the patch of stars, which spreads above us, just a few meters away, but all we have is just one meter or so, the size of our blocks, which is our own prison that covers the blue we bear only in mind.

Chapter 3

"Yes, I believe a true artist should do this, namely bring the sky on his canvas to show it to people. Yes, people nowadays need the sky and the light, lots of light or cool air, not the cooling of the air conditioning and the light from the light bulb, they need something as natural and beautiful as can be, something to be inside us and only in us, yes, because we bear something heavenly in our soul that is unbounded.

I often feel like I burst, like I want to escape into a new world, a abstract world of this world, to be as concrete as this one where I would not be so tied up to a device or a human or a situation. I want to be free from something only I know and only I understand, and I often feel that art can offer me this freedom, yes, if I were a painter, I think should enjoy this freedom and I should bring this freedom to people. Because it's the freedom of an idea, the freedom of a thought, it's the freedom of something only I know and which I cannot speak out. Yes, it's something that alienates us from this world, which lies within me and within us, which I do not know and I have no time to become aware of. Because my cerebellum contains other things and they rush to become present in me. Seems like my consciousness is always covered by something I know nothing about. It seems like I am somewhere and I don't know where, because here I try to understand myself as being into a world, this concrete world, as being in front of a computer or in front of colleagues whom I try to submit, because I make them submit one way or another.

I am often scared about how transformed and artificial I can be when I must make decisions, decisions for the company, decisions for me. Then I cannot defer to me but to a reason which is apart of me and it's extremely compelling as the human factor matters no more. In this empire where the only source of existence is embodied only in economic turnovers, and the blood is just the fluid called money, the human is just a point that needs to press some buttons. A surreal world in which I fear I'm a bigger point or a smaller point which accesses, in its turn, other points which, in their turn, make a vane of death and soul chaos spin, a vane I am afraid of and I am not so aware of. But what can I do? We all have to survive this absurdity to which we surrender our soul, our daily life incorporated in competence, professionalism and evolution. All these in the name of the idea of survival and ambition to be an important person in the world, among others, to be competitive, to be a perfectionist, what for, for a bonus to the wage. What is the purpose of so much sleep-deprived work, work up to physical and mental exhaustion? It is very difficult for the young today, they need to work more, more for a little more money, for some normal facilities, because we, the young, who are not stupid, live badly."

Maria shivered to this image of decisions she had to make at different times, decisions that she could not control and could no longer know their consequences once made. She was wondering "what has happened to the man I kicked out, perhaps I can only pray for him to find a better job elsewhere and a place to suit him."

She was afraid of these places, of this system where people do not matter as persons but only as individuals, where no one was irreplaceable. They matter as a bulk, what they do collectively, but not together as such, as a group or community, but together in a different way. They are asked to do something collectively, altogether to a machine or a complex of machines, and by the way those devices work one can say what these people do together, so they matter collectively by what they do and not by what they actually are taken together, it's only their action that counts, an exterior action and not an inner action. That is why this world is focused on the exterior, on what can be done and what can be seen, that is why this body can be so fascinating. But has ever the hidden, unseen world matter. Could it be that in primitive times, people behaved with each other as if the other would not matter unless he does me a favor."

Maria often said:

"I feel that each of us is put to work on such a war machine. I think of a whole army, they had to work to do something, so they would not die, but survive, to do something to fight. Well, that also happens now, you have to fight to make something happen, to make a big machine

15

work, move, not to stand still. In fact, this big machinery called work is a small machine into another bigger machine and so on, each has above him another machine even greater he cannot escape from and where he works and, that is why, the evening comes and then the night comes and you cannot see the patch of sky that you live in and have above your head. I think of a Byzantine image, or in the sense of Fra Agelico, because as we live on earth and have a piece of land that we live on, similarly, if we could look upwards, we have a piece of sky that we live in and we should be aware of this habitation, it's just we only see the habitation seen from beneath and we cannot perceive the habitation seen from above. But I wonder if I could imagine a flower which I would see as having roots in the skies and petals here under my forehead, shouldn't I have to stay bottom up, lie down over it so I can admire it. Maybe at night when I go to bed and sleep, I should have this wakefulness to something great and huge which is in my mind and, somehow detached from everything I am or what I can experience, I am just this immense sea of light that I should perceive. I often wonder what did Christ mean when he said that the kingdom of God is in your heart. Well, that's what I fail to make out. This kingdom which lies in me, in my heart, this light that I need and I cannot escape from. And I cannot get detached from, it is like a sort of longing to something unspoken, but, here, I can only see this land turned into intelligent forms which, in their turn, are put to work for something unknown, but we want to know and to think that someone holds control over us and we blame God when we are unfaithful to our own tendency towards eternity and we cling to simple and small things that we cannot handle, things we want to get rid of but we can't. What should I do to feel the presence of this sweet light which is God's kingdom in my heart. I believe something happens to the world I live in, it is quite interesting that I will never know exactly how people lived in past times when they created something so grand as music.

Due to the daily stress, our mind attempts somehow to escape from this day-to-day work through these flashes of maximum intensity feeling sent forth by subconscious, but I don't really agree with that. I believe that the soul wants to save our inner being and, then, it needs moments to relax and lives in split seconds beautiful things at maximum intensity, as much as we can experience."

That was what Maria was doing, she sent faxes, checked everything necessary in accounting, edited papers and documents in computer with high speed and, when she couldn't handle this pressure, from time to time, her brain would create other images, some extremely beautiful, brought from dreams, so she could relax. In a way, we are perfect as we are built, because if we don't take care of ourselves, there is someone superior to us, our inner self, which saves us from this constraint. So, Maria willingly or not, without thinking or realizing, was experiencing some states of maximum intensity in her moments of respite, as many as they were, for one minute, one and a half minute and she managed to fend off stress and save herself. She was praying in her moments of respite. I think we can speak somehow here about a therapy which lasted a few seconds. And to get such a therapy in the spare time, we have to store beauty, so that our mind can have something to collect in the moments of relaxation so it can calm us down with something during the stressful period.

Maria remembered the dream she had a few nights before. It's amazing how well the dream can relax us, even if the dream expresses our desires. Most of the times, the most terrible relaxation is there. And without being too much aware about that. She remembered that feeling from her dream, similar to a flash of maximum intensity, it seemed like she was walking in the rain, but a warm summer rain, she was strolling in the dark. Saying no words to anybody but herself, she put a hood on her head so rain would not get her wet, and, thus, under the street lights, she could see the drops hitting and crumbling onto the asphalt. But, ironically, she was not living this rain in a town, in Bucharest, but somewhere in the countryside, in a village. She didn't know where she recollected that image from. Perhaps when she was a girl and went with her grandpa to a villager to take honey. Those images are so vivid, a green garden and, then, another garden with blossom trees. Her grandpa used to say that honey from spring flowers, in May, is the best, that's why it is deemed today as the best medicine. All of a sudden, the rain from her dream was no longer an atmosphere of darkness but one of light, it seemed like it was not raining so hard in the night, but at dawn, when everything was clear before her eyes. And even when she looked at the computer which had been waiting for her to introduce data there was dark no more, but everything turned into something unknown full of light and beauty, serenity and she felt a little better, relieved, liberated, clean-minded and with clean soul.

In a way, Maria was very cheerful, she found that she was feeling much better from this dream which had brought childhood images back to mind. Her fingers seemed to fly over the keyboard and she wondered how free her mind and brain can be, even if she was staying in that confinement called work. How wonderful were those monks who did nothing but live in the isolation of a cave. They were busy only with prayer, contemplation and thinking about God, they wouldn't care about the problems of this world, they were there to pray for the world and people. Maybe we should learn something from those hermits who were really very isolated from the world, but used to bear the world in their heart to save it through their prayer. It is true that it's difficult for us to set apart from the world because we cannot fight against recollection, against the memory which saves us but also includes us in all sorts of fears and fantasies. This memory will have to be controlled and educated, that is our case, in the human being nothing is left to chance. We are the ones who must refine and control everything, we must turn something which disturbs and huddles our soul into something of a small beauty and, afterwards, into something of great beauty.

Just as those hermits used to stay isolated in caves, our soul is isolated in all sorts of nooks from which we cannot go out to be free, they used to find salvation in God, and we should also find in Him our refuge and fulfillment. He knows best where truth and salvation are, we just must mind His listening. They, those hermits, found out what they had to do, but can we really discover what we should do? Because we live in a world where our souls seem to be indexed.

Chapter 4

Mihai instead had some remorse, he was the kind of a tough person, who made no compromises and cut to the bone, he was drastic. She used to discuss with him about work problems, about employees, what and how to do, about one person or another, and his advice was always the same:

-Kick him out, don't even look back, he'll be ok!

-Okay, but he's a poor guy, he's in distress!

-Well, I don't care, it's his fault he's in distress, he doesn't use his brain, I couldn't care less he is like that, let him work his way around, fire him, don't even talk to him.

-Okay, okay, I'm also thinking of God, said Maria.

-You can think of whoever you want, I'm not thinking of God when it comes to this, what, isn't God just as hard on us. What, is God interested so much about our fate, we are struggling alone, is God coming to give me food or to make any of my contracts!!

-Yes, but we must not involve God in our business, we must deal with that.

-See, you have found the answer, kick him out and don't mix God.

-Okay, but shouldn't we prove some humanity to the poor man who can't make his way?

-People are is distress from their own fault, they are to blame for not making their way, they are guilty for being poor. They say Romania is a poor country, it's Romanians' fault for being poor, and it's true. It's our fault, everybody's, for accepting all sorts of nonsense and rubbish from others and we don't know what we to do to get rid of them.

-It's true, but there is something else, we must have compassion for the other.

-You can do that, I wouldn't complicate things and wouldn't have any remorse about this. You say Romania is poor, but look at the cars in traffic, would you call that poverty!

-That's opulence.

-See!

-But how many people have such cars, few people own such things.

-Many, few, it doesn't matter, that man has worked it through. Do you think that when I sign a contract I'm thinking too much of the one who comes to me, well, if I do not negotiate the required contract in the most advantageous way possible, do you think my bosses would give a damn about me?

-I know, they say about you that you are expert in concluding contracts, you are the best and, therefore, it's only you they send.

-Well, I am interested in obtaining maximum profit and minimum costs, I'm not interested in how others are doing. Don't you see that it's not about the person, don't you see that the person does not matter here, don't you see that it's not about any person, but only about the system that brings more money!

-Well, it's not about the person, but the human factor.

-You still don't get me, we speak different languages. Can't you see that there's nothing about any person-related I and the one I sign the contract with are the only persons here and that person is interested just like me, in maximum profit and minimum costs. If any human factor, it is just the negotiation.

-I was saying something else!

-Yes, I understand you perfectly, but don't you see that, in this system in which we all operate, the man doesn't matter, but only the strong one who created and runs the this system, the one who gets into the system has only one value, which is to produce, to bring maximum profit, as I do in the company where I work and I am not going to do that for much longer because I'll move to my company and I'll do the same with others, I'll be the system creator.

-Okay, but this is an evil system, where the man does not matter, all that matters is the one running the company, the one who is somewhat part of the management and the rest is not important. This system is guided by the principles of war. It's the financial war.

-Diabolical or not, it has always been that way, and you are too used to report everything to God. Somehow, God is the idea of weak people, who have failed and want everything to be as they like and, because of their helplessness and frustration, they seek explanations and refuge in God, nothing more than that. Religion is only a matter of imagination, so I heard one saying on TV.

-Come on, stop saying that, we'll end up fighting, because you know it's not like that, now you're speaking only with your mind, not with your soul.

-Isn't soul a part of the mind.

-Yes, but if we refer to the beautiful, soul-related, spiritual aspect of things ...

-Why do you bring up the spirit, is there anything spiritual here, where do you see that I ever think of spirit issues, don't you see that it's only competition, war, as you said? Don't you see that it's only the obsession to succeed, to do something concrete, to make a sale. If you're not the best, you disappear from the market. Therefore, you must hire the best. The weak must go. What will Romania do when it will have only weak people. You should see then, it'll be trouble. I hope we will not get to live those days.

-With the current state of education, we have all chances to reap the fruits of daily incompetence, in several years, or one generation.

-I heard a painter struggling for a year to sell a painting of many hundreds of paintings that has and couldn't sell any. Well, that's what I see as nonsense, why should he start selling paintings, considering that everything is bankrupt, he should sell donuts, because that's what makes money, they say he sells spirit, well, who needs his spirit in this world. Painter that he is a fool, how to buy your I's painting, I do not go to such galleries, painting their assholes, are only some doodles, sexes everywhere, drunks who painted their obsessions and dreams of being rich as Picasso and Degas as adults after death. Some idiots sexualized by television, reduced to dumbness by television, all their paintings will be thrown away by their grandchildren or strangers to landfill transported by those from the sanitation of Mr. Tilica Poenaru, present daily at fools' televisions, with the highest levels of audience. They all are scum of the consumer society, in any country they would be. Everyone wants to be like Michelangelo but none leads Michelangelo's life, how many live like him secluded and in monkhood. We will all have sooner or later this fate, to be thrown to the landfill of history and obliteration because we did nothing good. Those painters are drunkards, who drink not only from their own money, but they also want to drink from my money. They come to me to make sponsorship, that makes me laugh. Most of them are losers stinking of booze and laziness, who did nothing in life but they claim to have stayed in their workshops where all they did was to move the bottles of drink among paints, living in unspeakable filth and poverty. Their families are destroyed, they get divorce, they are allegedly misunderstood, and, because they are frustrated, they paint or carve, just to pretend they are important, well, how could I take such a drunken scum seriously? This is also the case of writers, a group of drunkards. Don't give me that look.

-You're wrong, just some of them are like that…

-Don't you see that this is not about any spirit, but about competition, strength and the ability to cope.

-You exaggerate. I don't understand you, Mihai, I don't understand you, you often scare me.

-What do you mean I scare you, haven't I always thought like this, how to be the first, how to get on top of others, it is like a mad rush for profit, for money, what, don't you run after money, but you pretend to be innocent.

-Well, it's not quite so, I sometimes joke when I say money does not bring happiness if it's little.

-The man has always been and will be preoccupied with money and fascinated by money, by this product which now has other forms of winding, but money has always been the apple of discord, some say it was the woman, the woman might have been in the past, because in the past the woman, that is the beautiful woman not just any woman, was seen as a very precious commodity, still a kind of reference to money, and that was the reason why they would fight for her. Or, nowadays, it is different, now you won't see a man fighting so hard for a woman, why, because they have loosened principles. The woman is no longer a property and, therefore, she is not of any financial interest, only to the extent that she can make money and, from this point forward, she has become equal to man, but she still isn't. The woman is also producing income, so she has not been weighed or compared with money so much. The woman is free to be compared with anything else, that is she is taken out of the game and that is why no one will fight for a woman. She, the woman, has been knocked off the pedestal where she claimed to allegedly be the queen of man's mind. Not completely, but the last fortress will soon fall and then something else will animate and enslave humanity. It is this thirst for power and supremacy, to rule the earth with everything on it, with all its breath, and to hold total control over others, who would have to obey you.

The entire stake is the absolute power and money. We are in full economic war which has been lasting for almost one hundred years since the great scientific revolution. The development of science has pushed humanity to the economic war and that is why the two support one another, all under the so-called guise of research and invention. And if it were so, then why the one who makes the discovery only gets the so-called copyrights. The one who gets the profit, who gets rich is the one who produces the idea and turns it into industry, see mobile phones. Stooges like you who believe in a better world work in research and science work. How many professors who made discoveries have you've seen on TV or getting rich. How about Tesla? None, because it's war and this war is won by whoever is stronger, more skillful, more cunning and more competitive. It's a matter of management, but war management because business means to annihilate the other so you can hold monopoly, to steal from him, to take everything from him, if not legally, then by bringing him to bankruptcy. This is happening now and will be in Romania in the future. Globally, it will will be increasingly difficult for those who lose pace, who want financial freedom, who willingly accept slavery. You cannot dodge the system like a fish in the ocean.

-Well, then, this was also the Communist ideal—to subjugate and make the other obey you and whoever disobeys must be eliminated.

-Why do you think the leftist policies are so well received now everywhere and the big countries did not vote for the EU constitution?

-Why?

-Because people have realized that whatever is being prepared is not for them, but for others, for the big ones, for the strong ones. Well, that's it, now the interesting part is not only how to have the most money, but how to acquire the strength to get to it and to control everything with it.

-Yes, I have always thought that every businessman is a supra-human and that is the reason why he has such a great power. I think of my bosses, they have so much power to intimidate you, as if they have something demonic in them, they smash you and you cannot have any personality in front of them. They bring you to your knees, they humiliate you for the slightest mistake, or a big one, they are almost capable to annihilate you psychologically, and what do you do, you cry. I experienced that state in front of bosses for so many times that I wanted to quit in those moments and leave. What did I do, I cried and started all over.

-See, you did not matter in those moments, she, the boss, knew that you could be replaced anytime, she relied on that, she knew that you would tremble with fear because she can kick you out. This is the source of power and domination, she was the one who proved you what the material and psychological power and domination were, could we still be speaking about morality?

-Well, but I've worked so much for her, I worked as if I were working for my own company.

-You see, she knew that because you're loyal and you work with pleasure and she has fed you with an illusion. It's as if everything had been for you, you are guilty because you allowed her to fool you. You lived in a dream, an imagination and she, as she has lived such feelings in her turn, could speculate them in her favor. You have not experienced the state she is now living and that's why you'll never know how to speculate these feelings in your favor.

-Well, I won't be like her, I will not be able to experience what she lives until I have my own company.

-If you will have it.

-Yes, provided I will ever have.

-But I don't see you doing so because you are too human. To have a company, you must have the heart of a dog and be able to make decisions in cold blood, and you take too long to make decisions! I don't see you like that, you consider so many factors, and that is not important in a company, sales, profit are important, as well as this unfaithful and inconstant development of the war. Because every company is in constant war, as it is a matter of survival. Do you think about what would happen to a company which would not make a profit at least one month, it would go in the red?

-It would be on the brink of bankruptcy.

-Now, do you understand why a boss cannot and has no time to think so much about the human factor. Well, the human factor has to make shift, what do you think, that we are really beasts, but this is the system, if you don't move fast, you die. It's worse than at war, because back then you would die walking and it took some time until you passed away, now you die riding the car, you get thrown out during the ride and that's it, the world has forgotten by the next sale.

-Do you remember the first company where I worked? That 29-year-old girl. Can you imagine, running a company at that age, it was her grandfather's company, but still, at that age, I was fascinated by her power, her strength to keep the people under control.

-Yes, but she states she went through, you were afraid of her, it was like she was crazy, she was hysterical, she was too young and not ready for such a stress, she needed some time to adapt.

-I was terrified, she was always making the sign of the cross, when she started to have some kind of shaking, people were saying she was on drugs.

-I don't think she was on drugs, I believe it was something else, she was so tired and worn out, that she could not sleep at night and had hallucinogenic states, she could no longer control herself. You know that I had similar reactions due to stress, as I worked so much and would sleep only four hours and I was working like a desperate. The doctor said then:

"Leave everything unless you want to end up in a madhouse and go to the mountains to get some rest for a month, I'll recommend you sick leave".

-And you did just that, you scared then.

-You see, it wasn't my company, but it didn't matter anymore, I was a Stakhanovite. I had so much confidence in my strength and I wanted to do so many things that I didn't want to know about anyone or anything except what I was supposed to do.

-That poor girl. How is she?

-She ok, last month I signed a contract with her, she recovered, but after two years.

-I still remember that image from the company, you know how it was, messy, chaos, some were screaming, others seeking contracts desperately, it all went down the drain in a few hours. The company was a mess, everyone left wherever they could and girl's mother was crying because the entire company was stopped, can you imagine so many people were not paid, were laid off, I had to leave because no payment had been made. No contract could be signed because she no longer had any right to sign and was admitted to madhouse, everything was stuck. Nobody could take her place as the boss was not in her right mind and then any document could be challenged in court.

-God forbid such a thing.

-See, you're still saying God's name.

-Yeah, but only in extreme cases, when you can't handle anymore.

-And why not pray to Him at all times?

-Well, thus, it's like I should get in with God to be comfortable and not be interested in others, it doesn't seem right.

-I went to the hospital, she didn't recognize anyone, she didn't recognize me, she was in such a state of excitement, you imagine, poor girl.

-Just like me back then, I could have got the same if hadn't taken measures in time.

-That's right, if you must suffer, you suffer, there's nothing else you can do, that's life.

Chapter 5

Meanwhile, Mihai got to where he wanted. When the loyalty contract expired, he had everything ready to start work at his new company with some of the clients. He resigned from the old company which raised him, brought him up and sent him around the world and he began working for himself with a German company. Act of courage, now he had to do everything by himself, there was the possibility he might make some mistakes. If he failed to do something back there, it was a normal thing, but here, if he failed doing something was terrible. He was struggling hard because, in his mind, he was in some kind of competition with the former company and he wanted to overcome it, but it could not be possible so fast. Besides, it was more difficult for him to conclude contracts now, it was different, the former company used to have an already created market, or he had to create his own market. His luck was that the one from Germany did his best to make things go right and forced him somehow to grow, brought him clients on the IT market so he had no alternative, he developed up to a level where he could be satisfied.

But as a boss, he noticed some sort of change in him, he was not as bad with the employees as before, he was more friendly and behaved humanly, he was not too tolerant but he had moments when he knew how to stimulate people, because, at first, he had no interest to make his employees leave so fast and end up with no one to do the work. He couldn't do anything without them. If the company had been bigger, he wouldn't have be bothered with that, employees kept coming at his door, but so, being a new company, he had to take care of people. This also changed the situation in his relationship with Maria, he was more lenient with her, but he always came home tired and only at midnight, they wouldn't not get the chance to see each other. When he had to go to bed and went through the door, Maria was already asleep. Being the boss, he went either later or the first to the company to take his employees by surprise, that was his strategy, they never knew when he would come up and where he comes up from, because he liked having everything under control. Sometimes several days would pass without getting to speak with each other. What a strange relationship, they lived in the same house, they slept in the same bed or in separate beds but they barely got to give a goodnight kiss or say good night. They managed to meet on weekends and to get to know each other, they were like strangers in their own house. They were so tired, the house was so big and empty that one night he said aloud in the villa:

-Everything is so empty, it's not what I wanted, I thought that if I have all these, I can sleep peacefully, but it's not like that, I barely get to see my wife, what life is this, as if I have estranged from everything, I think it's time we have a child.

Meanwhile, Maria had got up and heard his words:

-What did you say, a child?

-Yeah, a child!

-Well, I think it's on its way, I'm not sure but that's what I feel, plus, I had a very beautiful dream, I think we shall have a girl.

-How do you know?

-I do not know, I dreamed that I was holding in my hand something so delicate, small, beautiful, I could not even touch and I felt like crying for joy.

-You don't say, really?!

-Yes, I tell you, it would be really great, I don't know, here in this big villa, everything is empty without a child.

-I don't know, I'd like to have two children, said Maria.

-Until the two children, you must have one first and then we'll see what will happen.

-But, Mihai, can we be really happy, will we get to be happy, we barely see each other and we live in the same house.

-It's great to come and meet with you here and sleep in the bed where you are. That's it, I'm really happy because I wake up beside you healed, relaxed and with desire to work. This is where I calm down because I'm beginning with this company, I don't know, the problems are so big. Sometimes I regret that I left that company.

-Do not regret it. Now you have more money, more power.

-Yes, I make more money, I think I'll buy a new car, I'll sell this one and get another in leasing, so I can change it when I feel like it, but I am a slave, Maria, I am slave to my own desires, I read that somewhere at you when we were in college and it keeps coming to my head.

-Confucius said it!

-I do not know who said it, but he was so right!

-You got into metaphysics now, at midnight, when we have to sleep, Maria said jokingly!

-Yes, I remember I used to tell you that and now you got to tell me so, I wouldn't have expected that.

-The wheel is spinning, who knows where we'll get.

-But we are still happy, if we can talk at two o'clock in the night.

-But how long in a week do we get to see each other and we are happy?

-For too short, why is time getting shorter, as if I don't have time to do anything, as if everything happens at such a speed and so fast that I can do nothing of what I wanted.

Chapter 6

"I have to fight, to fight, as if I don't know what's wrong with me. My age is creative, brilliant and I must not leave it to fate, as if I couldn't do anything with anybody, as if I wouldn't have anything sacred in my heart. Having this ambition inside me and lacking strength to go on. Why should I give up, because I always quit. I must follow my thought and not be too impressed by these rubbishes that I don't really know how to get rid of.

Literature, how to drive away these thoughts of mine, what I do is not literature, these are all my inner struggles that I don't know how to get rid of and where to run away from. I've always known that I can only run towards God, I have this immense feeling that I should lie down at His great feet and never leave. This life I'm living is like a blessing. And I must always look for this feeling that my life is and must be lived under God's blessing. I'm not in the proper mood for that, what should I do? What am I doing to write so much, why all need to write, this writing is almost like an obsession that harms me. Why are these harmful things possible when I actually should sit quietly and not struggle so much. Who am I to judge this world, who I am, who, that I'm not so easy to be fooled? I am a person who thinks and who wants to fix something with his own thinking. So, what's the result, I often feel like I cannot have any strength in me, any mood, I don't know what to do and where to go in those moments, it seems so hard, with all the things that I do. I have to learn something else, to pass with indifference through the nothings made by people, to let no one trample me. And how to do this? There is only one way, I should let no such exterior moods affect my inner self, I should live in my prayer all the time and I should let nothing influence me. I should not take them seriously, I must focus only on these ideas which turn me about, which don't let me live adrift.

Yes, yes, I am a man of reason, who thinks and wants to lead his life according to his own thinking. I'm not denying that there might be other people who think that, it's just I don't have so much foolish pride in me, so that I despise everyone. I want to think and find this joy and satisfaction to create something great, a work in which I can show, show myself how important it is to live by the rules of the good God. But could I always be thinking about God, could I do that? What can I achieve and where to go with my own mind because I am worthless. I want so much to be able to understand the saints and their so beautiful lives and, especially, to adapt something from their lives and thoughts to my life, but what can I do. I really want to write this beauty which must be mine. I must be more patient with myself, be patient and not hurry, because we, humans, think so little and are so vulnerable. Nearly all our life is a huge waste of time and, actually, my purification and my life that I must take care of, with such obstinacy, are what's good for me.

Yes, but a monk's life is so great, so magnificent, that's how I would like to be, in a reality that takes me away. To keep God in mind constantly, but what is with this mood of mine? Isn't it rather an ambition that I cannot escape from. To explore my own mind, my thoughts, my moods, isn't that enough? It's not enough because I want something more than this reality that hurts me so much. I'm afraid of what I could do later, in the future, I am so afraid of loneliness, as if the good Lord hadn't been near me always in the most difficult times, as if my power and hope had not come from Him. Something is stealing my thoughts and my strength gets weaker in my moods. I see myself powerless before this greatness to which I don't really want to cling so desperately and to live naturally in prayer. In this state of purification, I should stop this unnecessary suffering and should have courage, to have the courage of the person who prays. Why do I want to probe so much into my suffering when those moods should remain so intimate and quiet that no one else finds them out, because one should not go into the deepest suffering, but one should stay on the outside, because if you go inside, it's even worse for you, you die without God."

Rafael was having these thoughts while sitting on the bank of the Cernica Lake. He had come to Saint Calinic to pray for his peace of mind. He was mad at himself because he couldn't mobilize to be different, to be better, to fight against the passions from his soul and body. Having the young and virginal body, his desires beset him and would not give him freedom to pray. These passions led to his frustration and he was outraged for having them. He was ashamed of himself before God and kept praying to get rid of them. These onrushes were not too frequent, he could not say he was too tormented by them, but they were so intense sometimes that he was amazed by their intensity and felt so bad, his desires drove him crazy and didn't know how to resist. He had strange moods that made him sick, but he wouldn't give up defending his bodily and mental virginity, he said to himself: "it will go away, I'll be ok within hours, the saints were also tortured and they resisted. I have those states so tough because I'm a normal man. It would be bad had it been otherwise. It means I am healthy and strong. I have to resist in this battle just as the saints resisted".

He was sitting by the lake and was watching the fish jumping out in the light. The church was in his sight on the back edge of the lake, like a place of blessing and salvation. The interior of the monastery was full of spring flowers and colors of old frescoes and they emphasized the holiness and greatness of those places. Saint Calinic was lying quietly in his coffin and this silence from inside encouraged people to pray and have this ambition not to give up the fight, the power given by prayer. Rafael was aware that, had he given up on one commandment, the temptation was so great that it would have rolled like a boulder down the hill and everything would have been lost completely. It wasn't worth giving up his entire life of virginity and prayer for his transient instincts. He will not abandon his life in case he doesn't ever marry. Marriage was sacred for him and his ambition was to step as a virgin into the church and in the God given marriage. No other life mattered to him and he was willing to fight with his states and desires. He was brave, not a coward who jumps from a height to die. He left the fish that jumped out into the light and went near saint's coffin, he knelt hiding in a corner somewhere where no one could see him and started crying persistently and ashamed of the lusts that beset him. He was crying bitterly in the saving prayer releasing the nervous tension which had defeated him in his own body. He was crying to free himself. The church interior was cool and full of warmth, it had something timeless. The church interior invites you to meditation and strength and tells you that the man is eternal and that this life is a shadow and that you, man, need to look for the real life which is Christ, the Son of God. We must look for eternity and be in prayer above all bodily and spiritual impulses that constantly assail us, to be above the world through prayer.

The sky's blue enshrouded the monastery with its interior like a spaceship towards the kingdom of light. The shades from the inside were proper urges for the outside light in which we shall live when God gives us this living according to the battle we fought. Rafael was so happy after this relief that he felt like crying in the holy silence which embraced him. He was even more determined and stronger because he was healed, he had chased away for a while those moods which had made him feel overwhelmed, ashamed and defeated.

Chapter 7

Rafael, tired after work, would get home, eat something and, lying in bed with his hands under his head, meditated and, if the thoughts burnt his soul, would rush like a robber to the computer and would start typing with unexpected measures. This time he was just thinking.

"I always have to fight with myself and not disgust me, to keep me at a distance, and at a certain height. I read in a magazine about a poet who published only one book and, then, he committed suicide. What an idiot, he made me sick, his poems were only about this desire for suicide, about hanged people, disgusting, I fear of such a mind. Lord, You must give me some much balance so I can live this life barely waiting to stay with Thee forever and live in serenity. The articles that I am trying to write and publish, and I did publish them, I believe they are doing good to those who read them. When I read the writings of others, I do not see them as something brilliant, but as writer's innermost and deepest issues, as something essential that concerns him, and I learn more about me from these anxieties or shallowness. Eventually, I believe that writing is an exercise of thought for everybody and it must be appreciated.

As for fear, I guess I don't fear anymore, but I have moments when I am scared that I could abandon God and my serene life and I could say that the life full of misery is better and more efficient to be lived. People living at the level of sin and body are already old and tired of life, sad people who get sick very quickly.

The humiliations you are subject to constantly as a person, at work, in society, in all kinds of relationships with people are states protruding consciousness, they are numerous and huge and suffocate you in time. You are humiliated in many ways, you're humiliated as a person and you're humiliated as an artist or writer. As for the rest, there's nothing to your advantage. It's very hard to go on your way without being influenced by the people around you and without making the compromise of allowing others to tread on you because you have no alternative, no other choice and, eventually, that's how you understand that you must do your job. This way does not suit you and requires sacrifices. Then, what is the attitude? Tolerance for everybody. It is important to be known, to be present in events, to be present in as many places, to have resistance to humiliation and not spend all the money on unnecessary things, not spend the mental time on empty ideas, not turn your time of thinking and praying into ashes ".

Rafael wanted to get in the literary world in Romania. He had some exaggerated and strange ideas about the truly great people, presented on television. He wanted to become one of them. He thought that these great people are right here in these cultural environments similar to the geniuses of humanity he had studied about in college. He gave them the same credit. To him, the personalities he was listening to had something special in their very special minds, they were truly important people and had lot of power, and he took them seriously in everything they said and did. The cultural world of Romania was select and heavy, really great in the country and worldwide, especially now after the revolution, nobody and nothing would stop you from being everywhere as you actually are, valuable. That's how Rafael imagined that things actually were. He deemed that everything he heard about culture was reality itself. He was manipulated a hundred percent. And he had no doubt in his unshakable belief. You should see when Rafael will wake up from the one hundred percent state. Meeting these intelligent people was a great honor for him, great hope. He was hoping that he will get one day to meet them and talk to them, to discuss with them the greatest ideas of today's world, he would have caught strength and wouldn't have been so lonely. He would have had a model. He wanted to feel togetherness along with the truly important people, with the brightest minds. He did this exercise every time he was writing, because he would write for the smart people of this country and of this world. How would he cross the border from his country to the world? In fact, he was only a Math teacher and a clerk in a company.

Those whom he watched or contacted some worked in ministries, doing all sorts of juggling at newspapers, or they were members of the

Writers' Union, otherwise nice people who published in literary magazines, published books, so they were quite smart, intelligent people, they would debate the hardest issues about the world today. He stared at them as if he couldn't believe that those gentlemen are so important and real. He often dropped it and said that the best thing in the world is to make it on your own, as you can, and to have around you people you can count on and collaborate with. That suited him for the moment. But where were those types of people? The truly great people were so far and he saw himself as being so tiny that he was eager to learn from each one, to be contaminated with their vast culture, their impressive erudition. At the same time, he noticed a world contrary to all these. And he was astonished, he wondered:

"Why is scorn so spread in this world and it seems that everywhere you go people's mockery makes everything dirty?" The views were so different that he barely got to see or find out something. He couldn't understand people and didn't know how to behave, how to express. Living in isolation in his own mind, he felt shy, helpless, he was looking at each one, everyone would utter his own opinion, thinking that only his beliefs were really valuable. Then, he got even more isolated inside and spoke only for himself that his thoughts do not matter to others and it's best to write. When he will publish his books, people will find out what he really thinks, but, for now, it wasn't the right time to publish, now it's the time of creation in silence. He would participate only as observer whenever he could and had time at exhibitions, cultural events and book launches or fairs. He thought he would have to see how things work first and, when he knows this world very well, he will decide then which door to open because he wanted to express by betting on the winning numbers. He wanted that all his thoughts be known abroad as well, but, for the moment, he had no idea how to cross country's borders with his writings. All he had to do for now was to listen and learn, he had to know how to keep his mouth shut, he needed great skill for such a virtue. Besides, he also knew he should not believe everything, everyone was right in his own way and the truth was somewhere near or everything could have been a big lie. He looked at each person separately and didn't know what to believe. Sometimes, when he would go to literary circle, at the writers' union, he said to himself:

"I easily recognize these the people's behavior as described by saints in ascetic books, in Pateric and Philokalia, because that's how human nature is, indifferent and evil, spoiled by nature and you are always instigated in all the relationships that you establish and then live. I feel this malignancy in me, in my inner self, in my character, in my way of being and I try to tame myself, to get rid of it. How to behave with people, how to treat the one who mocks at me, should I turn the other cheek and shut up, I should not be afraid, I should not have fear, I should not be scared, I should have this power to pray for the one who mocked at me, I should pray for the ruthless, heartless person.

But how is it to be heartless. I believe that when a man humiliates the other, especially his friend, he acts so because he is not ok, because he is not in harmony with himself, because he cannot get used to his new and fake condition, contradicting what he wants to be and is not. Then, what do I do, how should I behave, because I find it so hard and I don't know what to do, how to feel good? That is best for my life, to stay as far away as possible, to be impartial and to find people I can work with well and nice. How should I do that because every person has a good side and a bad side. Theory, again, what is important? How should I relate to these issues, to these truths that I cannot get off and I will no longer need. I have to do something to straighten myself, to shut up and be like Jesus, because He is the one who endured everything and went victoriously through the world. I have to find my resemblance with Him and struggle to keep this resemblance inside my heart. A man who does not believe in God is a weak man, is a man who has no power because he has nobody to lean on when he goes through hard times. Where should a man stay to get comfort? Only God gives us the strength to be strong and good and kindness is a constant battle of the soul which includes heart and mind together. I think I have learned something from these taunts. That they are transient, they have no consistency, they cannot make us obey as they would like. The world we live in is good, not bad, and, especially, what I live inside of me matters the most. The great victory of life is being just as I can be and being how I can dream of becoming. My good and serene dream is about my relation with myself, with the world and with God. If the world comes to me with its weight and errors, I must head its way with the beauty of my thought. What should I do inside of me so I can struggle to maintain the pristine condition of my mind which has to work hard. Thus, I have to flee this world and look more for the world of saints which lies above this world."

Rafael wanted to be somewhere as far away as possible from the bad things in this outer reality experienced rather by looking. He wanted to exist with human dignity and to find in this world something beautiful in being friends, in being human. But this friendship reality was so great that it often seemed it could not be attained on earth.

Rafael was confused, he was intimidated by the insults he witnesses daily. It was the election of the patriarch and he could not believe that there is so great mockery at the Romanian Church and at that monk who was supposed to be elected. And the Church has no reaction. The people can taunt nonstop. The church identifies with Christ who receives all the insults. What does it mean? The situation is similar at the presidential election. Well, what kind of country is this if you do not have respect for the President, for your Patriarch, for the Pope, for your teachers, your parents? What kind of a world we live in?

All sorts of allegations on TV and in newspapers, in the mouths of people ready to condemn, he looked and could not believe that you can hear and see such things on radio and television, where you might expect a different level from the public square. Who can be good in this universe then?

Rafael was disappointed because he didn't know how to react to the people who insulted him. He has such an attitude which demanded more insults, more mockery, and he was rather unaware of this. He would not speak, he kept quiet all the time, no one knew what was on his mind. How could he tell what is in his intimacy, considering he is busy writing and discussing by himself in that intimacy. Those writings were the secret of his existence as it made no sense to start disputes about ideas with anyone and, after all, who would he argue with, why and what for.

Oh, Lord, it would be nice if we could leave behind all this wickedness and would keep away from all this nonsense which means nothing after all. But where to find this strength to detach. Blending so much with the others, he could no longer find himself and he was sad, he felt hit around by other people's opinions and he wondered how he could have any own opinion and attitude, he felt sorry for this deficiency, this alienation. He felt sorry for himself because he was not as he should be. He remembered that he was not so weak when he was younger, he had fought with himself to be him alone and to remove other people's rubbish from his conscience, to pay attention only to his own actions, because that was really important, as for the rest, a waste of time. Yet, that attitude made him somehow revive and then fall again in this state in which he was no longer truly good.

Rafael was disgusted by these assails, insults he saw on television, ugly stuff told to one another, which was reflected in the day-to-day relations among people at work and children in school. He discovered in himself all sorts of contradictions seen in others then he wanted to understand them, to live them mentally like on a battlefield and then get rid of them permanently. He felt lonely and stronger at the same time. He will do something and somehow to find the strength to feel good and move forward no matter what.

Chapter 8

Rafael had a very good friend, Nicola, whom he considered an ardent defender of orthodoxy and an accomplished theologian who makes sure that justifies virtually everything linked to orthodoxy and church. Slightly fanatic, but very honest. That made him so strong and gave Rafael much strength. Nicola was a good kid who did nothing but pray all the time out of desperation, due to this world, as he could not find his place in it, as he used to say. He was suffering tremendously because his sister had died in a car accident. He had had a sister like an angel who had led a life so pure and pristine and he could not understand why God had allowed such a tragedy for her and him, for his parents. Why lose her if she was so pristine and had led such a beautiful life and had made sure to do everything by the word of God.

-But, perhaps there's room only for idiots in this world, you must be idiot and evil to live in it, if you're good, God won't let you stay here too long, he takes you to Him, that's how this world is.

-Yes, it's true, said Rafael, but God won't take to Him all the good ones, He lets the good ones stay here to do beautiful and true things, He lets them here to work and defeat the wickedness of the others, this is our existence, this is the only way to live.

Nicola looked very nice when he was well-dressed, as anyone would. Today, at the church, he looked great all dressed up in a light grey suit, with a purple-to-pink shirt and a dark gray tie to match the rest and not set off, he had a very soft, fluffy-like, coat over the suit, similar to a trench coat, fit for boys and young and sturdy men. The trench coat was light peach, suiting his yellow, light brown hair and his blue, small eyes with a penetrating sight as if he had looked at you from the back of an unknown distant heaven. Each of us has a heaven quite unknown that we carry with us each time we need much rest for the soul.

Was this person called Nicola a proud human being, was he an ambitious person, a great ambition conferred by much culture and the dignity you want to have when you want to really know something worthwhile? Nicola was a young thirty year-old man, who knew many things about life, unlike Rafael, a naive, and he wanted much more from his existence which he wanted to live properly and not adrift.

But Rafael felt a great, great perplexity and even greater disappointment about Nicola because he had begun to see him a friend in Christ, similar to Dragos, from the monastery. Rafael had met Nicola at the church where he would go every Sunday and they discussed about mathematics, philosophy, theology bringing him great joy. They would meet at the church where Rafael used to go and discussed ardent issues related to church, books, saints. It is true that Nicola was speaking so fast and passionate that Rafael barely got to say much, but it was very nice that they spoke and debated over an idea. Rafael usually asked the questions and Nicola answered with endless speeches, but very pleasant for both of them. It was some kind of ad hoc friendship, established there, at the church. They knew nothing about each other, but it was simply cultivated friendship. They used to laugh all the time when they met and greeted each other.

After a while, Nicola disappeared without a trace and he met him at church today. Nicola was standing next to a girl whom he had married, had said, and received a parish somewhere in the countryside and almost didn't pay attention to Rafael. He spoke with the priest, then he rushed to leave without saying goodbye to him, he acted as if he hadn't known him, unless from a distant memory.

Rafael felt so bad. When he saw him, he could barely wait to ask him what he had been doing, why did he leave so fast without giving a sign, God bless your marriage, I wish you both to be healthy, happy marriage. He looked at Nicola leaving so fast, seeming to run away from everyone and chased by something unseen. Rafael gulped and continued to feel bad, then he said to himself: "these are the people, whether they are theologians or Christians, it is equally hard to be human, for both believers and non-believers, it is equally impossible to be good. Perhaps he is frustrated because he left Bucharest and went somewhere in the countryside, he ran so fast as if he had been afraid I could steal his wife. He had the attitude of a loser."

He started laughing and went into the church, he sat down quietly on a bench and looked at the people who were praying and worshiping the icons. This is how such a great friendship in Rafael's heart and so small in the other one's mind ends. Simple words without coverage of heart. "We are all alike, just pottering about," said Rafael, while he made the sign of cross looking at Christ Pantocrator.

The service had long ended and Rafael was sitting in the pew, on a stool at the back, and continued to chew on thoughts.

"This is my opinion about what we live today, about this time which is morally degrading, fallen from world's order ever. We live this century so dark and far-off from moral standards, and what else do we need other than this road of self-destruction that we are walking on. Our way to hell is wide open and we follow it cheering and jolly, carrying the TV in our arms. I would repeat now everything that my dad laughing, when I talked to him last night: "the man digs his grave with his own teeth." Everything you do takes you to perdition with great ceremony and pride. Amid much fanfare as in major literary parties.

This is my opinion and I stick onto it, violent movies are shown everywhere just because they want the human being to forget the natural course of life and search sooner or later for his own decay. Keep away from this course of the world, this is my advice, and how to achieve this? But, then, where are the people who uphold ethics all this time, why isn't their voice heard? They are afraid, but why be afraid of what they cannot create, cannot have, cannot be as they intended. Do they have any intention to become something as long as the man of art, the beautiful and good art, is no longer promoted. Why do we destroy this existence and show no interest in a different kind of reality? Except the one of money? One of mind and spiritual ascension. The spiritual world we should live in does not include money and, then, where is creator's voice condemning human decadence? Where is Moses who wrote the tablets of law. Ah, I forgot that the thing with Moses is just a myth, a legend which has lost consistency, as some scientists claim today. What is the reaction of reasonable people all this time? Why don't people put their intelligence to the service of God and good, and beauty and why do they allow ugliness to be everywhere?

What will happen if we educate the youth with a mental war and do not educate them with beauty, what will be next, a general downfall as fascism or communism was, now that we have just came out of it. What's with this decadence that we are always forced to live in, this immorality that we are fed daily through movies, through games, a vile trade with death. We educate our children with violent shootings on computer, as if preparing for another world war.

And why don't writers and intelligent people of this country oppose but are proud to join this degrading trend rather than take a stand against it. What kind of mind spreads moral decay. Virtue means morality, it means health. What is the result of the 300-year period elapsed since Plato if we still have not raised above his reflections and, even worse, we live in exactly what he condemned, and we deem him today as being decayed, outdated and behind the times. Nowadays, we give no importance to philosophers and thinkers, who have become specialist's concern, reading books is now activity for school children and we, the rest of us, get together on television to be informed, to be up-to-date with the news, building further the great moral disaster in which humanity has been for some time now. What's the use for me to know some news that we all struggle to find out?

The writers in this world, in this century, as they claim to be more well-read, should promote a life of morality and virtue, but what can one expect from them since they are lecherous, drunkards who abandon their wives and children, leaving them to chance, just because they are artists. This is not everyone's case, but this is the set pattern, if you love your wife and you stand by your family and children, you are old-fashioned, they say you cannot be successful. You cannot succeed unless you have vices and you are full of passions, otherwise you cannot be a great writer. Then, what about the gap between a creator's life and work, why can't one be both genius and saint, with family and children, like the great patriarchs? Why isn't that possible? What's the use of so much brain and knowledge if you live so badly and so far from the normality of life led even by sensible peasants.

How could they promote morality when artists are so morally depraved, claiming they are beyond good and evil, because their art is beyond these two coordinates of life. What nonsense, well then, art must be primarily moral. Their art is one of perversity and decadence, as if we live in doom century, almost everything is a curse against God and human being.

How can you dissipate indignation when you constantly live in decadence, why be as we are now, when we could live differently. If God gave us a good life, why do we destroy this existence and do nothing good for it. The man must change the world and not the other way round. Moreover, we shift with the speed of light and sound apart from the good life and morality, which is the foundation of society and world and we are invited to live a borrowed life, as if we live other people's lives, not our own. I'm so sad and, by these words, I can only let myself drift, adrift, and yet, I have to fight back. On the other hand, I cannot tell others my thoughts for fear they might laugh at me and therefore I write them down, I write to find my dignity of man, this is the only way to stay awake in my mind and before God.

There is another aspect I don't understand, why so much scorn and to whose benefit. Why is this joy to divulge all kinds of rumors, which are nothing but fantasies and lead to nothing good, which are no use to anyone and take the world towards evil, as if your soul gets paralyzed by so much ugliness. Why mockery and scorn should be a form of existence. What world are we living in, a world lacking respect, honor, honesty and human dignity, what world are we in if common sense degrades by the day. In the past, people used to fight duels over a word, a mockery, nowadays we witness so passive and helpless to everything that's evil and blasphemous to God and people and we do nothing, not even oppose, we all live in this stench. The first act of protest would be people to give up watching television for good, as many as possible, just as I do. It only gives you negative energy and thoughts to destroy you in time. Morality, we do nothing for it, because this is the trend. Well, fascism was also a trend to which people passively submitted. If we educate our children in such a way, without fear of God to do no harm, what will come of us in the future? What we live today, a spiritual disaster, where could it take us to? What will come after this part of living history if not man's darkening and demonizing, his downfall to the animal level and below, seemingly back to the barbarism of the primitive man, dressed this time in the most expensive clothes and having the most beautiful body.

I don't believe that the elevation of today's man is so high anymore if we don't have the peace of joy, if we don't have the freedom of soul. The times to come will condemn us instead of praising as we do with the ones from history. We have nothing sacred to live for and fight for and, then, where are we going to and what are we heading to, if not towards the everlasting values of humanity which need to be values of these times, as well.

But one thing is certain, it is true that we are highly evolved from material point of view as compared to other moments in history. It's a fantastic step forward made by man, it is a great advantage for humanity, then why isn't he spiritually elevated as well? This may be the next step humanity needs to take and I have to work to this spiritual future through my writings and my undisclosed life, I am actually working to its future with everything I do and there are millions of people who think like me."

Rafael let the tears roll down his face as a sign of liberation and he stopped his thoughts and started to stare. Some time later, the priest came in the church from the altar, looked at him for a few moments and walked towards him. He laid his hand on his shoulder and asked:

-Are you still working so hard, Rafael?

-Yes, Father, I still work, if you knew how hard it gets, how bad I feel, I often feel terribly because I cannot make any progress with the money, with anything, not just that. I have so many things to do!

-But what do you want, do you want a villa, do you want a car, you have all these, you don't have a villa but you have your own dwelling, a four-room apartment.

-Yes, you are right, I have my own house in Bucharest, for which I thank God but what use if it's empty. See, I'd like to have something else, something more, to be mine, I want a family, my wife, my children.

The priest held his shoulder strongly and told him:

-Pray, pray for it in every moment, for your bride and you shall have plenty of these, you'll see. Do not lose hope, pray, cry and pray and God will give them to you right in the most important moment of your life. Don't you doubt that. You're too good not to have a happy life here and in eternity with God, we all must have the strength to fight and not let anything defeat us.

Chapter 9

What has actually happened to those two, let us recapitulate. Mihai and Maria, two, a man and a woman, are very much in love with each other, they get married in college, in their last year of college. They move to Bucharest. He gets a very good job in a IT company, she takes a test and gets to work as manager at an accounting firm, things go easier and faster since they've been married, they earn a lot of money so that have the opportunity to build a villa, each of them has a car, she gave up her husband's luxury car and bought a trendy Romanian car, then she gave up on the Romanian vehicle and bought a foreign car again. They have enough money and decide to have a child. The child to be born connects the two, unites them, they are happy in this waiting. She gives birth, but the baby nearly died at birth, including the mother who had an emergency surgery and is kept in intensive care. When she wakes up she wants to see her baby. She is told that the child was born with a major problem, he has no esophagus and will have to be operated. She stays with her baby in hospitals.

She gets back to work, she sleeps at the hospital during the night, the hospital becomes her home because that's where her child is. The man slowly gets out of the picture and finds a mistress, saying that he pays no money for a disabled, he doesn't spend money on medicines. She is crazy because she doesn't let the child die, because she makes him suffer so much turning him into a guinea pig, an experiment for doctors. That child has no chance to live, no matter how many stem cells would be discovered in this world, she must accept that she gave birth to a scrap. He will be a loser anyway, he will suffer all his life, just due to her ambition to keep him alive. She's making a big mistake for having this ambition to revolutionize medicine, it will be excruciating for him. That child is only a tormented human being as bitter as any disabled person who lives such a hard life. It makes no sense, she must accept her helplessness and let the child as he is without intervening so much.

Maria takes her child and moves into her parents' apartment, this child who was taken to the doctor one day and brought home the other day and his periods of seizure were so long and frequent. She could not stay in the villa where her husband now lives with various loose women who considered themselves owners of her work. She had no financial claim at their divorce, because nothing of his would have mattered any way, if there is no love, everything else is meaningless, she could manage on her own, she had the means. Is this man, Mihai, a single parent? Is this man a miserable father? We do not know whether he is aware of his misery, but, in the arms of his new lover, he feels very lonely and doesn't know why the void in his heart overtakes him like an endless night. Mihai began to walk only in the dark. How long until his birthday? How can we define hell? Is this loneliness of such a father who does not help his child, meaning he does not live his life near his child because he cannot help him spiritually and live. Because he lacks that essential something: love and humanity in him. This is his choice and once made, he can't turn back in time and pretend he was not there, time is irreversible, even with thoughts. This is hell, the helplessness of this love. Will he find it?

Rafael, however, has never married as because he hasn't found the right girl, he had a few attempts but he ran away, he now lives like a monastery monk, alone, in prayer, in chastity and writes books secretly. He is often mocked at, seen as sucker, some even think he is stupid in many ways in which he should have been cunning and opportunistic, not really stupidly good, but something like that. But, at the same time, he is even brilliant in many ways, he saved them many times from trouble with his unexpected solutions to problems. Everyone around him would acknowledge his brilliance, but when it came to dealing with people, with women, they all laughed at him and he did nothing to change people's opinion. There was something that made him special and spared him of additional effort in various situations, this mood allowed him the luxury of not talking, to keep quiet and think intensely. Even though he was rather laughable, he felt comfortable in this state. Everyone knew that he was very smart, he's the smart guy who cannot be the occasional slicker, he is that pleasant and trained guy who makes everybody feel good for having met him.

Rafael came to Bucharest, he took a test to work as a Mathematics teacher at a high school in Bucharest, he passed the test, he is tenure teacher, he is happy, he's proud of it, but he needs a house as he's had it living in rentals. He has no choice then, as a teacher he earns a humiliating wage, this is the policy of his country, whoever studied in schools must live in humble poverty. Since he knows how to use computers, he takes another job at a company where he does all kinds of work that do not require him to stay there with fixed working hours, so he also goes to school as a teacher, because this is what he likes to do, and also goes to the company, working on weekends as well. He's busy working all the time. In his spare time, he writes dancing on the keyboard at amazing speeds. He works hard but now has his own car, a four-room apartment, he is happy. But just as miserable because he does not have his own family, a wife and two or three children, in this loneliness. Everything is possible if you work and want with all your heart to have whatever you planned in your heart and mind. He managed to stay on the way of money and culture and spirituality. He is strong, good, reliable but dangerously lonely, silent and self-contained. He awaits his great love and he is sure he'll meet her soon.

Chapter 10

Rafael felt very much the need to calm down and wanted to go somewhere far away from this restless city where you could only be suffocated by congestion and so much dust, you could only get sick of a sure and slow death. On the other hand, he knew that these expressions were just exaggerations of his because he actually loved Bucharest so much that he would have stayed there all his life and would have never left. He wasn't planning to leave and he wanted very much to grow old here with his wife and children. But that's not going to happen anytime soon, he thought. So, he got into his car and drove off to the monastery to see how Dragos was doing and pray to God, to calm down. He was to on leave Friday afternoon and get back on Sunday evening. He enjoyed spending time alone in the church after the other monks left for their monastic cells to meditate, to sleep, to pray, to calm and rest, thus stepping away from what they have experienced or struggled throughout day.

The road to the monastery took about four hours, but that was not a problem for Rafael, he was such a good driver that he seemed to have been done that all his life. He felt great driving on the winding road. He was relaxed when driving and he was able to admire the gorgeous images offered by God in all His creations, so we can know them, encounter them. He was so delighted about the fir-trees which were so close to the road that you could touch them and the winding road that made you feel afloat behind the wheel that he burst with joy and laughed like a child fascinated by beautiful story-like dream. He was in a state of well-being when he could watch everything from the farthest distance and from such a great height that the soul grew wings and this state gave him strength.

"Is Dragos happy about his choice to be a monk in a large wilderness? I get bored driving up there, but what about the poor monks who climb

49

such distances on foot. Or maybe they have cars and, thus, it would be easier. Well, yes, the monastery has cars, they have a jeep they can use, they wouldn't stay without. Dragos has driver's license and drives it as well as he runs the monastery. Yes, the car has become requisite nowadays when everything happens at high speed."

Rafael got to the monastery in the evening and the monks were already at Vespers. They would always read the Psalter, even during the chuch service. That impressed him the most, this chain that monks can make with the prayer which surrounds mountains and perhaps the entire world without stopping. It was impressive for Rafael. So, he left his car at the monastery gate and went into the church in the deepest and darkest corner where he could not be seen by anyone, especially by Dragos, who was delivering service and didn't want to distract him from prayer and from the beauty of the service he needed so much. Rafael sat on a chair and closed his eyes, all he wanted to hear was the voice of the monk, or brother or priest who was ministering and attempting to put up these beautiful thoughts to God. It was like he wanted to be immersed in another world where he knows no one and nothing, no pressure, no worry, no desire to girdle his mind and heart. "Lord, by all the pain that I live in the world, You only make me come closer to You and Your words which I could not live without. I am very lonely and this loneliness used to hit so hard on me in the past, but now, since I've been trying to cure this pain through You, I feel so liberated. I'd want somehow to live in the world and be with You the same as these monks who live in this monastery. Well, I shall never be so pristine like them because I am tempted to see and think in a way that most often drives me away from You. But I have to come back and, if I stay here, I feel so good. Yes, Mother of God, I'm happy in a way because everything that I hear right now can only make me calm down and leave behind all that I've lived yesterday and today and in the days that past."

This evening service helped him relax and made him feel as if he were in another world. It was just him and God's world which was worth all the effort and all our endeavor in this world to be lived, as for the rest, it all seemed chasing after wind and illusion, he knew that if he tried somewhat to put hope in people, he would surely fail every time and would live illusion upon illusion. This doesn't mean that he despised people, but one could expect anything from people and he renounced then at relying on anyone. His thoughts and prayers were all that mattered. He experienced some kind of seclusion in his own mind and that was the reason why prayer was essential to him.

"God, this service is so beautiful, it is delivered because the soul, so confused in everything it does, thinks and lives, finds comfort in this prayer. In fact, if I don't have what I want is because You do not give me, because You want me to be with You and only You, because this is the best way for me. Lord, if I could carry with me, in my soul, when I go to Bucharest, all this beauty of the prayer and not be disturbed by anything that people do and what they are to me, because I must put my hope in no man except You, I'd be the happiest man. Oh, if I could stay so detached somewhere very far away from everything that people do, protected by Thee, how great it would be. When I'm around people, whatever they might do, I'll do so that they won't hurt my heart, for I am with Thee and I am the strongest, I need this exercise every day. For me, this mental monasticism is salvation, Lord, without this monasticism I think I would go mad. I think about these brothers who have their life time in Your hands, so I want to entrust my life in Your hands, because otherwise I feel I'm going crazy. Isn't Dragos feeling lonely? I think so, but he has much more than I have or he is just as confused as I am. And, then, he runs to You. These prayers are like therapy for me and for my soul, for what I need to live. Lord, give me strength to expect nothing from people or from women, because I always feel confused about this. I'm so addicted to a woman that I bear in me, in my mind and in my soul, that I try to get closer when I meet one and I'm ready to believe then that Thou hast sent her to me, but I'm so wrong. And now I'm in such a deception, I don't suffer, but I want to get detached from it, because I can only trust in You, because my life can only be as You wish. And I want to be well, not bad, because I'm the one who leads such a beautiful life and I don't want to lose this life. I'd rather be alone than be wrong, as my actions would set me apart from You. Lord, I want to be as far away as possible from this state that I've brought on myselfI must be as strong as I can be to solve this state of vulnerability, but I shall get detached, I won't give up, because I will leave healed from here. Monasticism is the best solution for my soul and my mind, it is the most comforting state. If I think I'm a monk in the world, then, any illusion or pain which could can come from a woman or from any other man would vanish. I should be primarily interested in prayer and let God take care of me. Lord, give me strength and let me be the way You want, if I can help somebody there's no problem, I'm glad I could do it, otherwise, nothing matters in this world, I have to go on thinking of You."

The service was so nice in the church. The only light came from the votive candles in front of the altar icons and the monks from lectern were reading at the light from a single candle which fell on the writingThus, they could respond to the ministering priest. They knew the service by heart anyway. It was dark in the church because the windows were small and quite narrow, covered with some curtains just to give the sensation of semi-darkness. Rafael felt so good getting this light from the votive candles in his prayer, he felt free from the illusions he could not escape from and which were coming upon him like unbearable obsessions. He knew that he will get rid of these states eventually because they would not last too long. He started getting closer to a girl, colleague from work, the girl even kissed him once briefly, and, one month after he had made some hopes, the girl told him she was seeing someone whom she didn't want to break up with. He was so disappointed, he felt in love with her in a way, well not exactly with her but with his need to love and be with that woman who would become his wife. He was feeling dejected, bad, but not so much because he said to himself:

"This girl is not from God, because if she had been from Him, she would have loved me, so it makes no sense to suffer, I do not suffer, because I was detached and relaxed, I did not get involved more than necessary, but I feel a slight feeling of discomfort, that girl mocked at me and I was misled like a teenager. How quickly people despise each other and hurt their feelings, poisoning the soul. I will get over it because I've always been a strong man. I've always been by myself and no woman has ever loved me, so I won't be able to be so sad. How beautiful is this state given by prayer's well-being, it's like a liberation."

Those red lights coming from the candles in front of the altar gave Rafael a sense of well-being and silence. He felt drowsy.

"I think, eventually, the most important for this life of mine is not being married or not, but be at peace and live in my mind and in my soul with God, devoted to Him, focusing on prayer and being connected to His world, to be as Christ the Savior said, <the kingdom of God is within you>.

But how to get to this peace other than praying all the time and staying here for prayer. It is more peaceful here indeed. but I cannot find that inner peace that I need unless I am somewhere, as I am now. Yet, I carry with me the noise of the world and of my feelings, like a water in swim into, or like the air that I breathe along with this image of the monastery and the sky embracing the cross from above and, thus, I will have something to return to, because it all stands in our mind, in my mind. That's strange, now instead of paying attention to the prayer and thinking of God, my my thoughts keep coming to my head. Appearance is everything in this world. I only seem to be quiet, in fact, nothing could be farther from the truth, I am agitated and I long to be relaxed. How is this quietness, is it when your mind goes silent and stops swirling everything in an infernal and uncontrollable mixture?"

The service ended and Rafael was sorry for that, he would have wanted it to last a little longer because, being on his way there, he could not feel at ease and pray properly or the way he would have needed. But the way he prayed was so real and spiritual that it seemed like the most authentic prayer ever because it came from a pure soul sitting before God.

Rafael insinuated into the church and he was fully convinced that no one sees him and no monk noticed him. Although he had phone Dragos to say he was coming to the monastery, he still wanted to make him a surprise. Still, he felt the need to sneak in and hide thinking about the prayer. He had this habit from work, when everyone would talk and laugh or work, he used to stay secluded and just watch. Most times he didn't feel like joining the conversation, he would rather enjoy watching his colleagues and learn by heart their behaviors so he could create his characters. Strangely, if the others had known that he was listening with interest for his books, they would have certainly become suspicious. He was praying so much for them. Every one was laughing or telling, between the lines, worries or problems, and then Rafael would pray for everyone from the company and would fight him to remove any wisp of envy, discomfort or harm that might have come from someone who would picked on him out of nowhere. The person who was making scandal was often right, as he who makes no mistakes, makes nothing, with or without a reason, everybody was wrong in a way and you had to stop this evil emerged from too much work under pressure. But any way, this undercover Balazac could be dangerous, as he was paying attention to details and wanted to know people's hearts.

He was so fascinated by the expression of the human soul through all these experiences that we call trivial just because they repeat themselves and we live them permanently, that he had a stronger urge to know God through this sacrament of the miracle through which He created us as we are now, with so much power to become, think or live. Everything was so fascinating in Rafael's mind who was fighting to his last breath to repeal hatred or contempt or other toxic moods which could have hurt him and everyone around, that everything took shape of a miracle. The wellbeing of consciousness is a form of mind and heart won through sustained effort, it is not an easy outcome. You need quite a struggle to get to love your neighbour as you love yourself. The state of mental harmony is the result of a long struggle, of purification by prayer of personal effort, it is not a state that we might all wonder that we do not have. But it's a great sense of our inner life, to stay pure as long as possible and surrender the mind before God who is at the center of your being. You must have the pride to live life with the dignity of having been created by God and to constantly fight to maintain this coordinate. It's something magnificent for each person. It is worth trying to become such a person in the world. It's so hard, but so beautiful, it is a constant miracle in our internal structures.

But, Rafael felt defeated most of the time and he had to return to the previous state. He felt better but not pure or healed by those spiritual states so toxic to mind and body. He was pleased when he managed to become harmless as a state.

Rafael thought he could be invisible and unnoticed if he entered quietly and noiselessly, but, in fact, all the brothers were waiting for him as a prince to come, because they all loved him and his arrival was always a true celebration. The entire monastery seemed cheerful. He was a model for those monks who would say: "If this boy is standing so firm and steadfast in the world, having just the prayer and thinking of God, we should all the more be cleaner and worthy of being children of God and God's followers with all their lives. The monks represented a mental model for Rafael and Rafael was greater motivation for monks.

It was Dragos' turn to deliver service and, when he saw him coming through the door, he felt a great joy and began ministering more carefully not to disappoint Rafael who comes to him to grow stronger, not weaker. They all felt such an emotion because they were praying for a layman like Rafael and they are not alone in the top of the mountain. Rafael had no reason to think he had been unnoticed and he was just an ordinary person who stepped into the monastery, because his arrival brought an extraordinary joy in everyone and they all started singing even more intensely. When being together, everybody seemed to find himself in the other one, finding out what had been lost and everything made an unexpected sense. Rafael had no idea about this, he was with his thoughts and neither the monks were too aware of their state, of their childly joy. They were all so beautiful in prayer as if they reached heaven with the prayer of their soul greeting God's eternal infinity.

The service ended and Dragos quickly came to Rafael to take him, to talk to him, to go and eat because he might have been hungry. Rafael unloaded from his car many gifts for the monastery and brothers, it was a true joy for either of them. After dinner, Rafael and Dragos spent time like brothers, until morning, chatting about all sorts of theological, philosophical, scientific issues, as current as possible. Rafael brought Dragos several hundred books in English and books about electronics which he was going to read to keep abreast with what is written and debated in the scientific world, with respect to this dialogue among science, philosophy and religion, a highly-debated theme in the cultural environment from all over the world and every man who is fascinated by reading could not help but be intrigued by these issues especially those living in the middle of such reality. But all in due time. For now, meal in refectory and the joy of meeting again.

Chapter 11

Mihai could not resist the restrain he was living. He was having problems at the firm, which he wanted to solve by himself. He was having all sorts of meetings that could not refuse because otherwise he would not have been able to conclude the contracts that kept him going. Had he suspected that it is so difficult on his own, he would not have started his own business.

It was terribly hard to resist by yourself on the Romanian market, even with the help and support from a foreign entity. He would be held responsible for all issues and was supposed to take care of everything, that was the cause of his sleepless nights and that baby thing was something he could not accept nor solve. He admitted his defeat. It was inadmissible to him, he could not believe he fathered a child so ill, born without esophagus. Moreover, he was going to stay in hospitals from that moment on, he could not stand Maria who would only speak about the child. She would obsessively speak only about the child and nothing else, and she would cry her eyes out in front of him, it was like she took it all out on him, he was disgusted at this woman who has no dignity in her suffering and takes it all out on him, as if he were who knows who, why stay and bear her crying all the time, he was no psychologist, he thought. She would only yell at him hysterically whenever they met, as if she had gone mad and what was he supposed to do, where to go and who to tell, especially since he was staying home alone and could not even solve the problems at the firm. Had he not constantly seek contracts, he could be on the verge of bankruptcy on the following month. He could not afford to go at a loss and with no sales or cooperation agreements, as he would risk destruction and disappearance. He could not admit that he had waited so long for a child and he was born with so many problems, a disability, that he would not enjoy his child as everyone else, just like everyone has a baby or child and does not stay in hospitals as much as he does. Moreover, when he would go down the hospital and see Maria in that state and the baby lying motionless connected to machines after the next operation, his heart would petrify and he did not want to see that any longer, he felt he was losing his mind, he felt like running away, screaming to death, he wanted to disappear and not see again any of that ugliness. All he wanted in those moments was to run away as far as the eye can see and not meet anyone in his way, whoever that was. He felt the urge to fight God and he would even swear at God and often said to God:

"You do not exist, how could You exist, if You gave me such a child; had You existed, this child would not have been born like that, since he is so, why is that happening and why to me? It is true that I aborted a child and I had many women, even prostitutes, a long time ago, when I was young, but what is that got to do with me, I was stupid back then, and that girl did not know much either and I did not love her and did not want to even look at her, all I had was instincts, why did you endow us with such instincts if they are not good, to fight them, You should not have done such a thing to us. Because I'm not the one to blame, but that girl, she should have been careful not to get pregnant, and what's a child got to do with another. Why punish me like this through the child, and why haven't you punished me, You punished her, Maria, no, she is not to blame, neither is this child, You should have punished me, Lord, You are unjust, Lord, in fact, You do not even exist, why should I speak about all these. You have given her such a child to her, You have given him to me, I cannot see this child anymore. However, I not want to see him because he will die anyway and I do not want to see such things, I would rather break up with Maria, break up with her and the child, because they are not mine. I believe that Maria slept with another man since she gave birth to such a child, I could not have fathered such a child, he is not my offspring, I am a perfect man, if he were mine, he could not have been born that way, I am not to blame, Maria is fully responsible. I am not involved in such things. As I did not want it, I wanted things differently. My marriage should have worked just like this company, a company which is entirely mine because I brought it around. When I see that child in hospital I could just die, I'd better run and not see him again. Besides, Maria is unrecognizable, she seems to have gone crazy. She speaks to me as if I were the only one responsible for all this and she blames me, she tells me a million times that it's my fault, she shouldn't have married me, a womanizer, she brings back my past experiences since college. As I had a life of prostitution before marriage, I got my body sick and I alone have genes damaged by the disease of lust, and my seed spoiled by prostitution fathered this child, the illness taken from whores destroyed the baby from the very beginning because he did not have the gene to develop his esophagus. I told him that the nonsense has no scientific basis and he yelled at me that it shall be discovered. Such gene, cell and blood damage, such diseases are transmitted only by sexual intercourse. She keeps telling me that I do not get involved more, that I do not go to doctors to give them money, as if they can do anything more in case you give them money. I am so tired and upset, I have so many problems and I do not understand why should I take care of the child, why should I go to the hospital so often, to do what, I can only see that child in one way, and then I seem to go nuts. I don't want to see such a thing, I don't understand what she wants from me, anyway she is not making any money and I must be the one to bring her money, I give her as much money as she needs to be able to live and I don't understand what I have to do because I am so helpless, moreover, I don't want anything, I want nothing from life, as if I am crazy.

I wonder why I got married, because I used to have some ideals and I was convinced that if I fight for them I would become somebody, now look at me, I got so big that a bottle of whiskey is enough to knock me down, to sleep and think of nothing. Could it be that this is what this woman wanted from me that she blames me for the state of this child? Could it be that this woman wanted this from me, only one child and she has never loved me, had she loved me, she would have behaved differently with me and I don't understand why I must stay with her for the rest of my life. That's silly, there are other women in the world and, thus, perhaps I will no longer have this child who will die anyway. I have no ideea why she didn't let him die, I don't understand why is she keeping him agonizing with so many operations, what should I do with that kid who is a retard, but this is it, he is my child, I fathered such a child. I feel so stupid, anyway must go somewhere to have fun, to find someone, a friend, a colleague at the firm, a business partner, a place to go on Friday night, because if I continue to stay in this house anylonger, I will go mad. My own house has turned into a tomb, it would have been great to have my mother here with me, I wouldn't have felt so lonely."

Mihai felt the need to go out, to talk to someone, to stop being so lonely, so he would not see the house so empty and unbearable, he couldn't sleep anymore, he felt the need to have someone with him to pull him apart from what he could live and cut him off from whatever he had and could experience. He had no courage to tell anyone about his problems, nobody from his firm knew about his anguish, he kept quiet all the time and was so edgy that all the others thought he was nuts, but they said nothing to him because he was the boss and was invincible, plus, they could end up jobless. Everyone thought he was the most powerful man on Earth who succeeded financially, who stroke gold as one might say. Nobody, absolutely nobody suspected what he was going through and his feelings, the hell he was living, no one could suspect him because he knew very well to conceal it and plunge into his work with the desperation of a sick man.

Since it was Friday night, he asked some younger guys who worked with him more often and he kept sending them to run checks, they were young people who had just graduated college, one was still a student and, in a way, he had trained him in accounting and business issues.

-Where do you go to have fun tonight?

-Well, we go to a nightclub.

-Where is that?

-We can't tell you its name.

-Why not?

-Because it's an ill-famed pub!

-Tell me, I'm interested, I want to join you.

-But, you know, boss, it's a club with high-class whores.

-It doesn't matter, I'll join you.

-Ok, boss, we are heading there right now, before things heat up, we must find seats forehand as it gets quite busy and you won't even find a place to stand.

Chapter 12

There are places in Bucharest that the average Christian or the regular guy has no idea about, he just comes across signs such as "nightclub", "sex shop" or "cabaret" when passing by down the street, but he does not see them. A normal family guy with everything he wants to do good pays no attention to those street mockeries, to decadence shops. There are also many casinos where young, brainless fools come to bet their money gained from their work or rather their parents' work, or traffickers, drug addicts and the motley world of fools from everywhere. A man who works hard for his money would not want to lose it all in one night. But which world do we want to deal with now, this world of losers may interest a rational person only insofar you learn not to be like them. Similarly, a regular man, with problems, with family, with burdens, who works hard, passes by such locations of decadence as if passing by garbage, he doesn't even notice them, he acts as if they were inexistent, he pays no attention to them.

Neither Rafael gave them any importance, he was concerned about his company, his school and he wanted to make his family happy, to be the best wherever he was. As for fun activities, he didn't even consider them.

Rafael was only interested in the church, where he went to attend service, his house, his car, which he used to be on time to his two jobs, and that was it, he would not go to areas he considered quite diabolical. He knew what was going on there because he tried to imagine and he had brains, he had no curiosity to see or know, Rafael didn't like to listen to music turned up to the max, he enjoyed Byzantine music, sung by monks, he enjoyed services and classical music, he used to sing some popular song but he was not interested in that.

He rarely liked a popular singer and was very demanding in terms of music, he would watch some movies which showed the atmosphere of a pub or a disco and he considered those people barbarians, those who go to such places of debauchery, primitives of the modern age. Living in the era of the greatest scientific discoveries and not be interested in any of these and lead a life as if they were inexistent, as in primitive times. That was the place which gathered, concentrated that state of frustration that could not be practiced in public or openly, instincts repressed in time were exhibited there. In his opinion, the human–animal attended those places and he had no intention to get contaminated with those aberrant states, he did not want to see something like that. He kept repeating in his mind, "how blessed is the man who does not walk in the counsel of the wicked, nor stand in the path of sinners, nor sit in the seat of scoffers, but his delight is in the law of the Lord, and in His law he meditates day and night".

This was the first of the Psalms of David, he only had time for something like that. These ill-famed places in Bucharest were so repugnant to Rafael that he was almost outraged when passing by them. He didn't actually even see them because he got disgusted instantly. He passed many times by a sex shop, but he never thought what were those objects displayed in the window and what could they be used for. In fact, he did not even notice them, he would only see what he was interested to see. He did not know that something like that even exists until a colleague showed him, the one who kissed him on his mouth and he took her seriously, he thought that this may be a sign that she likes him, that something beautiful could be between them, that something divine could happen and he was waiting for the miracle to happen, but he waited in vain as it did not occur.

He thought she wanted them to get close and he even tried to follow this feeling, he had invited her to the movies, to have dinner at the restaurant where he used to eat frequently, but not the way she would have wanted, straight to bed. All the girl wanted was just an affair for a few nights with Rafael, as revenge against to her partner, but for Rafael, as a boy and man, that was unacceptable, he was not looking for the love called sex of the youngsters nowadays, he was looking for that unique, true, holy love which is God's gift to man, not this mockery at our bodies, this denigration and demonization of the principle of life. Rafael was searching for love without sex and she was searching for sex without love, a terrible contradiction of this time and of the two in search for love, because they did not know each other's thoughts, they lived in their own assumptions and expectations, until everything fell apart. Rafael could not admit that a child is no longer God's gift in people's minds, but an accident, a mistake, an error, a perversity and, eventually, a murder. A child is the fruit of love, not an abortion. But if the two no longer share love but instincts, whose fruit is it if not sin's. If love is inexistent and the child is only a piece of meat which must be in decay, the same as an ingrowing nail and, therefore, the child must be cut, eliminated, what world do we live in if not hell? This is not the world that the mind perceives and wants to be in, this world is estranged from the soul, what to do then? If you kill a child by abortion, it woman's guilt because she is the one making the decision. But isn't it a man's fault? Is the man just the cause? This is common thinking.

Let's be serious. The guilt belongs to both woman and men, equally, a woman's guilt is visible, a man's guilt in invisible, but God knows them all. And he, the man, rightly blames it on the woman, because instead of thinking about God and virtue, she allowed the degradation in her mind and, then, in her body. "But isn't the man guilty, Rafael wondered, for this murder, no, he is not guilty, as he blames the woman. He is very guilty, the man bears the most guilt in case of an abortion, had he been more careful with his principles and with his own body, it would have not come to the murder that he causes, he pushes the woman to comit murder through his animality and indifference, his lack of love and when he gets ill, he has no idea why and runs to the doctor, therapist and his despair grows because the sin howls inside him. People don't like the word 'sin' nowadays, they stand fiercely, full of hatred against whoever utters this word giving you the creeps, you are not allowed to pronounce this word. Sin means error, serious mistake upon life, it means total separation from God. Lord, why do we live in such a world where the freedom inside me allows me to do me harm, Lord, take away my freedom and let me stay bound near You. Freedom is the most terrible state, the biggest test in a man's life."

Rafael saw in sexuality the principle of life and love, and if God put the birth of babies in sexuality, we should not hoax sex, that is to deviate from the sexuality that He left, up to the pleasure of hormone discharge, as they say, in a degrading libertinism. But what's with this visual prostitution which surrounds us all over like air. Why does this serious phenomenon happen, mental violation of our children and their feeding with the aggressivity from computer games. Are we getting ready for a world slaughter? What's with this corruption of a baby's innocence? You must fight, we must become spiritual even in sex, a lay brother once told me. But, people live nowadays a deviation from normal, from love, from the sacred love and union between a man and a woman. It's a decay, two people who love each other are almost abnormal and shut off from society and friends, they are no longer up-to-date, it is sad to love your wife, you must have mistresses to be happy.

A man who is in love is a fool, just like me, people no longer place their love into Christ, but in something degrading. They make love, they do not love each other, and that sounds awful. It's come to this, instead of dreaming and living the true love which is God's gift and our likeness to Him, you see how everything slips into the invitation to the daily prostitution or we could speak about the daily prostitution or daily rate of prostitution.

The decay which is permanent, overtakes us all and why is that, just to mock each other for a pleasure that lasts so little and is so repetitive, but creates such big problems. Well, this is a decay greater than animality, because animals have their time and their rules of living and they obey, but we, oh, yes, said Rafael, we have free will, we can kill each other and sell our soul, and so what if I have something in my belly, it is a piece of meat, a cancer that must be removed, this is the child, this is the principle of life, just an empty pleasure. And the man always says, "What, is it my fault?" This is the outcome of lust and the spiritual death is one step away from physical death". Rafael shuddered when he had such thoughts.

He would often feel that if continued seeing those fallacies of human life, of this hell, he felt he was losing his mind and, therefore, he had to think of nicer things, he thought of God, that was all, He was the only one he clinged on and, all of a sudden, he said, that idea came to his mind: "God is the only benchmark in mind's chaos and the chaos of the world". Yes, after all, thought Rafael, I'm exercising this dignity, this honor of thinking, of being clear-headed, of judging the world and its decadence we live in day by day, the profound promiscuity and prostitution, and thus, the taunt is increasingly higher. I wonder where will we get, because, according to my knowledge, refering to pedagogy again, if a child is not educated to be good, to be clean, to work, to learn, he will become a scoundrel, a primitive. If you feed him with decadence, he becomes a fallen person, in some rare cases one of them gets rebellious and wants to be something else. Or, if this world is living in this level of moral and psychological decay, what will become of youth in the future, a schizophrenic world, capable of even greater wars, decadence, just like fascism and communism were possible.

People were not educated to be good there, fascism and communism are the fruit of the Enlightenment culture or a false interpretation of the Enlightenment, a diabolical Enlightenment, when man took God out of his concerns and turned Him into something measurable, to be at the level people's understanding, they turned Him into a principle. That is, they have gotten out of Kant's paradigm, they contradicted his philosophy, they argued against him, claiming that man can use reason to think of God, and here's where they come. Perhaps Kant's philosophy should be rethought and his philosophy should never be allowed to be turned into idelogy, whatever that may be.

Man is no longer a mystery but a quantity. Therefrom, everything is permitted, man can be defined in terms of the power of measurement, he is in relation to the fluids and substances contained by his body and nothing more, love is pure chemistry. If you cannot prove his spirit, well then, this means He does not exist, the man has an ego, he has consciousness, he has intellect, he has whatever he has, all sorts of layers, but he no longer has soul. This word started to bother in modern culture because it alludes to religion and everything that is religion must be liquidated. Or, moreover, if they saw that this term could not be replaced or changed, they try to give it all sorts of definitions, any other than its well-known definition in Christian religion and tradition, immortality of soul, the soul is immortal and we go with it before God to be judged and receive reward for its life.

The soul is whatever remains of a man after his death, or rather said, whatever a man becomes after death, namely what he is and what he becomes, deemed together. You cannot prove that scientifically because you are still here, in the pot of life. Or perhaps, science is heading that way, that's its purpose, and now only false interpretations are made, creating ridiculous ideologies. And if you cannot prove scientifically anything about the soul, you deny it, it's the simplest way. The hypothesis is plausible, we are not researching anything that does not exist. How many mathematical truths were only theories, and here they are now! Man is a mystery and his soul carries all aspects of life and immortality, he is responsible for all things and he is the one to be judged and placed before God and in His order.

You cannot take away a man's eternity, you cannot deny the immortality and godliness of his soul. This reality is totally absent from this period and from the science of these times which weighs everything, takes measures and then labels. It's not a bad thing. It's bad when they deem that this is all and there is nothing else besides that. But it's not about the scientist who makes the research, he is the first level, but it concerns the other levels, the second, the third, of those who come with interpretations and turn scientist's results and his books, his torments and his discoveries from knowledge to multiple interpretations up to ideology. The advance from level one to level two and level three triggers a disruption of understanding which gets to the population, then the deviation and interpretation occur, the scientist knows that things are not as interpreters say. But what can you do, one is the genius that makes the discovery and another is the scholar who teaches about the former's discovery, it's all a matter of understanding, one is Kant who wrote down the philosophy, he's the first level, and another is the one who read his philosophy and turned it into a school knowledge, these are the other levels of understanding.

We are moving in a dualistic reality, I cannot identify with it, I cannot accept it. The good and evil go together. Let me think of a reality, I'd give the example of fascists and communists—they are one world together, they had the same means of killing people and, eventually, they killed among themselves. We can create a better world if we destroy the existing one. Well, where could so much current decadence lead to if not something similar, such as Hiltler, such as Stalin, anyway, anti-Christ theories are inceasingly fashionable, a growing number of people spread them around more than ever. Politically and culturally, people behave like pagan hordes where animal instincts are released, you can see so many street protests with all sorts of claims for rights. Those people have such faces, just like in computer games. This can only lead to the necessity of a totalitarian regime and setting bounds to human freedom, where the right of the most powerful supersedes the law, and the most perverse and greediest and the more primitive is entitled to dictate and command. For now, until they get to the totalitarian regime, they begin with minority rights."

Chapter 13

Involuntarily, the wedding of a popular, homosexual singer came to Rafael's mind, he couldn't remember the name, ultra-publicized on all television channels all over the world. He thought that marriage was the most bizarre and comic event, just like Andersen's Emperor's New Clothes. That man was a transvestite wearing a wedding dress with a train I dont know how many meters long. That man imagined he was a woman. There is nothing uglier and more grotesque than this. He saw the pictures on the Internet, he saw them on television and he was gobsmacked because such a thing could happen. A lot of people from the world's high-society gathered there to celebrate the great wedding. That fifty-year-old singer had all his fingers stuffed with gold jewelry with diamonds, jewelery worn by any luxurious woman, but he seemed to want to be more than that, he wanted to wear a woman's jewelry, to be more of a woman than any woman in the world, to have a woman's eyes and gestures, wearing earrings, rings on his fingers.

He was fat, having a big belly like a round and red bell-pepper, in a countryside garden, surrounded by a large and white cabbage sheet used to make cabbage rolls. And that huge belly wrapped in a wedding dress with thousands of pearls gave him away in all his wretchedness and his splendid wealth which is just the most exact expression of time's emptiness that we consume without morality. A fatty dwarf, a swollen, square, old toad, dressed in a wedding dress made of the most expensive fabrics in the world and sewn by the most spectacular fashion house. In Praise of folly, once again, bless the one who wrote this book, which is still the book of today's world.

Bravo, Erasmus, have a look! The world lives in your book, your book is the stage of the world. I think those who sewed the dress for him had quite a laugh. You can't believe your eyes, you get dumbfounded by such a conduct and mockery. Everything was so grotesque, as never seen even in the great empires. Not even Nero, I believe, in his madness, wouldn't have dared to marry his partners, in public, to have a Christian wedding ceremony at the church, to marry before the altar, where the priest was gay as well. Even worse, can it get further from Christian point of view? Yes, why not, things can go further, but I don't want to imagine. To dress a bridal gawn with a tremendous train carried by ten girls dressed in white, like a very fat, poor-hearted and fancy-dressed woman. He even had a wedding announced worldwide, because, hey, he is the greatest singer of the universe, and everyone had to know that he is gay and that he can marry Prince Charming. And this event will be forgotten, no matter how much they have struggled to spread the word around. People had a laugh and got back to their lives.

Moreover, they went to the church to get married with wedding rings and that is the greatest contempt at the holy word and the holy book. Such a thing has never been heard of in two thousand years of Christianity, but it seems it's democracy and everyone has the right to live their own intimacy as they wish. Well, in such conditions, can he still be called a normal human being, let alone morality? But why do we need morality, if such mockery happens under our eyes and we cannot say anything and we cannot take a stand. That has never happened in the past, it's outrageous, it makes you wonder whether the law in this world protects madmen and normal people have no more right to life. How long does it take until these anomalies become mandatory? Well, what world do we live in, a world in which looking at other people makes you sick. Rafael stopped his train of thought, gazed, as if looking for someone, then he resumed the unseen flow of thoughts.

Well, then, it's great to be in trouble, it's a blessing to be poor and have nothing to eat, because you're concerned about having, pulling through, doing, finding solutions to your problem. You go to pray to God so He takes care of you and you have no time left for debauchery and degradation. It's great to be a peasant in the field, to mow, your only thoughts to be about your home, your children and your wife. People have gone crazy in villages as well, but normal people speak badly about those who marry like that one in the wide world, a man wearing a wedding dress, fancy that, people call them "queers".

Such a true word for them, judging by consonance. So much normality, simplicity and beauty are in the people who have nothing special but than their work and cleanliness and their everyday life. Villagers are no longer as kind-hearted, just like people from cities. It's good to be poor and have troubles, troubles strengthen you unless they drive you mad. What can you do in this world, it seems you have no choice but pray to God to keep you in your right mind, and nothing more, pull back and flee from the maelstrom. It's the same, just like you couldn't do anything during Communism or war times, you can only live your life as secluded as you can, and obey the times, you have no other choicePerhaps we should thank God for having this option. Yes, but one is not even allowed to think. Well, you can think and nobody prevents you from being strong and having great faith inside your home because nobody controls you, at least for the time being. No one can enter your mind. Not yet, there used to be hard times when one got killed for being Christian, now they pull your leg, they say you are smoked and outdated, they humiliate you, poke fun at you, they call you zealot, idiot. So what, nobody could ever stop you from believing.

No one can keep you away from lies, from dishonesty, from hatred unless you do it yourself, but if you are a genuine Christian, then things are different. The more people around you, the more they will appreciate you as a fair person, but only to themselves, and that's all, they will feel they can trust you, even loafers will know that. This is the advantage of being a Christian, you can actually and practically live in harmony with everyone, as the song says: "Seven villages can be warm, If I pass through and do no harm." If you are a Christian, you are a free person and you can sleep by yourself, if you are a Christian, you can be happy on your own, if you are not a Christian, you are desperate by yourself, if you are unhappy in love, you are happy with Christ and you have found the solution, the only thing is that you have to hold tight to Christ, because if you break away, you go mad, the mind cannot rely on itself, but on God, just like the body has its foundation in the light or the neurons have their basis in light radiations.

This world is driving you crazy, you end up in a madhouse if you take for granted everything that you come across with.

Stay calm. Well, how could I be calm in the midst of this war in which the soul is decimated piece by piece. I thought you said the soul cannot be measured, quantified. Oh, yes, I contradict myself. You know how I see things here, Rafael said, look, I am reading "The Three Musketeers" and, in that book, people were killing each other, the corpses were thrown into canals and the man was history, he was thrown into the night of oblivion, he was worthless, the man was an object, the dead was just a corpse, rottenness. When alive, he was only good to be killed or kill, like animals, such horrors were happening, just think about what the human being was in wartime. The instinct of war is maintained nowadays through PC shooters games. If all the possible techniques were used to kill the body during wartime, as the soul was going to God, now man has become much more primitive, fallen and smarter, more diabolical and better dressed, millions of techniques and methods to kill the soul are studied and now I remember Christ who said, "Do not fear those who kill the body, fear those who kill the soul and you are thrown into hell." I must read again this fragment in the Bible because I don't know it by heart. Well, this is what happens now, there are all sorts of means to kill man with his soul and he is pushed into the abyss of madness, as Jesus said, mad and blind. Well, this madness and this blindness are systematically studied in a lab, how to bring people to blindness, I think there's some sort of organization in this respect. I believe that the phenomenon of globalization and uniformity paves the way to that, one leader, one country, one religion. Globalization is an ideal and it's not a bad thing, in my opinion, although there are voices that cry out loud that we will die, it's good for humanity, the thing is how to get to it, what paths to follow and not at all costs. Considering the philokalic writings, there were seven deadly sins, described by the holy fathers, seven great sins, or more, I don't know exactly, described by St. John Climacus in "The Ladder of Divine Ascent", where man is pushed to the death of soul and hell, one of the most feared is, as they say, the demon of lust.

Well, something like that is happening now, as if this demon is unleashed and the people are staring at it and getting more and more contaminated, they want growingly more pleasure. Then there is the gluttony of the womb, people talk more and more about weight loss, about all sorts of food, about the struggle against growing fat, increasingly sophisticated diet recipes, food recipes, which are still disguise of the gluttony and the food that weakens the inner spirit and pushes the soul towards hell, that is, to decay. Because this world no longer speaks about souls, it speaks about consciousness, about me, but no man would tell you about soul, this term is obsolete and it has been replaced with all sorts of expressions, I, ego, consciousness, spirit, but that would be all, the soul is always forgotten, eluded, as it cannot be touched, it cannot be weighed, but there are levers for its destruction. If you deny all these, you will find the meaning of soul. The method of negation applied to this world, by elimination, you will have little left, the soul. The most straight forward is the quest for pleasure and avoidance of effort, pain, insistence, strength, all these are now turned inside out and the man is slient and mute spectator at the spectacle of world's degradation. How? By mocking at everything that is holy and durable.

How to get here and how to do this, through specialized literature, promoting it on all channels. Why is it possible, because the greed for money is big, prostitution makes the most money, so they say. If a man lives in mental prostitution, he can no longer pay attention to himself, he pays attention to something outside of him and he can be manipulated, controlled, turned into consuming and producing cattle. How can you make more and more money? By putting someone else to work for you, who is the one who works for you, the one who is inferior to you and who is attracted to pleasure, the pleasure that creates addiction, he will work hard to produce it, that is to work for you. If he is debauched, he is easy to manage and for him to be at the farm, that is in your company, he should not have a family, so this must be destroyed as well, quite simply, debauchery, always the safest and most productive way, and you give him other models, you cannot control him without that model of vulnerable loneliness, you cannot manipulate him, but why and for whose benefit? We will declare that this is the new course of the consumer society. And there are also the models of homosexuality. Where will such a system lead, to a more diabolical dictatorship than ever before, if it cannot be invented yet, I suspect they are working on it right now, a new dictatorship, that is of the few, the great, the powerful, who own everything and which will be called arbitrary dictatorship.

A new Nero, but one who will do whatever he wants for real. We, who are here and now, what can we do, we, as a minority, submit to the majority, we can oppose for us, for our lives, and we can think, thinking is our only weapon left and it cannot be controlled, to think and not lose God who is the only fixed point in this chaos, and since He is very far from here, He is not caught in this world and He is the only one who sees, the only light in our blindness that we can cling on, God help, for those who read.

Why are these people like that, because they are for each other into something as primitive as intercourse and momentary pleasure.

He got sick when he heard that sex is nothing more than a discharge of hormones and that love is nothing more than a chemistry of fluids, he felt like throwing up when he heard these strange, ridiculous, demonic, paranoid explanations for this century, it is completely false biologically and mentally because it's much more than that.

But his colleague thought that if she hits on Rafael, she will get pleasure and ecstasy from him, as if the man is nothing but a sex machine. How dehumanizing. You make sex with someone, namely your colleague, after which she will be able to pretend that she doesn't see him, she doesn't know him, we had a good time together for a few nights, we have exchanged fluids, we had strong sensations and nothing else, we can pretend that all we did there was honorable, what two mature people should do to get rid of sexual tension, we have released it and we feel great and it's done, that was all, just that. Next time, I'll look for another. "Who does she take me for? A gigolo?" he said with disgust.

Rafael realized that this was what the woman wanted from him, but could not believe that it was actually so, he could not accept it in his soul, such dehumanization, not even at the level of perception, such degradation, such an extirpation and annihilation of feelings of love, such elimination, so low and painful, of the highest soul experiences, how not create from such pains or states of indifference towards you, at the level of body and mind, blockages that lead to incurable diseases. Lechery leads to illness, that's for sure. Afterwards, you go to the doctor, to therapist, you take a bunch of pills.

In fact, the woman was attracted to Rafael like a butterfly to light, but she deeply hated his way of being. And since he was giving her the back, he was apparently ignoring her, always keeping quiet, secretly examining her, wanting to find out everything about her, without her being aware of that, measuring her every move and gesture and he would not cling to her as she wanted, that drove her mad, she could not put up with him anymore.

And then, out of frustration, she despised Rafael and considered him a wimp who could not make a woman happy, and Rafael had no idea that the woman was laughing at behind his back. Why was that, because he did not respond immediately to her invitation to sex, but he wanted them to fall in love with each other, he wanted to love, to dream, to write, to take walks, to go boating in Herastrau, like two teenagers, to walk around the park, to recover the lost time, that is why, when Rafael asked her if she was accepting his invitation to a walk in the park or to the monastery, she burst into laughter, in terrible mocking roars, and said to him:

-Well, then, Rafael, is this all you can do, you invite me to stay on benches, hahahaha.

Rafael did not understand why the girl was roaring with laughter, but it did not matter, he had begun to have some feelings for her and he would forgive her mockery, teasing, although he did not understand them, he did forgive them until he braced up and told her he was fond of her and he wanted to take her out to town to know each other and, why not, even get married. The girl made a weary face and told him the story about her boyfriend, whom she did have, but would not consider him as good as she had wished. Rafael got very sad, he had lived the moment like a blow to his head, but everything was happening inside him and nothing was visible outside. Total opacity. He was ready to tell her so many things, as though he had done many times this exercise of his exteriorization, his sensitivity and now he was prepared to tell her about his love and his feelings and that intimate and beautiful baby-like tenderness which touches our heart and we want to tell the other, to plant it in the most beautiful garden, to be with us in this beauty, in the completeness of feelings. But one can be in such relationship with God alone, he said to himself as a final solution and slowly came to terms. Even if, all of a sudden, in Rafael's mind that beauty had been thrown away and trodden on in the mockery of human relationships. The monster of mockery seemed to have invaded his soul once again through this illusion of happiness. Rafael blamed himself for having been wrong again like a fool, how come he had not checked that woman to find out things about her and fall in love afterwards. What, can you give orders to love? No, you can't, but you could be more careful. He should have been more careful, to find out what she wanted and who she was, her mentality, how could he have fallen in love with a stranger, like a teenager, and it hurt so bad, once again. He had always felt for her a sort of rejection, even if he had fallen for her, he should have been be careful about that, it was rather a subtle rejection, but he had not listened to his inner intuition and thought he was wrong, that one should not judge a man, a woman, by the looks, by one's first feelings for her, without knowing her, that one may be wrong, but he had not been wrong, provided he had followed his instincts of complete inner rejection, he wouldn't have suffered so much later on.

However, he was thirty-five years old and, at that age, a boy like him, a man like him, so special, who had had no relationship with a woman because he had not wanted to, he was alone because he wanted so with ambition and persistence, all he wanted was that unique beauty lived along with his wife, the one given by God, no more than that, he was expecting that beauty, without half-measures. He was interested in no other woman but the one in his future, and if he never found her, he would live like a monk in the world, in cleanliness and beauty, in bodily and mental chastity, in prayer and sapience and his day-to-day work. If he encounters his wife and sweetheart, his life so far will seem the greatest beauty and the grimmest struggle given by God. And he will bring to the world the most beautiful and smartest children made out of soul's love and body's purity.

All his frustrations were not related to sexuality, everything was clear about that, he knew how fight those inner desires aroused when he got near one girl or another, quite rare moments though, he was fighting them as recommended by Saint John Climacus in his book "The Ladder of Divine Ascent" and, with the help of God, he was able to calm down, he would confess and communicate in the four fasting periods and he was interested only in the beauty of his inner life, but he did not accept these betrayals, this mockery that he got into due to naivety. The colleague from work was very annoyed by the fact that Rafael had not fallen for her, she was attracted to Rafael and she did not know why. It's true that Rafael was particularly handsome and well-knit, he had the figure of a strong, tall, blue-eyed, dark-haired man, with a white, milklike complexion. He looked like a real, but intangible man. And she did not have the slightest idea that he had had no relationship with any of her kind, furthermore, she thought he was some kind of a macho, who gets off with every lady he meets, and she felt some sort of frustration and spite for he had refused

her. She did not even suspect he was a virgin. She could not forgive him
for not having received her in his bed and for he had not come to her bed,
he had refused any intimacy with her.

Rafael used to dress very elegantly, he had expensive clothes, even
brand clothes and he was very stylish and refined, with a perfect haircut,
with a well-cared beard, when he had one, and very well shaved when
he was not wearing a beard, he used very fine fragrances, specially made
for smart and wealthy men, and he had class, he caught the eye instantly
when he walked through the door. His nicknamed at the company was
Alien due to his appearance and because he was often absent-minded. He
was respectable by the expensive simplicity of his clothes, as if he had been
working in a London firm, and by the loftiness of his figure and look. Some
women were shivering of pleasure when they saw him, but he remained
impassive to all these. Children used to call him Londonai in school, from
The London Eye, they said he was an eye coming from London judging
by clothes and his perfect English.

His pronunciation was impeccable, almost native. He was respectable
and, since he never spoke about any woman, they began to suspect that
he was gay. They all even gave him a fisheye due to his refusal to gossip
with them, they started to hate him with an unuttered hatred. During
discussions about women, he was the one who never spoke about that. He
stirred up the interest of his lady colleague in him, rather a mockery at him
for he would refuse to talk, but they all were seeing him as a lady's man, she
never suspected his purity of soul and the naivety of a man awaiting only
that intimate, mental and spiritual beauty called love, that force that binds
two people and they never grow apart. That was what Rafael expected to
get and experience, it was the force that brought him even closer to God.

People nowadays do nothing more but argue, despise each other, it's
a greedy fun made by one at the expense of the other, rather concerned to
betray as often as they can and, therefore, they always end up so lonely.
Rafael believed that the loneliness which does not destroy you is a good
and beautiful thing and it makes you strong.

The girl was holding a grudge against him and was angry because
Rafael had turned her down that way and she even hated him, she
considered him a fool and a redneck, a human being who could never be a
man since she, such a beautiful, perfect woman, la femme fatale, cannot get

his attention and he was not attracted to her. She felt like laughing at him, therefore she was teasing him, making all sorts of innuendos, she made him feel bad and Rafael was saying to himself "this is sexual harassment" and he would giggle by himself, but he considered them innocent jokes, sometimes he was going along and responded to instigations, an attitude that became the delight of colleagues who were waiting for something spicy. They sensed that something was or had been between them and were laughing behind their back, the two were constantly a gossip topic. Rafael was previously detested as they had suspected him of attraction to men, but now they backbit and bad-mounted him due to his lady colleague who was now playing Rafael's victim, when, in fact, she was the one who had turned him down. All of a sudden, Rafael was a charmer now. This time he had no idea though. He did not think that the girl was playing double role out of frustration, being the one who was judging and treating him that way, with so much contempt and disdain.

But Rafael had not turned her down, he was having pure, clean feelings for her, not physical attraction but something spiritual, but she cared less about his feelings and his body was attracting her like a magnet and that was why she was so uncomfortable when Rafael came around. It was true that she was having a boyfriend whom she had argued with and she was not too happy, she was suspecting her boyfriend of cheating, she was creating in her mind all sorts of scenarios and that was the reason why she would have wanted to retaliate somehow through Rafael, because she was not content with the one who did not want to marry her, but to stay together without any plans. Because marriage was not important to him as he was a modern man. She had said to herself that if she retaliated with the help of Rafael, she would restore her pride, but that didn't happen and now she was experiencing frustration and double disappointment and she was actually even more affected. Rafael, on the other hand, felt cheated and dishonored in his most salient and precious feelings, in his most beautiful ideals and in his beautiful, Christian lifestyle in the true sense of the word.

Eventually, Rafael realized that the woman wanted nothing but a love affair and his body and he suddenly felt like a soulless object and he was disgusted. He was feeling nauseous again, he was experiencing the indignation felt each time when someone wanted nothing but sex from him: "they want to hit on me just because I'm a good-looking guy to satisfy them, but, hey, am I a gigolo, a mating bull, well, this woman is not too smart if she thinks so, and why was she hitting on me if she already has a boyfriend, what does she want from me, what was her intention when she kissed me, she jumped on me, better say … … she wanted to touch me all over, but I stopped her, "wait, wait, take it easy, I said, you've seen too many movies, this is different." I took her out several times, what a fool I was, I'm sorry about the money spent at the restaurant, in Herastrau, near the lake, eating seafood, I will ask her for a refund, and Rafael burst out laughing loudly.

He was watching TV, but had no idea what was going on in the movie. He was analyzing his situation on thousands of sides. She was shouting to meddle, just for fun, to scoff at me. He wanted to go to her and ask her questions, to clarify things, to give him some explanations, but he thought he was so ridiculous, besides, he had gone through those sensations many times before and now he had been had one more time, because he was stupid, what could he do, beat those who treated him like a rich sex toy. You cannot beat them all, but at least one of them, and he burst into laughter again. This animal sex drive in women blocks and disgusts me. I can already see a whole battalion in their past who have slept with them. I am so disgusted that nothing, besides a prayer, can erase it.

Well, this is the biggest dishonor in the world, what, was he an animal, not even animals have such behavior. Why so much decay, how disgusting, a mediocrity of ugliness, decadent and disgusting feelings in this world, the sin of fornication is so ugly, and why is that, because I want to be with God and His commands? And, look, I'm not giving up, I'm stubborn enough to do that, who can stop me, no woman in this world can stand in my way.

People of this century have succeeded to destroy concepts such as family and love through this constant incitement to fornication and prostitution. But I don't give up. Where could so much lechery lead to if not dementia. A passage from the Bible came to mind. In fact, Potiphar's wife tried to seduce Joseph as well, and what did the poor boy do, he ran away naked leaving his clothes in her hands and he got to prison later on due to the woman who accused him of alleged attempt to seduce her. Some women and some men are really ridiculous and primitive, and what can I do, to forget, to clean myself of this mockery and this illness. Truly ugly, mediocre, decadent. Now, I would like to quote what I have heard from an older man: "What is permissible to the bull, is not permissible to the man." But this century is more decadent than that. Man's decadence, not even the bull can do, so low. What is permitted to man, not even the bull in its decadence can do. The man has gotten worse than the animal, we could say that what is permissible to man in his lechery is not permissible to the bull. Considering the the life of emperor penguins, I almost envy the penguins and I am sorry to be human, I am ashamed to be a human as compared to those royal animals.

Chapter 14

How derisive, how horrible, to be dragged like this into such prostitution vulgarism. You actually see them, people have something in their mind but you do not know what, you know nothing about their expectations. That woman wanted me to give her a night of love, to rock her world, while I wanted something good, true, eternal, coming from God. I bring God's name too much into this human cesspit. I'm looking for a woman to marry, not a mistress, what could I do with her, and that's exactly what she wanted, a loverboy, when she has arguments with her boyfriend or whoever she was with, I suspect she has more than one, all she could think in her little head is to come to me to fix her hormones, what am I, a gigolo. This is the biggest insult you can cause to a woman or a man, seeing him as a potential surrogate, as an object of your pleasure, does she think I am a male prostitute, a pleasure machine, does she think I am scallywag. I think this woman is not in her right mind, and how could I pray for her because I can't, I let her be. How could I pray, I feel like running away, not praying, perhaps when I am over it, she hurt me so much that I don't know how to get this harm out of me.

There are so many miserable women, not like this one. Many of them are divorced, the divorce rate is so high, and everything starts from sex, from pleasure, from the damn uncontrolled and incomprehensible state. Well, in this case, this physical pleasure is nothing but a drug, it's something harmful if it destroys your family, life, health, you always need to get the drug with someone else, so you don't go crazy. This is pure slavery. Could God have been so cruel to have put us in this salvery of physical pleasure and not being able to escape unless you get satisfied and the only solution is madness or cancer? Could it be? I don't believe that. This is human being's exaggeration. Can't they live without it? Check this out, they say that if you do not make sex, it will drive you mad, you'd better do some sport, go to the gym and work out, like me, until you get over it. How absurd, if you have nothing else to do and you keep thinking about that, of course you go mad, but if you think of God, you get over it.

Pray and the structure of your cell shall change, your body shall get modified by prayer, the pure thought from God cleanses the body of any tension. The sex strain disappears if you constantly pray and wait to get over it. You must not satisfy yourself in any way or catch some sexually transmitted diseases from a woman, all those who go to prostitutes have venereal diseases, they surely get infected. That's for sure. Whatever precautions you may take, if you play with poison, you will surely get poisoned, you will definitely make mistakes at least once and once enough it's enough to get AIDS.

You will not go mad, well, well, allegedly sex is a physical necessity, it is if you have produced and trained this necessity and you rack your brains all day about this, but if you have something else to do, you'll see that the need is not so strong. If you don't get aroused, it's easier to keep under control. This is the great gimmick of contemporary science, the same as the one with homosexuals. They allegedly have a gene I don't know where. They are like this because they want so and because the society instigates them to be as many as possible, this is corruption of morals and, therefore, you can be whatever crosses your mind, just pay your taxes to the state, that's all that matters. They have something special in their bodies, some genes that make them homosexual. Well, I don't care, it's their business, it's not normal to put them on the index, to kill them, to put them in prison, there has been a lot of injustice, but now, coming to the church so that the church calls them normal, it's far-fetched. This is utmost insolence, they want the church to stop being church and turn into a political party with a change of choice. If the Church no longer respects its ancient laws and keeps changing them, then it is a democratic state, not a church. If the church changes its laws as it pleases, it's no longer church, it becomes something else, none of the churches can do that. If it surrenders the principles revealed in the Bible, it's finished, it has been compromised forever in history, which will not happen unless they dissolve it altogether. But it will live in catacombs, they cannot dissolve it because they can't take Christ out of people's hearts.

Church's mission is to keep God's revealed laws alive in the history of mankind, which are unchanged. How can one falsify Leviticus? And that happens whether or not the world desires. What's so hard to understand? Why would you ask the church to change the law given by God? This is exactly what it's doing, it defends the law that you incriminate, it cannot remove a thousand-year old law from its structure, whether you like it or not. Go and run riot elsewhere, wherever you want, but not here. God's revealed laws in the Bible are unchanged, the church cannot change its laws depending on historical or political trends. If it does, it will be an ill turn, it dies. It's not a state institution, it's not a political party, it provides the one-way historical unity of the world, God. You can neither destroy something that has been lasting for two thousand years nor change it. Whoever tries is making a great mistake, because he will fight God himself, just like Nicodemus told the Jews when they were prosecuting Christ, or as Saint Paul said, "If I come myself to say that what I have preached is not right, you must not believe me."

Therefore, I do not deny this reality of the human being, because it is the only one that makes sense to me. Here I find salvation for my soul. I don't want to think about what the martyrs did to die for Christ, it's too hard for me and scary. But I continue this way and I do not give up. The good of mankind is here, in these truths revealed two thousand years ago. Ever since the Old Testament.

So, that's with the new theory that their body contains some sort of structure which allows them to be as they are. The purpose is to explain their passions. And another new theory, concerning sex, is that you have to make sex so you don't get cancer. If I take this seriously, it gives me the chills. There are women who have had normal sex life and got breast cancer, how about that? But if you live without love, don't you get cancer, don't you get depressed, don't you die, don't you get inner suffocation, how about sexually transmitted diseases? Nobody ever talks about love, everyone talks about sex, body, abuse, this body which is temple of the spirit. I give here the declaration of body rights and soul rights. Declaration of body rights: 1. the right to live in harmony with the soul, 2. the right to nutrition, 3. the right to morality, 4. the right to cleanliness, 5. the right to health, 6. the right not to be tainted by sex without love, 7. the right to rest, 8. The right to avoid excessive medication, 9. The right to respect for natural aging, 10. the right to live in harmony with nature, 11. the right to resurrection, 12. the right to not being hit, 13. the right to privacy, 14. the right to love in harmony with the soul, 15t. the right to harmony between marriage and love. Declaration of soul rights: 1. the right to love, 2. the right to prayer, 3. the right to learning, 4. the right to eternity, 5. the right to unlimited knowledge, 6. the right to perceive the infinite, 7. the right to dream, 8. the right to intuition, 9. the right to resurrection, 10. the right to live in harmony with the body, 11. the right to loneliness, 12. the right to friendship, 13. the right to saying yes or no, 14. the right to harmony between love and marriage, 15 the right to communication, 16. the right to thinking, 17. the right to creation, 18. the right to self-improvement, 19. the right to meditation, 20 the right to spiritual food.

I want to love with that passion given by God to people to experience, prostitution is useless to me. Courts for violation of body rights should be established similar to the courts for human rights violations. Oh, so many people would come here. How could the spirit live in a temple dirty with passions, agonized by lechery. What is sex without love, a great frustration, a huge void and a death-like desert, human soul's lack of beauty and grace and a lack of human dignity, a different death of the soul. Sex without love is a vice and vice leads to self-destruction, it's like a tank filled with thousands of tons of fuel that you set on fire to burn, it gets re-filled and you set it on fire again, and it gets re-filled and you set it on fire again and so, until you run out of energy in your body and you go strengthless like a dry leaf in the wind. And these are not my ideas, but so many philosophers and saints, so many people have always condemned the exact issues that we claim nowadays on the streets that are good and, above all, by the laws of science, by specialists in our laws. This is ideology, not science.

Lord, Mother of God, these people now claim that Christ's words are a great deception, that God's words preached through the commandments of Moses are fallacy. If you tell them about the Ten Commandments, they burst out laughing, but they don't know that the Ten Commandments mean total freedom in this world. So, let's recap what they say: if God said 'you shall not commit adultery', he was wrong. They claim nowadays that if one does not have sex, one could go mad, get cancer. Now, if you use the word fornication, you are primitive, you are no longer up-to-date, if you do not have sex, you go mad, meaning that if you do what God told you to do, you are crazy and you will become mad because you will lose your mind anyway, meaning that God gave us commandments contrary to our lives, therefore, God is not good. We have come to think so due to our sin, due to our alienation from God. I feel like shouting and yelling like Jesus, as He said that we are mean and we are blind even if we have eyes to see. I feel like repeating "Lord Jesus Christ, the Son of God, the right mind of those who are pure in virginity."

It means that God's word is wrong and what they say is true. What did that woman want from me, to sleep with her, I haven't lost my mind, if I had done that, I wouldn't have been able to communicate, I would have been away from church and God, I wouldn't have been able to worship, I would have betrayed God for some instincts, I would have felt guilty before Jesus and I would have had nobody to come back to, I would have had nobody to talk to. I may even have catched some venereal diseases. I don't want to have these feelings of betrayal to God and to my pledges, I want to be like Joseph, I don't want to betray God, I can see when people betray me, how bad it is, how hidous betrayal is. Well, my betrayal and my promiscuity are much greater and uglier to God. I don't want to be like Judas. In fact, as the people betray me, so I betray God, I'd better stick to my prayer. The words of Jesus about what a man's life are so beautiful that I want to be as He said. I wish this with all my heart.

What was that woman thinking, had I satisfied her with multiple orgasms, wouldn't she have left me to go back to her partner, they do not have a limit when it comes to sex, they can't help it, I would have been the big fool who was paying her attention. They allegedly want you to sleep with them on the first date so they see if you are good and, afterwards, they will see if they come back to you because they have no time to lose, and if they get to love, but that never happens because there is no such thing, whoever is thinking about love when it comes to sex. They examine you, they try you, like a dryer, like a pair of socks. What if love is not reached, but who said anything about love? Another one on the list, we're splitting up, farewell, we're trying first. This is pure illness! I mean, my soul is like a sock; I'd better not have such a thing. I mean, let's see if he fits me, if not, I'll throw him to the garbage, he's not good, and we pass each other in the street, as if we had never met."

Rafael gazed in front of him and saw the woman, in his imagination, like in the moment when she told him she had a boyfriend. Sadness overtook him instantly. When you think he was about to tell her that he was in love with her and, at least, he had solved the entire mystery. He was seeing her as a thief who had stolen something very expensive and dear from him and had thrown it into the fire, just for the mere pleasure of doing harm, of stealing. His soul hurt and tears started rolling down his cheeks and he kept crying until he got a headache, but at least he let it all off. He couldn't believe that the woman was so infamous, all she wanted was his body. If I'm a handsome man, does it mean that I am for sale to any woman who lays eyes on me, am I the pleasure of a woman or several women or men. When he mentioned that, he suddenly remembered that a male colleague, who was gay and had left the company, had hit on him once. He had grabbed his ass, when they were alone, he punched that man immediately, fast, in the first second, when he had touched him, that Rafael still felt his fist tight and tense and felt like throwing up. No one has ever suspected him of being gay ever since. His colleague had his face all bruised up for a month or so, he had hit him hard, his hand was big and heavy, strong, he had muscles from the gym, his new colleague was impressed by his manhood, but he had no idea about what was awaiting him. Rafael suspected him, he realized the guy was from the other world by the way he was fawning like a dog. Though the others were avoiding him subtly, rejecting him tacitly, he behaved normally with him, pretending he didn't understand anything, without any inhibitions, saying, "I won't intrude, it's not my business, it's God's work to judge, I must follow Christ. As long as he leaves me alone, I don't mind, I cannot change the world, everyone has to change himself. "And the guy understood from Rafael's natural and normal behavior that it was possible, until he got knocked down. They were alone in the office, and the guy sprang into action... he received such a strong punch from Rafael that he was thrown up against the wall. When he remember that, as he was so upset, because that's how things go, one bad one brings on another, his stomach started aching and he felt like throwing up. "Oh, Lord, I go through such ordeals in this world, I believe today's people are crazy, they are as you said, Lord," fools and blind ", I can't stand these people anymore. I want to get out of this world, where to go, where to go, I don't want to see that woman again, in fact, what happens if I see her, now she seems like a cloth, faded, lacking strength and intelligence, heartless. Oh, and in was seeing her in such colors, I even wrote poems about her, how ridiculous, I can't take them back now, I leave them like that. I was seeing her so beautiful, it's true that she's beautiful, she's very smart, she has money, she has her own house, her car, expensive clothes, she goes to Vienna during the discounts period to buy shoes and clothes. She's stylish, I must admit. I wouldn't go there to buy clothes, as if I hadn't found cheap and good things. I buy my brand clothes here.

I cannot believe that people are so small, so wretch, some, not all, so mercantile, in fact, what's the use of so much opulence, so much money, so many expensive things that we put on? I use pretty expensive clothes as well, I can't just dress like redneck, but still, I must also focus on other things besides that, not just being concerned with my body satisfaction. I feel humiliated, offended, trampled on, in my dignity as a Christian man who wants to be with Christ, not with those little people who follow their instincts. Stop boasting, I thought. It's true that I boast, but I am also sad in my manly pride. In fact, that thing with the instinct is like a TV commercial, it suits the people in these ads, "follow your instincts, follow your thirst," yeah, be animal, drink until you drop."

That was a commercial promoting a soft drink, but, in fact, the subliminal message was different, a commercial telling you to live your life instinctively bears a sexual message, according to Freud. Fancy that, for these people nowadays living your life means having as many women as possible, countless, and I can't believe when I hear them saying such a thing, as if I were from a different world. I know it, I have heard that many times, but I have never been more confused than now, that is living your life means having as much sex as possible. You have many women, much wealth, you take advantage of this moment, of whatever life offers you now, you take full advantage of everything. Okay, okay, but how about tomorrow, what will you do tomorrow? This is the attitude of uncle Gheorghe, it's his dream, the dream of the drunkard from the pub, who sits and watches TV and nothing else, he makes the pub sales grow, it's a primitive attitude, it's not the attitude of a man who thinks and makes long-term life projects. If you refer to life as a finite and marginal thing that results from limited moments, surely, the best attitude is to live your life and do that to the fullest, to have whatever you want right now, because who knows what could happen tomorrow. However, this short term carpe diem thing can be an alternative for a man on the brink of death, he still wants something in this world so that he won't die with an unfulfilled wish. Or, if you are young and you have the entire life ahead of you, why would think on such a short-term, you see life from different perspectives and this attitude, namely that you need it now because anything could happen tomorrow, is so restrictive, God, you don't care if you are strong, the saying becomes a stupidity, you just want to have many things in the long run, but that reduces you to nothing, at some point, it sows the seeds of death in you and the idea that the end of life could happen anytime, this is highly destructive. This is the attitude and thinking of an old man, not a young man. You are old from the very beginning if you are guided by the expession "live the moment".

And it's even more painful if you want to know and grow. If you relate to God and know that life does end now, you have nothing to do with such a matter, which only lasts for a few moments, you need something durable which does not change, you need something unlimited to lay the foundation, to last, to be stable, similar to the base you want to build something else just as durable, as this is the foundation of your own evolution and not live the moment to run away. What can you do with things or states or people or feelings that last so little and are so insignificant? You are the only one who gives too much importance to useless things". Rafael stopped his train of thoughts and went to put some tea.

In fact, the two mutually rejected as they had nothing to do with each other. There was nothing but a clash of two strong characters and two ever more powerful egos. Anyway, each one gained something, they were gossiped about at the company for a while, after which no one suspected them of anything, everyone was received and adopted as trustworthy.

Rafael was laying down in the armchair, listening to classical music, ready to type, with the computer in front of him, thinking about what to write and considering these states of indignation against the times he was living, he was breaking completely free from the lost love. Even though he was still unable to break loose from the woman he had fallen in love with without realizing, almost unnoticeably, and still feeling one disappointment after another, thinking that there had been nothing of what he could have possibly imagined to be, since he had no idea while staring at the computer, he decided to go to sleep. Tomorrow is another day. He turned everything off and went to sleep, a long, deep, restful, dreamless sleep. He was reborn, he was fresh the following day.

Chapter 15

In one of these barrelhouses of lust where people spend money and life, Mihai, with his employees, goes to have fun, to escape his obsessions, to forget about what he had at home and inside his soul. It was a very large bar in Bucharest's old town which has all sorts of strange places, with truly vicious people who attended the areas of decadence. He went there for one night only, but there were some toxic places in the area where serious money had to be paid for a coffee or an exotic drink. They came across an alley, went down that alley which had tables and all sorts of people standing and smoking one cigarette after another, having cheap beers in front of them, the tables were full of young men, women, usually men who had nothing to do with their lives but spend their money and savings or who spent it out of boredom, because they could not think or feel to do anything better for them.

Mihai hadn't been in such places for a long time, since college, when he was lady's man, he used to buy drinks for everyone. He suddenly felt young again. He had no more worries. He wanted to sit at one of the dirty tables, but the two young men said:

-Boss, we can't stay here, it's ugly and it's too cheap, thugs and opportunists come here, racketeers, we go somewhere else, where it's high-class, for us. If we stay around here, there's a bad smell of urine, those people go to relieve themselves wherever they get, from booze. "The primitive commune is here", Mihai thought. They don't have other place to go, the employee continues, they are not allowed in pub's toilets, they are known for their filth. Some of them are too lazy to go to the outside toilet as they are too drunk, these terraces are the filthiest, if we stay longer, all kinds of pimps will come to tell they want to give us some women and we don't need to be tackled like this, like second-hand human traffickers, with less money. We go some place where it's more expensive and fewer people, less exposure, some place for us. He bloated in his mind, "just wait and see the look on their faces when they'll see that I bring them a big fish, I bring them the boss" and laughed with satisfaction.

-Ok, guys, let's go where you want, show me what you know about this hidden Bucharest and about nightclubs, because I have no idea about such an important thing in a European capital like Bucharest. I used to know many such barrelhouses when I was in Iasi, but I haven't been curious to see how things are here because I already know what it is. I can see that things are quite similar here, people's faces are same. Equally destroyed by indifference and alcohol.

Mihai burst out laughing. Poor people dressed badly, who were leaning over the draft beer and holding a cigarette, as if you were in a madhouse, something specific to the poor and fallen man in the third millennium, the primitive era of the third millennium, and these people have been living here in downtown for a long time, others maybe just come here. They have always lived there and, even if they stay downtown, they barely have money to live, but they drink, this is the vice of the century, they drink and smoke all the money they have, and those who have wife and children, though few still have such a thing, don't give any money to their family, poor woman, because that man barely has the money to drink. Such barrelhouses are everywhere in Romania, I believe that some similar ones are also in other countries, just a bit more stylish.

But Mihai seems to disregard these appearances, he had something in his mind that he wanted to forget, to escape from and he even succeed. They walked carefully along that alley so they would not get dirty or step on syringes of drug addicts, a church was to the left, crammed between apartment buildings as Causescu used to do, he used to hide churches behind buildings so they be out of sight, so was this one, with scrawled walls, even dirty words written on it, but they had been scraped, probably by the priest who served there, so that the writing would no longer be legible. Mihai had also seen such vandalism on church walls in Venice, so he was not appauled, he thought it was normal here in Romania where many people seem to care less about religion. Even the cattle have a certain ritual of their life, when the cow and the sheep go to sleep, they make a sign similar to the sign of the cross on the straw bedding, that's what the granny told me, but the human being, such a shame of so much decadence in the full era of technology and boom of scientific discoveries.

Looking back we can say that humanity has evolved so much, it's like a miracle, but, morally, we seem to be in the primitive commune when people used to live in caves, although I believe that men did not leave their babies and wives so easily back then, even if they would go work elsewhere. He felt the need to go somewhere else, but he gave up the idea and Mihai followed the lead of his employees. During the night, church surroundings were a place of depravity and prostitution, of gangs, discotheque, decadence, because everything was out-of-sight, just like the church was out-of-sight, and they would go wild since they could not be seen from the street as they were surrounded by apartment buildings. During daytime, people would come here to pray. It seemed to be Satan's work that luxury bars, cabaret, pimps, drugs were right near the church because the land in the city center was very valuable and expensive, it had to be used to the maximum at any cost and everyone did exactly what he wanted and what or how he could, nothing else mattered, just to make much money.

They arrived at a better venue after crossing the alley on the other side, right across the street, it was a very stylish location on Victoria street. Some sophisticated, very expensive rails with some sort of red carpet plunging down to the sidewalk invited them to show them downstairs, to the basement, a sign saying 'Cabaret' being placed above. Mihai's eyes started glowing just like in his youth, he suddenly understood where his so-called employees, who seemed quite unadventurous guys, were taking him.

Mihai asked them as they went down the stairs, because the venue was, and everything was going on, in a huge basement, and, from the inside, you had to go up some escalators to various rooms and to upper floors, it was a real fortress with the message 'strictly confidential'. Mihai started whistling and thought "can you imagine if the police come here with dogs, appearances can be deceiving," and growled as if he had made quite a discovery and said loudly:

-Do you come here often, guys? What a luxurious place, the owner must have made some investment here!

-But he's also making a profit!

-Not necessarily, he's the only one who knows what the real gains are.

-Eh, boss, you're asking us how many times a week or a month we come here, because it's the place where we have fun at night, especially on weekends, all we need is money, that's how things are, the fun comes at a price.

"Where's my money going," Mihai thought, full of disgust.

Immediately after they started going down the stairs the smoke grew thicker and they could hear music turned up to the max that people could hardly understand each other's words, and the lights, which were controlled from a server somewhere, were flashing and swirling in tens of colors creating the feeling of dizziness, the noise was unspeakable, the ideal fun venue for people who earned above-average montly income, as well as for those who earned less and came here to spend all the money earned in one month, just to brag. Mihai looked around and saw that the place was offering everything that means fun and pleasure to the fullest, all you need is a strong body to bear all these. He saw that the basement of an apartment building built in the Ceausescu style was so smartly set up, renovated that, besides being a huge space, it was well partitioned, with dancing floors, hotel-like fun rooms for girls, with numbers, with blonde chicks queueing up to be seen and bought by those who were paying them and got heated up, with a stage in the back where the girls were pole dancing showing everything, there was another stage for men, or male and female dances were performed alternatively "The pole dancers are slaves", thought Mihai, and everyone is showing whatever has for sale in the body, everyone is selling himself as a commodity. The strangest smells of smoke and aphrodisiac scents were coming from a corner and Mihai gathered that those who intended to take drugs could go there.

He headed to their corner and saw those laying on sofas and armchairs as they were high and shouting all sorts of strange words seeming like the dead of Dante's hell. They almost passed out from so many drugs. Freedom is atroceous, Lord! Mihai was getting dizzy and suddenly felt an uncontrolled desire emerged from the depths of his subconscious, similar to hypnosis, to take drugs, at least to smoke a cigarette, as he used to, just a little. But, all of a sudden, somebody else seemed to be screaming inside him: "Are you mad, do you want to destroy yourself altogether, you're not like these losers who have no money, you have a company, you have a prosperous business, do you want to end up in the street like a beggar, do you want to mess your head up, you have a child to raise! Hm ... child ... a dead child. Hello ... what kind of happiness do you want to experience, you'd better take one of these whores and have fun with her, it's a lesser evil rather than getting high, do you want to lose your mind. No, no, no drugs, no, especially since I know how it is, I know from college, you feel so sick afterwards that you'd rather die", and he was suddenly disgusted and a strange desire overwhelmed him, he had the impulse to go away, to spit, to run away, but something stronger than him, like a demon, stopped him. He went to take a look at the twenty girls waiting for their luck to be bought for the whole night or for a few hours and he didn't like any of them. They all inspired him revulsion and contempt, he asked the price for one night and was amazed how expensive this fun was and turned nose up, and the pimp said to him derisively:

-We have maximum fun here, but you have to pay big money, it's a bit expensive, boss, of course, but you also pay for the fact that we keep the secret, and laughed just as derisively.

Mihai wanted to say something or ask something the two employees who had accompanied him, but lost sight of them, he looked for them but couldn't find them, he had the urge to leave, but sat down in an armchair by himself and ordered something to drink amid that uproar. He had some drinks and, when was drunk enough, one of the girls who hadn't been picked up by men decided to try her luck, went to him and sat down in his lap, she did what she did, Mihai gave up and took her to one of the rooms specially prepared for such things. He had been chased for a long time, but he had no idea about that.

Chapter 16

He woke up the next morning with a hangover, in an unknown bed, alone, and managed to remember what had happened. He turned the light on and the room he woke up into was of unprecedented, unseen luxury, mirrors made of the most expensive, eye-catching crystal, curtains made of the most expensive silk, the room seemed to be that of a sultan or prince, he felt like in a tale, in another world where the money-giving pleasure gave him the illusion of one-night happiness. He put his clothes on and, when he was all dressed, the girl whom he had spent the night before and who had brought him there asked him to give her some money, he took all the money from his pocket and handed it to her without any reserve, he hugged her, kissed her and promised he would come again. He had no more money left, but he had the credit card to pay the huge price for happiness, pleasure and fun of the cigarette smoke moment. The girl was holding so much money in her hands that she wondered about her luck that night without doing anything. The client had been so drunk that all he could do was to fall asleep.

Mihai looked at his watch and could not believe how late it was. He regained his senses when he got home, he realized what he had done, and he got drunk to get rid of laziness and pain, he fell again into a dreamless sleep while watching TV. He spent Sunday at home without going out, he hoped that Maria might come over, but she didn't. He had some more drinks, phoned a catering service to bring him a copious lunch, he ate, then threw everything into the trash bin, he got drunk again, watched TV until he fell asleep and woke up on and off. Sunday night passed and Monday morning came.

The next morning he went straight to the company where the two employees were waiting for him, without any hint, any smile, or any caprice that they knew anything, everything was kept in silence and secret which amazed Mihai and he respected them for that. The next day's work went perfectly as if Mihai's life was having a new turn, his life took a new direction and went straight ahead, giving signs that he did not want to look back anymore. He would have wanted to wipe off everything he had lived so far, as if in the mere ten-year period he had lived and experimented something, got to a new level and he wanted to be a new person now, a new, important man, with his own secrets and privacy which no one would know about. To become, why not, the richest man in Romania, by any means, it did not matter.

Towards the evening, he had a strange reaction to his two employees who had taken him to that venue, he dismissed them without any explanation and paid them for three months in advance so they can find work elsewhere and, thus, he got rid of those who could have suspected his way of life, the way he would have liked to have fun from then on.

Mihai put an end to a period of his life and considered that all the people from his past were dead, he didn't want to hear about them anymore, all that mattered to him were his money, his company, the business and contracts he was signing, and the expensive escapades he had in the ultra-secret brothels of the Bucharest nightlife or from somewhere else.

Chapter 17

Once, he left with some friends to a party, he was making friends ad-hoc, friends from the pubs he went to, he met them and chatted for hours in the dead of the night. He would always go to the old town of Bucharest, which is full of barrelhouses located in basements, he would go in and see all sorts of decadents who spent their money on everything that was most expensive for them, drinks and cigarettes, and they mimicked in their dances the ugliest and most obscene aspects in the appearance of a man, and Mihai encouraged them, he would give them money to go on the loose in front of him and he would have fun seeing their looseness, a grotesque circus paid by him, and he did that only once or twice a month, until he got tired and bored with this rubbish, he was considering other types of fun but he couldn't think of anything he liked and came back home and got drunk, and the following day, even if he was having a hangover, he eventually managed to be in the best shape for his firm. Eventually, he gave up such parties. Women were the best fun, altogether, the ones he had met or the ones would meet. He used to call two or three women he already knew in his villa at the same time and they were having the most terrible orgy one could imagine, as in Sodom and Gomorrah. He did all these constantly until he forgot that he had a child in hospital or a wife he had left. His main concerns were the company and the money he was supposed to make, the development of his firm and the most profitable collaborations with foreigners. He realized that the West considered Romania nothing more but an outlet market, therefore, he had to be the best salesperson and exploit best this situation and he kept searching for all sorts of strategies.

But let's go back to the party in one of his evenings. Apparently, human sins are the same in all times, debauchery is identical, nothing has changed in this area, the world we live in can be changed by the good imposed by the bright minds, but who can understand that. They were having a drink and discussed all sorts of things from politics to dirty and horrible jokes, from movies with murderers and busting bones to unimaginable violence, to horror movies that could mess up your brain, or porn movies, when the bartender told Mihai:

-If you don't mind, the bar is closing, it's 2 a.m. and we only have license to operate until this hour. If you want to stay longer, until 5 o'clock in the morning, we expect you tomorrow night and Sunday night because we can be open all night long then. Thank you very much for spending your time with us and we expect you some other time. Please again do not be upset with us, but these are the conditions and we can't do otherwise because the police will come and will give us fine.

This was owner's speech who was looking forwad to get rid of the revellers who had had fun and didn't want to leave. But the pub was really closing and the owner, a young man aged about thirty, could hardly wait to go home and tuck in with his wife, because he was extremely tired and the employees were also tired of asking clients who didn't want to leave the venue.

Who could have been in the group of revellers but Mihai, who was holding a woman he had just picked up from the bar, he doesn't know how to got her, but that was not important because he had already gone back in time in his mind, he was no longer the boss of his company, with so important things to solve, but he was the twenty-year-old youngster who was a student at whatever college and would spend his nights in pubs. Oh, it's been so long since he had done such things, so many years, he seemed rejuvenated, because he was already feeling very old with all his problems and these were the best ways to get over them, alcohol and women.

And that girl was unhappy in her way, neither she had any idea how she ended up with Mihai in her arms, they liked each other from the first moment and neither of them asked any questions, who was he or what did he want, but she realized that he was a rich guy and she was going to have pretty good time that night and, later on, she would decide whether she would meet him again or not. She was alone, she had just come out of a divorce and she came into a pub to forget about her pain, to listen to music and stare at the walls or talk to someone or even pick someone up as she hadn't done that for quite some time. She believed that was the solution to her problems and that was what happened. Anyway, she had had a shot of vodka, she got pretty tipsy, but she sobered up in the meantime and could walk by herself. Mihai, on the other hand, could hardly stand on his feet. He was with a company employee, a thirty-year-old youngster, who was quite miserable and didn't know how to get over it, so his solution was also alcohol and night bars. Mihai, even if intoxicated, it didn't mean he was not conscious, he was tipsy and he was feeling good, the problem was that he kept remembering what he had, he remembered that obsessively, he could not speak up, and said to himself:

"Look whom I have at the company, I had no idea he was a frequent client of bars and used to trust him, you can't trust such a person, I shouldn't become too close to him, not because he wouldn't do his job properly, but he could do some idiocy anytime." A group of ten people was sitting at their table, they met that night, because each one had come with one or several friends and bonded there. When they left, they went through the door and passed the bar on their way out but, imagine that, the waitress who was in charge with their drinks cried out:

-Hey, hey, why are you leaving, you haven't paid the bill, please pay up.

They all looked amazed, stunned, confused that they were caught in red-handed and they turned their eyes to Mihai. He started yelling:

-Guys, haven't you paid for your drinks, awful, very awful, it's the first time that something like that happens to me, it's my fault I left that way.

-You pay, Mihai, you pay, said a few voices.

-Let me pay, I'm buying, how much is the bill? Mihai paid for everything and the others thanked him servilely, like some dogs under the table of their master, just like in his good times when he used to be a student and went to bars and bought drinks for everybody, as he was having money from his parents. Those from the bar were jumping up for joy as they had fooled him, Mihai paid triple the bill, ha ha ha.

They walked away from the pub which was just closing and Mihai insisted to the girl who was with him and his employee:

"Let's go some place else, let's continue the party, I don't feel like going home, I know a bar where we can stay as long as we want because it's open around the clock.

-Yes, boss, we'll go wherever you say.

And he spent that night like many other nights, until one day when he realized that, if he went on like that, he would go bankrupt.

The company needed him entirely, in his right mind, not half or a quarter.

Chapter 18

Maria was always crying and was sad because it had been some time since Mihai had stopped by her, by the hospital and she didn't know what was going on with him, she went home a few times and felt some strange odors, mixtures of smoke, ladies' perfume, alcohol and when she looked at Mihai, he treated her like a stranger, he gave her a frenzy-like look, as if his eyes were shouting at her to leave, to vanish and a sword thrust her heart. He had an ugly, doubtful, faded, frowning face which seemed darkened by something dirty. He did not pay any attention to her and he went out the door very quickly without telling her good bye, without saluting her, without kissing her, he treated her as if she had not been in that room, as if she had been invisible. When alone in the house, Maria started shaking and fell nearly senseless on the carpet. She was struck by such aloofness from Mihai, as if the spirit of death was pointing at her and coming between them. Maria felt like throwing up, a knot settled in her stomach and has never left her since then.

She was spending time at the hospital, then at the firm, she tried to call Mihai several times a day but he didn't answer the phone, she lied to herself thinking he was busy with the company, and the phone was turned off in the evening, he was nowhere to be found when she stopped by their house. However, she went there one morning to catch him at home, she found him lying on the bed, seeming disfigured by bad dreams, she wanted to tell him something and got the same reaction, silence, rejection, she no longer existed, he said no word, she came towards him, calling his name, crying: "Mihai, Mihai, what's with you, what's with us, why don't you talk to me?" He suddenly grabbed her and she didn't put up any resistance, he madly started to undress her brutally, lay her naked on the bed and possessed her with an animality and anger that Maria had never seen in him, as if they were two beasts and she got stabbed.

She was petrified. After taking his breath, he took a shower, got dressed and left without saying a word, all in a gloomy muteness.

Maria was glad for the moment of pleasure consumed between them, she hoped that everything was good and it would go away, but something froze her heart, her soul, she was lying on the bed, staring and having no more tears to cry. It was as if their love had ended and all they had left was only this physical attraction turned into something so ugly, even diabolical. She had the feeling that they were dead for each other, that their love was gone forever. He hadn't even looked at her when they were making love, as if they were two bodies without faces, hiding from each other so they wouldn't see, wouldn't look in each other's eyes, their kisses seemed to be the bites of two soulless bodies or two dead souls. The man she loved to self-oblivion shut himself down and became mute for her, living a slow disappearance like moving away to the horizon until you no longer see him. He got into the SUV without saying a word and vanished, seeming to be walking out on her for good.

When she returned the following day hoping that a miracle could happen between them and everything was like in the beginning, she couldn't open the door to get in the house, the lock had been changed along with the entire door, she called his number, but nothing, she sent text messages, nothing, not a word, no explanation, as if she were a stranger to him, a nobody, a death-like nothingness. When she went home to open the door, she was determined to wait for him until his return. When she saw she couldn't open and get in, she leant against the door for two hours until she came to herself, she couldn't believe what she was going through, she felt she was pulled out of her world with such brutality, in a deep, tense silence, with hatred, desperation, trembling from her frayed nerves strung out like metal ropes girdling her brain and skull she was about to go off, she felt she was losing her mind, that she was in a hell-like horror movie and she will never get out of there. Everything was like a disappearance, like death, without any explanation, any word, he wanted to leave, to disappear and he also wanted her to leave, to disappear, to vanish from his life. She and her child, but why, what did she do wrong, what was her sin before him, just because she, better say they had together a sick child, who doesn't get better after one year of surgery and treatment, and he is leaving her so brutally, horribly, primitively, like an animal, without words, without anything, why, why, why, what did she do wrong, she couldn't be blamed for everything that had happened. All she could do was cry in front of the door until she passed out and what would she solve if she passed out, nothing. It seemed to be night although it was in the middle of the day. She understood that Mihai is breaking off with her for good, that he doesn't want to see her again, that he chose to separate from the two, just so, because he felt like it, because that was normal for his way of thinking, because that's how he felt comfortable, to know nohing of them two, who were lost, sick and destroyed by suffering.

She and their little baby connected to medical equipment had to go on. There was no way back and they had to live. Period. With or without Mihai. But she had no idea how he had chosen to live his life, about the decadent ragtags he had chosen to spent his nights with, about the losers and scoundrels he had gathered around him. And when you think that Maria had put her entire happiness and her whole life in him, and what she was doing now, she was lying down on this cold pavement in front of the door, at her billion-dollar villa she could no longer use because it wasn't hers anymore although she had invested there all her money, all her work and life so far, and her money saved for their happiness. He didn't even allow her to take her things. She knew she would have to go back to her mother and stay at the apartment, to be strong there, to cry, to let off and fight this obsession which is worse than soul cancer, that death, because she was experiencing death in the true sense of the word, brain death, death of heart and soul, and why was that, for the man she had loved and she had given everything to.

But isn't this love, total sacrifice, total dedication, isn't that what makes you be like God?

Chapter 19

She stood there leaning against the door of the villa she had won by the sweat of her brow, because they had made the money together to buy it, they had both borrowed the money from the bank and paid the bills, why would he ban her from entering the house, that was her house, too. She was staying there, squatting against the door of the house, staring, she couldn't believe such a thing was happening to her. That Mihai had gone through such a major change in just a few months, as if he had become another man and another person. How could he have treated her that way, the man she had loved, how could he have changed so much and not come over to see his child. That was animalic, subhuman, she could not admit such a thing, how could he lock the door and not let her get inside the house. He had changed the door entirely since she didn't come home because she was staying at the hospital, and what had he done, who was staying in her home, she once saw a pair of panties and a bra thrown around on the carpet but she thought they were hers, though she didn't remember buying such expensive underwear, but she thought she may have forgotten, but the idea that those things belonged to another women didn't even cross her mind. She seemed to understand everything now, his silence, he had someone else, but why would he treat her like that, with no word, that silence burns like hell. Why, because he's feeling guilty, but why feel guilty. Yes, he had betrayed her and left her in the most terrible moments and she had make a mistake because she was putting all her despair on him and all they would do was fight, because he had some sort of hatred, loathing at the child who had been born so sick and had taken away their happiness.

Mihai thought he had the right to be happy considering he was working so much. Maria thought what a woman is going through when making an abortion. She had seen a bunch of documentaries with the fetus drawing back from doctor's knife inside mother's belly and trying to avoid to get killed until the doctor reaches him with the knive and the fetus dies. There are several-month old babies who already have a face and they are thrown out, they are killed, Maria thought that was exactly what Mihai was doing, killing his child, aborting the child from his life, from his body like those women who kill their infants, she suddenly becoming the baby from mother's belly ready to be killed and living this imminent death.

There is no difference, because we, beside the body, also have this entity called soul which makes the experience even more terrifying, the separation and death perceived at its level are much stronger than at the level of epidermis. Maria stood by her door like a beggar, in her own yard, in her own house, when the one she loved became the killer of her life, the one who killed her, killed her love, her life, her thoughts, her hopeless days and nights beside her child. All those had died because they no longer had any reason to exist. Because all she could live was death. What could lack of love be but a slow cancer that eats you inside, a cancer of the soul, what could this destruction and disappearance of love be if not a form of death, and this death is so tough and unbearable at a subtle level, in this state of consciousness called soul combined with our need for love, with this need for love and beauty without which we become dead, stiff, robot-like, without which life is narrower and more destroying with all its nonsense, and, from this point forward, the no-return direction called destruction, decline, death, beggary, promiscuity and, eventually, the daily prostitution we live in.

Mihai was living his life and he saw this as liberation, he had loved and died at the end of the love that he refused to live any longer, that deliberate inability to fight to be whatever you have to be, namely human being in the world, seemed like a suicide. The freedom and joy of the lecherous who ceases to have any holy thing is a state of cowardice in front of life. Do you know which is the paradox of the one who cheats, who lives this death, inflicting so much suffering on the other, worthy of courts of humanity, courts that do not exist but which should be. All the ones who cause suffering to those whom they once said they loved should be held accountable. And, most of all, that person also inflicts suffering on others whom he does not think of. You inflict pain but you cannot control the extent of that suffering you have generated and the number of people you have destroyed. But Mihai and those like him do not think about that. The greatest sin and the greatest crime on Earth is this attitude of a father who dissapears from his children's lives as if he had never existed. This is the cancer of the society we are heading to and we're living into. Increasingly more women and men and children live without the love of those who have given them birth, and why? Why, why God, so much death, such indifference, so much betrayal and so much suffering just for the concept of freedom. Freedom is not above the pain caused, just because you are free to do that.

Crouching down, leaning against the locked door, Maria started to develop the self-defense instinct, to sharpen and grow like a protective tree, pointing her back to this cataclysm.

When love is traded for sex and marriage for fun and one-night stand or one-day, one-week or several-month affair, love doesn't matter anymore, it becomes a street name or a newspaper headline. This is the darkest age we are going through, when more and more children are killed before being born and a growing number of those who are born get abandoned. In the past, boys would die in wars and girls lived alone, mothers would bring up their children on their own and lead their lives in indigence. They would die in wars back then and now they abandon their children willingly. Statistics are horrendous. What hatred, what passion lies inside the human being that makes it live life in the death of love, and all this before the great God which is the true love and eternal life. The man stands with his back to God and looks in the dark while the light of God is everywhere.

What kind of world are we heading to? To one of death and despair? There is only one attitude. The chance and salvation of the one who is defeated by neighbor's monstrosity is Christ, the light and self salvation are and come through Him.

Maria, after going dizzy and numbed in front of the locked door from her own house, perfectly understood that Mihai had returned to his former self, the one in the past, and realized he had taken to the road to perdition, but she didn't know how, a path of no return, with death as his only escape. He had turned into her greatest enemy.

She was disgusted at that house, at their wealth, his and hers, she was disgusted at so much fortune, so much wasted money which was of no help for them. Oh, but that money would have been so important if he had struggled to transfer the child to a clinic abroad, but he wouldn't care less, saying it was useless. She would have been able to sell her villa just to get her child well, she trusted doctors in Romania, doctors whom she understood and who behaved so nicely with her, who were healing some of her wounds. The thought that she could go to another country was terrifying. She had a feeling of despair, suffocation, as if she was gasping for air, like she was dying and fainting there in front of her door, behind a fence, built up so no one could see inside. An endless loneliness filled her heart.

And, after she got over the crisis, she came to her feet slowly, smoothly, barely managing to stretch her legs, her head was spinning and she propped against the door, her tears were coming down, she has been crying quietly that her clothes were soaked all over her chest, but it didn't matter anymore, she could cry and let it all out, and leaning against the wall she took one step, then another one, as if her steps were taking her one hundred years away from that place, time was expanding, dilating, fading away, as if she was vanishing from that place for good, it was a place that had never deserved her. She slowly recovered to her senses, she took another step, and so on, until she reached the gate, opened it, went out the gate, closed it behind her and she had the feeling she would never return there in her life. She got on the backseat of her car, closed the doors so no one could see her through car's tinted windows, lay down facing up, raised her arms as if clinging on God and heaven and let the tears roll down until she fell unconscious. She cried until she passed out. After regaining her senses, she started praying with some white, redeeming, powerful tears, which, though burning her face, chest, cheeks, lips, hands, reminded her that she had just overcome the most difficult moments, the toughest test for her, but she still has one more, the child, she had the feeling that the child will live, she was sure at that moment of awakening, of revelation, of power, terrible loneliness, that she and her God will breal through and her child, who is hers alone, shall not die, he will live and she must live for Gabitu, who is only hers and, as he is named after an Archangel, he will be more powerful in life and will survive, he will not be defeated by any disease, no abandonment, just like she will not be defeated and even if she is now the most humiliated person on earth, she will not be defeated ever again, she will be so confident that she will defeat all the mockery and betrayals in this world, altogether.

She wept quietly, eager to forget that humiliation and mockery, she will manage to forget, but she will be a different person. Hardly had her tears dried on her face, when she got up on her feet feeling determined, relieved, peaceful, she looked ahead with firmly, just for herself, just for her, the most powerful woman in the universe. She took one step, than another, as if those were the steps of her inner endlessness, she opened the car door, got out confidently, closed the back door, opened the front door, climbed behind the wheel, looked straight ahead, turned the key in ignition, the car started rolling by pressing firmly the gas pedal, she never looked back. Just ahead. She drove to the hospital where all her love and all her strength was.

She was the one who had defeated and left the defeated behind.

Chapter 20

Rafael came home from work, he had a few bites, put a cup of lemon tea, sweetened with honey, in front of him and started writing. The words flew with an indescribable speed coming out from the computer keyboard and the white pages filled with thoughts from his soul outraged by everything happening in the world.

No matter how hard you strive to be different, you have no argument in front of a man who has no God and beauty, just like those who used to stand in front of Communists in prisons, who used to kill the young or the elder and laugh afterwards. Everything is permitted to these people. A scoffer has no limit, especially in mocking about God. This is the most enjoyable these days. You stand no chance in front of them, you have to fight them or, better said, run because they defeat you anyway, it's a waste of time to enlighten them. But as a writer, you must take a stand without being ardent, but how not be ardent about your ideas, about the words you utter daily?

I tried once to clarify things for one who was mocking me, we discussed for hours, even days, I tried to tell her that it made no sense to waste time with such things, but it was useless. In the end, it all comes down to this struggle to separate the good from evil, to make a clear distinction between good and evil. Where's the good? It's wherever your soul feels it's Jesus. But Jesus? Yes, yes, we have to go wherever He is, you know what must be, that unique something, it's the secret message of the soul.

I don't know, I'm afraid, I have such a fear that we will no longer be allowed to believe in God, that people's reproach with regard to Him will be ever greater that it will get to such terror, as in Ceausescu's time, and people will no longer believe in God and holy books will no longer exist or will be altered and falsified. I'm afraid people will be so primitive in their hearts that they will not love each other any more, as they don't love each other now. Some people are so opaque that you wouldn't believe and you see how illogical is what they truely believe in. Which should be true love. Which is true forgiveness? I'm sick of such things, this daily mockery which is everywhere, in newspapers, on television, in books. This is a century of moral decadence, what can I do, I retreat into my home and I stay with God as there is nothing else I can do, I have no choice, I always pray like hermits in the scariest wilderness and I get on with my life. I'm only with God, that's the only way I feel safe.

The worst attacks are to the church and its servants, ei are attacked by God's people. But could it be without reason? We seem to live the Old Testament times, like Daniel in the Den of Lions. Well, that man opposed the regime, opposed the system, opposed everyone and believed only in God. St. Elias was so forlorn, just like all the saints. Well, you don't stand a chance in front of a scoffer of God, there is nothing to say and how to say, you have to come up with evidence, just like in court, to prove that you are right. But, how can you prove to someone who only accepts blasphemy and mockery that he is not right when the justice of the strongest, of the one who does not know how to do anything, other than to mock prevails in this world. I'm sick of such things. I'm sick of this battle I have to fight against people without God, oh, they are so many, but I live with this fear that something horrendeous will happen in this world and people will stop believing, they won't be permitted to believe in God, believers will be brought down. Could that be possible? Can you imagine? I already see myself being born without this joy of thinking about God, because no one told me, no one spoke to me about Him, in that case, wouldn't He come to me to rise my soul, to make me know Him, could God do that, I wonder, seeing these times we live in. In times of the harshest persecutions, in the days of true Christians, the more Christians were killed, the more people believed in Christ. He was the hope and reliance, the same as nowadays, perhaps, the more the church and its people are scoffed, and God, the more people are appaled and outraged and their belief gets stronger. Just like I am outraged now when I see but mocking around me, but lack of love, of faith, and still, people in their inner being think of God and pray, but why is there so much contemp, why is this terrifying state of decadence so spread out. Scoffing the Bible, the holy book, and Christ the Savior, just because you want so, just because that's the time, and just for your love of money and glory, just because your intention is to make everyone know you through scandal. But, why and as what, why would these ideals be so good, and good to whom and what for. These are people's ideals to have the glory of the world, to have what, how does it help him to be known by the whole world as an asperser and forgerer, because he mocked at people's ancient belief.

I repeat what Jesus said, "And what do you benefit if you gain the whole world but lose your own soul?" What's with this huge mockery, who can stand it, who can oppose? Don't you see that there are no opposing voices, most of them do not oppose because they are afraid, they have a Communist fear in them. Those who keep up with the times, who want to be with the world are now popular. And why is that? So they be earnest for places, for favors, for the destruction of everything that is beautiful and replaced with a short-term apparent beauty which rusts immediately and you have to buy a new one.

Yes, this is sad, most people don't obtrude, don't meddle, because they are afraid, they have much to lose in front of people, in front of the others, in front of their colleagues and they could lose their revenues, they could lose their social position and they would rather keep quiet and live with it because they are afraid, and priests find it hard to speak up as they are always bespattered. There are monks who go on the street dressed in their clothes and others spit on them, mock them, hit them. Oh, yes, people fear they'll lay themselves open to ridicule, you can hardly see opposition voices on TV, voices who don't take action, do nothing against what's always happening to them, but if you want to become a great writer, you must take a stand against it. In fact, I'm not a writer, I'm trying to think, I exercise this right to think and meditate, yes, I have this right to think, to write, because that's how I express best when I meditate about this crazy world I live in. It's my way of taking a stand, I'll see what I will do with my writings. I write things down for the moment and their time will come when I send them somewhere, I will publish them but there's a long way to go until then, besides, I don't want to come out yet as I want to investigate for the first time this phenomenon of thinking in Romania. If one doesn't take an open, direct stand wherever he is, it doesn't mean one is not thinking.

In fact, I'm always offended and I feel the need to gulp back every time I turn on the TV, I must consider whether the things I see have an impact on me, because most of the times they make me sick, seeing horror movies makes me sick. Why isn't a Christian art being created, why isn't something extraordinary being created for God. This is what I feel like doing, something to praise the Lord and to anchor my mind in this beauty of His.

I mean writing those poems, those thoughts that can be read in the church. Until I get published, I want to make myself known, but in a different way, I want to go to various literary circles and see how people are there, what they write, what they think and how they think and, if I deem it proper, I will read from my writings, if not, not, I will keep these beauties of my thoughts for myself so they would not be defiled, besmeared and taunted, I could not take that. I might decide to write something, I have searched and found out that there are some good circles at the Museum of Romanian Literature and the National Library. I will go there when I have some time, so I don't get into trouble. When I find some spare time, I'll go, it will be okay, I'm sure of that, I'm really curious to find out how people think and what they say, what's their state of mind. I often think this poem is a sort of mendacity, I believe you are false when writing poetry, the falsehood is noticeable. I believe that mendacity is the reason why there is so much low-quality poetry. People don't go all the way in poetry with their need for beauty and experienced truth. I wonder what people think, how they write, which are their uneases, I am glad to see a person having axieties just like me and telling them nicer than me and I appreciate that person. Because he thinks, but I resent if that person just utters nonsense, if his speeches are some sexual nonsense as I have heard about all sorts of so-called poets, who produce all kinds of absurdities, you wouldn't believe it, such nonsense, such baloney. Well, how could I agree with such things, one must come clean before poetry because it contains the most sincere word spoken before God.

Yeah, yeah, I'll say it out loud to those who mess things up that the most beautiful, the best criterion for a good poem is to read it in the church, it's only then that the poem can be beautiful. If I read one of Eminescu's poems, it can be told in a church, well, not all of them. Vasile Voiculescu's poems, yes, they are clean. Actually, I'm not interested in what others want to write, I want to write poems which can be uttered in church, yes, if my poetry can be read in God's house it means it came from my heart. My poem is beautiful at that point, it means it contains love, grief and pure thought. In fact, I go before God and in His house because that's where I put my thoughts at His feet. Well, until then, I have to write, I am determined to do so. Do you know why I actually like to write? I write because I like to think, I like this state of thinker.

I believe this is what's missing from this century, from these times: only some think for others. Thinkers and doers are very few, all the rest live the moment, lacking projection, lacking insight. Worries seem to overtake you and you start thinking then. When you say: "Lord, what can I do?" that's the moment when you think, until then, you don't feel if you are too far away from the memory immediacy, the existence immediacy, from your daily activity. You go to work, do your job, earn money, return home and go to sleep, you watch TV, which has become people's most exciting and cheapest entertainment because it's ready-made, it doesn't need too much processing, we live in a world where only some people think for others and that's very bad because it's not like in school where everyone thinks for himself. I believe this impression is false, but so I feel, the boss thinks for employee, the school principal thinks for pupil and teacher, the mother thinks for baby and her man. I wonder when to think, when do you make a person think, when do you make him take a stand and change himself? That's what should happen here, to a writer as well as to a generation or to a people. One thinks when capable of being creative, when capable of something extraordinary. As I would like to do something with my poetry? To make it something so good, so pure, to be like a praise to the Lord and to the powerful and victorious man who is his own master, who does not exhibit his perverse desires. More and more I see that men are brainless and women without attitude and turned into maids and, how can you think when you are a servant and you think you are the servant of your children or your man, and especially how to allow yourself to think considering the man is the thinker, he thinks for you. And if the man does not think, then you won't think either. This is the attitude and women thinker are mocked and scoffed, women with attitude are considered dangerous and male thinkers are deemed despotic and frustrated.

It's a very strange world, as if you should always keep your thoughts away and live driven by instincts, as they say in commercials: «Follow your instinct, follow your thirst.» I was wondering: «Thirst for what»? Because there is a spiritual thirst but, you see, money cannot buy it, you have to make the effort of thinking. Thinking about your passion is truely destructive, but so encouraged nowadays, ridiculous, I mean, to spend the entire day in frustration and to whinge about your frustration, you could end up in a madhouse unless you get out of this vicious circle, your passion could lead you to destruction. The vice is the one that destroys you, crashes you, strangles you, you don't have the priviledge of feeling freedom as in the case of the pure thought about eternity. In reality, it is a form of prostration, lack of power, because vice eliminates love and the only true and unlimited force is love, but as a spiritual feeling, not a physical one. The love preached by Christ, but as God's gift for the humble man as well as for the most powerful person in this world, with its millions of facets, is the only power we have to develop.

This is why this world is so dry, because man in his naivity believes this is a commercial area. Well, love is out of sight, it only lies in the pure soul and, since the soul is placed at the index in our world, actually at footnotes, there's not much to relate to as it stopped being unit of measure for human actions. Or, if I think of my soul, which is the infinite that vanishes and is not subject to measurement, everything is allowed in the world that I measure with instruments of hatred. What is the soul? It is the indestructible part of me. It is that strong part of me, in my heart, in my innermost being, that helps me express, it's a sort of mystery of my life, and I am the only one who lives it, feels it, I am the only one who sits and meditates, who thinks, who dreams. I stand before God with my soul. But driven by fear and loneliness, I run, run away from him, hiding due to the sin, just as I hide from God, it's Adam's condition after the fall, I kept saying that all the time. We do not feel good if we stay with us, we are fearful just as the child is afraid of darkness, we are afraid of loneliness, of this so beneficial state in which we discover new meanings of our life which are not seen on TV. Or, if this time has been emptied of thinking, it is filled with these fragments of spare time immediately consumed. We find ourselves in the situation that another person is thinking for us. Another one make decisions for me, the TV and breaking news make decisions in my self-consciousness issues because the news programs take all my time from work to sleep. The latest news, from TV and from anywhere else, is time wasted so you can keep up with world's daily trifles, it's time burned and turned into ashes in soul's kitchen, it's the time when you not only do nothing, but you also stay hungry, hungry for spirit.

This phenomenon with the news and the latest world developments is some sort of global sickness, it's a way to waste time, you just sit, have some tobacco, you spend time in pubs or in front of the TV, at home where your wife cooks in the kitchen. It is unfair somehow for the woman to work and the man to watch TV, but these are the times. The poor woman toils as always, but this saves her as she has no more time left for perversity since she works. Isn't it wonderful how work keeps the human being away from the extinction of the soul, just like work protects you from a certain death. But why so much wretchedness, the horridness of desolation is high up in the lead, the whore who knows nothing but to get aroused by her passions. These are now on top of ethics and consciousness. But there are unwritten laws of nature that will never fade away in the human soul and what can you do when these laws lead to indignation in some people? You, the one who promoted decadence? In dealing with this mockery, you can only hope that better times will come. But you can't just wait for these times to come until you get old. How can you sit and wait, let others make a future and... expect what? Better times and more chances, from others. They will never come unless you create them yourself.

I do not think this attitude towards life is any good, you have be ruthless and fight, never give up, oppose to the ugly lees, this abjectness that penetrates all the walks of life, you must never give up on what you have to do, never take God out of your heart. If He is there, you cannot join the world prostitution which wants to stay in your mind permanently.

I always relate to Joseph, he lived in the Egyptian empire where everyone worshiped idols, they bowed to idols both for pharaoh's fear and on their own, their beliefs were irrelevant at that time, it mattered less what they had in mind and soul, or perhaps it's the other way round, it doesn't matter now and we are the ones who interpret that way. And Joseph had the courage to face that mass of people who kneeled down before some statues, and he said no, he opposed, he claimed to worship God who is not human creation, he worshiped the creator of heaven and Earth. Isn't that fascinating? So much courage in that boy, that young slave, this is the right attitude in front of lechery, in front of the day, in front of the destiny, the promiscuity which infiltrates everywhere, even in your daily intimacy. Yes, the attitude of Joseph of Egypt is the right one and the one that gives you strength, that matters, it's worth obeying this man's idea, with his attitude and doing just like him, that's how I want to be inside of me, inalienable, incorruptible and unbeatable.

Nowadays, people worship the god of lust and they are locked into their own slavery, this is the master god of the contemporary world, embodied in immediate pleasure and rapid gain, the power of this god governs people's minds and this attitude brings destruction to the soul and so many children separated from their parents live their lives by themselves and learn from an early age what chronic loneliness is, soul's taciturnity and silence, the deep silence caused by the lack of paternal feelings, so many poor children born and living with this emptiness in their heart, that of being fatherless, of lacking that male love which is the force of love. As if the male force, which is a creative force, is missing from the world and it has been converted into a bad, destructive, warlike force. Oh, how strong and great is a man who loves one woman, who is his wife who loves him, who hugs his love, his children and those children grow big and vigorous, just like as the Bible says. Oh, Lord, so much scoffing at saints, monks, family, love, as if they all were compromised, how is this contemp possible, this daily blasphemy brought to the holy. That reminds me of the vandalized churches from Ceausescu's time, when cattle were brought into the church, churches were turned into stables, they turned some of the sketes into horse stables. I visited such a skete this summer. Animals were brought into church to live there because people were not worthy to worship God, animals were kept in God's house, cattle and sheep, as they were kinder, more worthy than humans, Jesus Christ was warmed up at birth by cattle and animals as well, we go back in history, when Jesus was born, animals received him better than humans who wanted to kill him. It was the same during Ceausescu's communist regime when churches were turned into stables, just like the skete I've seen. When opressed, people do not oppose, they obey and, therefore, they have no power to fight against the oppressor. This is still the case and I still cannot see what is happening, why is this happening with humanity and I cannot understand, I cannot defend nor react, except for myself personally. I am part of the world and its mechanism which suffers in the ruin of the world, because I feel how a part of me is broken, dies, turns into matter, a clueless matter. Oh, because the human being is weak and I have to learn from these weaknesses. We live so horrible times, so much mockery, these stupid people who can do nothing but scoff make me sick, yet I have to raise my mind to something truly beautiful and wonderful as I won't get stuck all the time in the daily ugliness of others, I must rise in my inner beauty, there I find my strength, in the prayer that becomes creative, as in Vivaldi. Oh, that man composed so beautifully, the same as Beethoven, or all those great men, so beautiful, so wonderful, their hearts had so much beauty. Their creation was exquisite because their life was exceptional. I must do the same and lead an exceptional life so I can create wonderful things. I have to go to bed, it's too late, said Rafael and he tucked in bed for the sleep that solves everything.

Chapter 21

Maria was still at the hospital near her baby. "You see, there's a woman here in hospital, Maria thought, in the other pavilion, who has a hip surgery and is confined to bed, she cannot walk because the postoperative period is very long and her husband left her, he does not come visit her, just her kids, and she is so happy when she sees them, but so sad that she hasn't seen the man since she left home. That's how I will be, too. Oh, Lord, give me strength to move forward and don't leave us. We are too important to die, I don't think everything is so meaningless, however limited my and other people's understanding may be, I must not allow to be influenced by those who do me harm. Some people do me harm without realizing, others make it out of stupidity and others because they are weak. But, I must sleep because tomorrow is another day".

Her emotional state was very hard to describe because she would switch fast from a state of calmness to anxiety, fear which she could not control or she could hardly control her destructive emotions. She was wondering at those moments:

-Am I a normal person? I'm afraid all the time, I wonder if other people are as fearful? Or maybe men are not afraid, it's only us, women, who are so fearful. I have always imagined that men are particularly powerful beings who can protect me and my children. I have always imagined Mihai as being strong, powerful, a person who can solve absolutely any problem, but I was so wrong, I often wonder how could I have lived in my dream for so long? I lived in my imagination. I was young, when you are a child or young, you live very much in your dream and imagination. I think this is the true growing up, when you live in this immediate reality and you can know it, as long as you live in imagination, you are not aware of the day-to-day reality. That's what happened to me, too."

She felt pity for Mihai because she began to understand that he had so much to lose for he had pulled out from her and the child, but she lost sight of the fact that he was not thinking about her anymore and didn't want to see her again. She could not find an explanation for his behaviour. She thought he had been so inhuman, oh, so inhuman! She would often argue with him in her thoughts telling him everything she could not say to him until then and she would never tell him because her present feelings will not be the same later on.

Her state is amazing. She tells him all sorts of things and has an imaginary dialogue with him, without him actually being present. Had he been present, she would have certainly had a different behaviour towards him, in a totally different way. She was arguing with Mihai in her mind, but not with the real Mihai. She was arguing with that Mihai from her imagination, who did not actually exist. She was having an imaginary dialogue with that Mihai whom she had met, that person she had perceived and had lived with. Had she really lived with the man who was in reality or with that image she had made about him a long time ago? That opinion had faded away and she was living a state of nothingness, a state in which nothingness is complemented with explanations and questions which may not be answered in this life.

Maria realized she lived her life only once. She did perceive this state that she could not explain, she could not put into words, she really perceived that she was experiencing this reality in a unique way and not in many ways, and this uniqueness of life could not be changed as much as she would have wanted.

When she was in love with Mihai, she used to feel she could change reality as much as she would have wanted, but now this reality could no longer be changed in her favor and, therefore, it was unique and irreplaceable.

Her heaviest struggle was with loneliness. She felt a terrible, unbearable pressure when she was in front of her sick child, connected to medical devices. Her suffering in those moments was so great that she felt she would lose her mind. She had never imagined she could go through such things. If we knew in advance our future troubles, I think we could die.

Why was she feeling the greatest pain in those moments? It would be natural, you might answer. But this is the question: how can we understand our pains? The pain that we cannot explain.

When desperation grew dimmer and a new wave of hope crossed her heart, she analyzed her states involuntarily. She suffered so much for useless things which had seemed important. Yes, those pains were so useless, everything seemed so illusive. We wake up and realize life's importance only in case of a great pain, but isn't suffering changing us for the worse? Didn't Maria have all the reasons to be a bad person, or maybe she could not be bad anymore, she did not have the strength for that because she was too busy with her problems, more than she could even handle.

What were the people around her doing? Some big-hearted colleagues helped her as they could in the beginning, mainly by encouraging her, because she needed that. But, then, they forgot her, because they had problems of their own.

She needed to be encouraged for an unlimited period. People around you get tired of your pain and feel the need to clear off. Who wouldn't run away from other person's pain so he won't be affected. How many times each of us felt a state of instinctual satisfaction and joy for the trouble wasn't ours but of the person nearby. Even if that person feels very sorry, he rejoices in his innermost being because he is not in the place of the one who suffers the misfortune. You feel better to keep aside and look from a distance and even forget about it.

In those moments, we could say that Maria was very lonely and she was looking for something essential for her life, for her child's life. All sorts of images crossed her mind, as if she had never thought so profoundly as now. She had never had time for these states. She was having such thoughts during sleepless nights. The doctor had recommended her to take medication, but she didn't want to take them, she was struggling with her forces because she was afraid of their addiction.

We often try to think when we suffer, when we are in a no way out situation, we look for solutions. But how prepared are we to think about us and about the persons near us? We might say that life is quite complicated when we do not understand it but who could fully understand what is happening.

Maria is afraid of this misunderstanding. She felt that her mind was quite limited.

Why did that misfortune happened to her just when everything seemed to be going perfectly? Could this be the reality we live in? But there was one thing she could not understand: why all this suffering?

Her imagination saved her and drove her crazy at the same time because it made her live in her imagination. The dreams disturbed her even more. She often dreamt she was running with her child, holding hands and playing in the park, but now this state was forbidden. Who forbade her to enjoy this happiness the same as everyone else, she is the only who cannot enjoy it? Why, why, why Lord? We often wonder the same, so shaken by all that's happening to us. We cannot explain our and other people's suffering.

On her way from work to hospital, where her child was lying among life support devices, she would often sit on a bench in the park in front of the University Hospital so she could rest and gain strength. She would park her car somewhere and headed across the park to the entrance which had become her home for a very long time. She would admire children and imagine, she simply dreamed of how she and her Gabriel, just the two of them, would dance in this reality which was just theirs. She knew that this kid had recovered and had no more health problems.

She was looking at those smaller and bigger kids who were walking in the park, laughing, riding bicycles everywhere and bursting out with joy or getting upset for trifles which turned into the most important thing in the world. She suddenly remembered that she and her mother had not strolled in that park or any other park for a long time. She didn't have time, as if someone was making her go faster and faster towards something unknown. She had never felt such a strong need to sit, just sit and walk without doing anything else. Oh, she would have wanted so much to be a little girl, to walk with her mother holding hands and without worrying about anything. She realized how important it was to be able to spend time with mom and take a short walk, talk, just stay as if that was just the most beautiful state you must have, you must live. Why run so much?

The children running around and supervised by mothers were magnificent. They had so much strength to grow up and become adults. Just her child could not recover and she was on the verge of tears. She often wept quietly on that bench without being known, noticed by anyone, her tears rolled down wetting her chest, she was suddenly cold and she knew then that she had to go some place else, to move. This sensation of cold saved her because, otherwise, she would have fainted from crying and wouldn't have gotten to the child who was lying unconscious, on i.v. and had no perception about her. That was what she thought or seemed to her although Dr. Andrei had told her she did not have to cry because the child had a terrible capacity to sense everything around him. It's something exceptional, it's like a miracle because devices, movements and diagrams have a different configuration when she is around and she is not allowed to come tense to the baby. That made her revive, come out of her huge, unbearable despair.

The baby was so small, he was almost one year and a few months old, he had already undergone five surgeries, because he had been born without esophagus. There were times when he was feeling very well and she could took him home and hold him in her arms, just the two of them. She was the happiest woman in the world in those moments, as if heaven had descended on earth for her. She often said that heaven surely must be similar to the irreplaceable joy of having Gabriel in her arms after surgery.

Chapter 22

Dr. Andrei, who attended the child, a young man who had been doing all sorts of studies in Italy, Rome, Vienna and Germany, preferred to return to the country to treat Romanians here and, why not, foreigners from other countries who come to Romania especially for such purpose. Why should Romanians go to foreigners instead of foreigners coming to us for medical care and surgeries. He worked with his wife in the same place, they performed surgeries together, studied together, worked together, both were exceptional and they were as one. Had he lived with his income as a doctor, he probably couldn't have had a house or car, but they had been abroad and managed to save some money and buy a four-room apartment, their home was some sort of hospital, and a car for each of them. Every Romanian's dream is to own a house and a car. The house, so he wouldn't bother with the rent, and the car so he wouldn't wait out in the cold, to travel by public transportation after having operated for six hours and barely standing on his feet. A doctor must have good living conditions but, in Romania, where all the money is stolen from Government down, intellectuals are forced to live to the limit of maximum humiliation, there is no more money left for doctors and teachers, for universities and research.

Had those means of transportation been faster, it would have been great, but a 15-minute car journey took an hour if travelling by city's means of transportation. The doctors who have succeeded in Romania are like those two. Not everyone succeeds, but many of them who are very smart make things change considerably in this country and they make you feel good living here, they make you think that you have made a good choice by staying in your country to develop and that you did not left elsewhere. Yet, I believe that as long as you work, you can lead a good life wherever you may be. He was a pretty tough doctor when it came to the right to live.

Maria was struggling hard, she had to breastfeed the baby and her torment was even greater when he was sick and connected to life support in hospital. Her breasts swelled and hurt terribly. She had to resort to all sorts of methods to take the milk out of her breasts, so she wouldn't develop mastitis. She wanted to have breast milk as long as she could to breastfeed Gabriel. The poor child was so ill, it was best she breastfed him as long as possible. So far, Dr. Andrei had been very affectionate and human with her but, this time, he called her in his office with a very serious, grave and accusing voice. He looked at her very frowningly and his first question was:

-How long has it been since you breastfed the baby?

-I fed him yesterday.

-Madam, I understand you have sentimental problems, that you're single, but you did something very serious. I think you should abstain from sex or... I do not know. It's very serious what you did. You are infected with a very serious illness which gets transmitted only by sexual intercourse. This is the only way I can explain how this hard-hit child has been infected with this venereal disease, you were his only source of infection because you breastfed him. Please don't take this personally but, to make it clear, you should abstain for a very long time, until you are fully healed. You will have to keep away from your child, as well. You won't be able to breastfeed the baby until you are completely healed and he will be able inoperable. Let us hope there will be no serious consequences for him. This is the last thing we needed considering all the problems we have. Your actions are very serious, you are going through a very difficult period, you are so irresponsible.

I'm telling you as a doctor. How do you feel, have you done any gynecological exam. You obviously have a very serious health problem, you have been infested with a disease that develops into nodes which swell all over the body and, especially, in the throat and on heart. We were lucky to have found this early in child's case as we run tests constantly. But what about you? Have you been examined?

Maria felt sick and nearly fainted, being on the verge of throwing up. She started crying and said between hiccups:

-I made love only once with my former husband, before breaking up. Half a year ago. I hadn't done it before either, as I had other things in my mind. We weren't seeing each other before the break-up.

-Are you sure?

-Yes, I'm absolutely sure, I'm not seeing anyone and I don't feel like having a partner considering my situation.

Maria took a seat and started crying, holding her hands in the lap, and her tears were rolling down incessantly and uncontrollably. She was crying in front of the person whom she totally trusted. He was the only man in her life she could rely on, she could let it all out without uttering a word.

-He took it from whores, said the doctor. But what is your husband's life, what did he do, where did he go, because it means he has something more devastating. You should not let him get closer to the baby because it's very contagious, it's a kind of leprosy. This form of sexually transmitted disease is supposed to develop certain forms of cancer, I hope we don't get there.

Maria was crying and sobbing and said:

-I think he was visiting brothels. I happened to meet with one of his former employees whom he had fired and he told me he was going to prostitutes in brothels from the Old Center of Bucharest and they are not cheap, he visits some of the most expensive whores. He spends lots of money there. But I didn't want to believe that employee, he told me he had joined him there once, the employee had taken him there, and he got fired the following day. I thought the man was telling me out of despite for he had been fired and to widen the gap between me and him.

-He told you the truth, madam.

Maria did not have the courage to look into doctor's eyes who said:

-You got it from there, if you say you didn't have nothing with anyone else. This is the only was to catch such a disease. How about you? I believe your husband is already in hospital under quarantine.

-I feel awful, I have some lumps all over the body, I feel horribly but I thought this is stress-related and it comes from this endless pain.

-It could be that, too, but surely it's from your husband who infected you. Let's be glad it is not AIDS, such people should be taken to Court. You should thank God you don't have AIDS. There have been cases when the father infected both the mother and the child. If your child has it, you definetely have it too and it's and advanced form, I don't believe it's an early stage. You must be examined, get tested and we put you on strict medication because you risk making all sorts of ugly complications and we don't need that, your medical condition is not very simple. Let's hope the body gives the expected results. Please pull yourself together physically and mentally, get stronger with a proper diet and take your medication regularly so we get rid of it. We didn't need that now.

The doctor examined Maria and indeed she had some huge ganglia around her neck, on her chest, all over the body, she took some tests that the results confirmed the diagnosis. She was very ill because of the venereal disease transmitted by Mihai in that morning of savage intercourse. That was the last time she saw him and left him with this superb gift. And the baby got sick too. The father gave his child not money and love, but his venereal disease he was having and spreading around. Any comments are superfluous.

The child had to struggle, beside his illness, to make the matters worse, with the disease coming from his father, who was sick rather mentally than biologically. It's like the Bible says: the parents eat sour grapes and the children's teeth are set on edge. Everything is possible in our world.

Maria now had to keep away from her child due to this venereal disease. She wasn't allowed to breastfeed until they were fully cured, both her and her baby. She was facing another torment caused by the breast milk she was supposed to throw away instead of being the best baby food.

Thus, a few more months passed in Gabriel's life, fighting with a new disease, until he was cured and was taken home, to the great joy of Maria who had gotten rid of the ganglia but still had great sensitivity to the heart. The grandparents were so glad, especially Maria's father, who didn't say anything but sighed now and then with an unspeakable pain, he was watching everything in a silent muteness.

Chapter 23

But the harships started to get their claws out. Maria's torment did not change and time passed while being at her parents', where her mother helped her with everything, at the hospital where she had to take the baby for checkups, at work which was essential for her to live. Time passed so fast that she didn't realize when her child had grown up so big, he was one year and a half. That imaginary Mihai from her mind was slowly fading away, he had lost the stridence. There is a saying: 'Out of sight, out of mind' and Maria had the right to take it all out of her mind. The word Mihai was not painful anymore, his face was fading away and memory was blurring him. Those were signs that she was healing.

They had to face a new challenge, very difficult for Gabriel, for all of them: he was supposed to undergo a new surgery, the sixth and final surgery. Doctors said he needed another operation because the transplant must be placed properly and it takes time, the body grows and it must accomodate the transplant all along. Everyone said those malformations children are born with are due to the radiation from the atmosphere, especially those from Chernobyl and not only. This child is growing up and he will surely recover, children have a fantastic power to recover, to grow and to heal, it's almost a miracle. He has good chances to heal, he is a very strong child and God does wonders with His creation, He won't leave us defenseless, we must hang on until then, until we get well and, afterwards, we have to take care of our health throughout our lifetime.

The surgery was done and Maria was in panic. The kid was on life support in a deep sleep and was supposed to regain consciousness. His prolonged state of unconsciousness worried her so much and she felt she was losing her mind especially as she saw that doctors were quite tense. They would not show their doubts, but a mother has her senses. Fear was so overwhelming at night. She wanted so much to take Gabriel into her arms, to caress him and hug him tight, to protect the kid from any harm, but she was so helpless! She wanted so much and she started praying desperately:

-Lord, don't take him away from me, let him, let him live! Don't take him away from me, I want him to live, I don't want him to die. You let him live so farm why not live further on. Please, make a miracle, I know things are as You want them to be, that is the only way, but why does it have to be so hard, why does it have to be so hard, can't it be otherwise?! It's too hard for me to go through this. This suffering is beyond my powers, why does he have to die, I don't want my child to die, I want him to live and play with him in the park. Even if his father doesn't want to see him anymore and pays no money for his medication, calls him handicapped and says I am nuts, please don't take him away from me, I want to hug him, I want to sleep with him at night. This child, so helpless, is my only meaning of life. Lord, do I want too much? You, who raised that five-year-old girl, Tabitha, please, raise my child as well because I cannot live without him! I beg You, I know I'm so bad, I have made mistakes, but I cannot believe that this child no longer exists, I cannot live with this emptiness where nothing happens. If he were taken away from me, I'd feel I live in the abyss of an unimaginable agony, I feel exhausted, Lord, I feel so lonely, so lonely and as much as others would come to encourage me, regardless how much my mother would love me, I am still lonely. I beg You, Lord, give me strength to move on and get my baby healthy because I cannot live without him." Her father came many nights in a row and took her in his strong arms and held her tight. He also used to hold her like a baby when she was at home, without saying a word, just to defend her, to protect her from any harm that could come over her. Maria became a child in her father's arms. He gave her strength. Her father's silence, when holding her, made her of steel.

That night was horrible for her because she did not get any rest. She was supposed to go to work the next day but she didn't feel up to it. She could not eat, when she would sit down at the table, images of her child in hospital struggling between life and death came to her mind and tears were dropping without her being able to hold them. She felt a lump in her throat and got stuck, she had to cry so her head would not burst. Besides, she was used to feed her baby first and then she would go eat, but, now, the baby was not there and food got stuck down her throat, having difficulty in chewing, then she stopped. Can you imagine that there are people who laugh when they see this, yes, unfortunately such people exist and are everywhere. Even people close to her who knew her pain and agony. That night, she knew she would have to go to work in the morning because she was not allowed to skip work too many times as that was a different world, a different reality which ignored her reality. She had to be efficient and carry things out, she was not allowed to make mistakes and, if you fall ill, you must leave, you must hand it over to another one who is better, because we have to move ahead, the company must not go in the red, you have to make a profit, but not just any profit, maximum profit, if not, you get replaced. There is even a saying that goes among colleagues: "No one is irreplaceable in this company!"

She was afraid for her future for the first time on that night. She had been criticized many times by her colleagues and by the head of department who had told her that she would have to be replaced unless she got efficient. It was true that the top directors have never said anything to her, she even liked the big boss who had given her money to buy medicines a couple of times and bought new clothes for the baby. Money was no issue for her, but any gesture could be so important. Maria got hired in the company immediately after big bosses because of her fairness, she was very honest and competent, she had never done anything wrong and always worked long-hours, as much as she needed to do the job right. The bosses considered her to the most hard-working of all, and that's why she has been promoted to the highest position that an employee could hold without being a company shareholder. That's why she had no fear, her boss was a God-fearing person, but she still had moments of doubt. Since she has had such big problems with her baby, she couldn't handle the higher position and gave it up, filling now a more modest job, well-paid but incomparable to the previous one. Anyway, she could not handle the fatigue and some colleagues used to talk behind her back saying she was chief's protégé, claiming she was not working, that she was making mistakes, some persons could not forgive her, could not stand her.

Let's just imagine that she was the most influential in the company, after the big bosses, and, deep down inside, all the others would have wanted her position. She was highly respected but not because she was loved. We are aware of such situations: you have so many friends-foes that you wouldn't even guess. Now, when she has fallen professionally, those who once respected her step aside and show respect to the next person who fill that position, nobody is interested in her anymore. She was feeling sadness and struggled with herself to forgive them, but she couldn't. She felt hatred growing in her soul and she felt she was losing control. She felt like arguing with everyone, as if she had sought revenge against everybody for her troubles. All these were inside her soul, not outside, because terrible battles of moral and mental survival were being fought inside her. Moral survival had turned into a principle of life for her, she could only fight to respect it because she could not live otherwise, she felt that she could not understand her pain and her attempt otherwise. That was the only way, relating to the holy and the durable in our existence, one could cling to God and live another day, another hour, another moment, another second. Hope alone becomes and remains a force for a no way-out situation in this life. That was the reason why she struggled so much with herself, I don't know what she would have done otherwise, she would have abandoned her child just like her husband did, she would have left him at a special care center, she woud have left him alone in a hospital and never come visit him again. As she was making that list of attributes, she felt her hair raising from fear and her mind went dark out of despair and incomprehension.

She would ofter wonder:

-Does this life of ours have anything holy in it? Do we live randomly without being able to understand anything of what happens to us. Do we have such a limited mind? I can't live like this, I want something more, I need something like I need air and, I do not know why, I need a meaning, a new meaning of this life, I can't live adrift and not think for myself. This life must include something else beside this very expensive car that I bought and which made me so happy. There must be something else than what I do at work on daily basis. There's no use in being upset with my colleagues who criticize me and have a bad attitude towards me, they can't understand what I'm going through after all.

She stopped thinking and stared at a fixed point, feeling a void in her mind. Then she said:

-Yes, but, at least, they could be nicer and stop talking behind my back so much and they could look at me differently, I feel somehow mentally attacked by some of them, that's because I lost myself in my inner states. It is true that it would be better if they hadn't claimed to know-it-all because that's the truth, we know so few things about us and about others. But one thing is for sure at my job, I work hard and I get detached from my troubles with Gabriel. Oh, Lord, what is my little baby doing now, Lord, I leave him under Your and my mother's protection because I have no power, because I cannot go any further, You take care of him, Lord, because You see how hard I struggle and You are the only one I trust, if you exist, but don't You exist, Lord, because everything that I live makes no sense and I cannot survive without these prayers.

When Maria went to work during the day, her mother took her place at the hospital, doing her turn, and when they got tired, Maria's father would come in and take care of that little baby, while at night, Maria was sleeping there as she could not leave the baby alone.

Maria had those thoughts while at work, in front of her computer.

Chapter 24

Rafael was sad because he had visited his sister and had an argument with her. He was crying his eyes out when alone, he was crying while driving and he kept crying like a fool when he got home alone. He was annoyed by her insults, she, his sister who stepped on his soul. Why did she do that? There are occasional quarrels between brothers, tempest in a teapot, initiated by all sorts of nonsense and meaningless vanity. Rafael kept on crying sitting in the armchair with all sorts of thoughts coming to his head, remembering various things since days of yore:

-Is this world really so bad and twisted. Is it so hard to be kind and generous? But my soul lives a great dilemma. Human malice is so great that it encompasses all the corners of consciousness, all the edges of my being from beneath, is it so hard to be kind, this is an exercise that I no longer want to do. I'm tired of being kind, because the kind is a strong person, but everyone hits him, it is very beneficial for others and not for me, there is no other way. But I cannot be a strong person, I don't want to be kind anymore because every time I try to help someone, I get nothing in return and all I want is that person to be nice and show me respect, not to mistreat me as if I were a low life.

But why is the good done to another forgotten so quickly and the evil is kept in mind. Because this is how we are built, could this mean the salvation of the soul? But I can no longer stand this mockery, how can my own sister be so cruel to me, though I do my best to help her. But what I want to do for her is so bad and ugly, I do not matter to her, she wants me to do it all, I've never seen such a selfish manner, she wants me to give up on everything and stop existing:

-Bring me the car tomorrow!

-But I can't tomorrow, get that!

-I need the car tomorrow!

-But I can't.

-Bring it to me tonight and take the bus back home.

-And I will get home at eleven o'clock at night, do you know what that means, I will have to wait out in the cold in bus stations, don't you care about me, or I don't matter!

-You come to me, bring my car and get back home.

-But what will I do tomorrow?

-You'll find a way, you take the bus, I must take some papers.

-But why don't you take your husband's car?

-He won't give it to me!

-Well, let him take taxi to work and leave you the car to run your errands!

-No, I can't do that, you don't want to help me!

-But doesn't my life matter, my fatigue, 'cause I work so hard, don't you have any consideration, be patient until Monday.

-I can't wait until Monday because the year is soon to be over.

-But there is one month to go before the end of the year.

No, it's not, I must take them sooner.

-No, I can't give you the car, I'm sorry, you have to think about me, I've got my own life, this is too much, it's a banter. Isn't she taking me into consideration, don't I matter, all she is interested about is her thing, to make me obey, but her attitude disturbs me, the gesture itself, I may be overreacting and maybe I should not care, maybe I shouldn't care that much, but I'm a human being. I wanted to take the baby in my arms, to hug that beautiful little girl who was only a few months old:

-Let the child be, don't take her in your arms, she'll get used to it and what will I do with her then? You hold her too much, go and wash, have you washed your hands!?

-Come on, don't act like that, what if I hold the baby in my arms?

-You should talk when you have your own family and your baby, until then, you have nothing to say.

As if I were guilty I don't have a family and child. Is it really so bad that I don't have all of these all together, am I to blame for having such a fate? But why would she brag about it, is it so hard not to offend another person, to treat him nicely.

Many times, when I go there, I feel how stressed she is, how she is struggling to behave nicely, but she can't, because she has to make an effort, she's so brutal! Is it really so hard and so bad to have a family, you no longer care about anything, neither about brothers, nor sisters, you throw them out of your heart and they no longer matter to you, they put you to inconvenience. I may have misunderstood that, I may have not realized that she didn't want me to come over, she only needs me when I am supposed to shake her carpets and wash her dishes, that would be all, I believe this is disrespectful.

Human malice is so deep, it's like a plague, like a disease that contaminates everyone. One must strive to be kind all the time and she doesn't, but I do, I'm trying to do this and I ask too much from her. I may be very demanding, perhaps I should not hold on to her, I should not be so dependent on her family and children, I should stop going to her for a while, a long while, to be even lonelier than I am now. Her words truely hurt me very bad, she has no time to think because she has a family, she has someone to love and there is no more room for brothers, because brothers turn into strangers, we become tools, do we really? That is human malice, why wouldn't I accept that she is also touched by this malice, that these are the times we live in, that I live in a regular family of these times, when siblings only visit each other several times a year. It's true, why should I go to her place and waste my time because I don't feel good there, as she's constantly hurting my feelings. She probably has no one to hit, but why hit, why always let off steam on the other, why should you be so agitated all the time? Is that really impossibile for you to speak nicely? How can this human being be so evil, in fact, she's like my dad and my mom. My father hasn't visited his sister for a long time, they have not seen each other or even phone called for years and they don't speak a word to each other, they meet once a year and dad and his brother have been at odds with each other for years. Why wouldn't this microbe be in her heart now. But mom has never has any quarrel with her siblings, they have been calm, such disputes have never existed in her family. There were some issues with her big brother because his wife had a bad, really bad attitude towards us and she could not stand us. Why does she want to do this with me, with us, I wonder why? Doesn't she have any feelings, I wonder why, she does whatever she saw at home, at her dad and mom, but her mother would

131

not do such things. Why is this human being so wicked? How do I solve this problem, because I really have no idea how to do it, it is beyond me. It is best for me to stand aside, because if I go some place where it's bad for me and I don't feel at ease and my feelings are constantly hurt, I shouldn't even stop by there. But that thought hasn't vene crossed my mind, not now, not ever, my visits there bother her and she gets hysterical as soon as she sees me, I must stop going there. If I could be strong enough not to care, I have to attain this power. The mighty God will help me because this is my fasting, I'm going to take communion, to confess, because I'm so scared of all these dangers. I can only pray for her and stay as far as possible, these are the times we live in, I must accept things as they are, this is her evil nature and I go over the top, because I visited them too often and I got plenty of kicks and slaps. I have exaggerated, you should not help a person, be it a sibling, so often because that person makes you kneel down, you become his fool and, after all, everyone must do his job. In case I need anything, will she come and give me a hand? I think not. Judging by the way she's treating me, I must never put my hopes on her, because you never know.

Lord, how could I find a solution, give me the necessary wisdom to be nicer to her, because I'm also nasty with her and I insult her. My attitude disturbs her and, as soon as I refuse doing anything for her, she goes off, because I'm the bad guy who cannot and does not want to do whatever she desires, she wouldn't understand me. No, no, absence makes the heart grow fonder, and I have gone over the top, I must see to my own business, there's no other way. Human malice frightens me at all levels and I don't know why I can't accept that such things can happen, that I must break off and be by myself, lonely and strong. Even though I'm upset now and I feel like crying, it's because I feel the urge to let go of everything. I've accumulated so much I'm just getting tired and I don't know what to do, how to proceed, how to go on, to let it out in a way but when your own sister is calling you names and makes you feel bad in her presence, I almost don't know how to react, I find it difficult, I have my own dignity and pride. She insults me and, normally, I get upset, but I'm to blame because I got upset. I must break off and be by myself, I have interferred too much with their life and I am an intruder, I've learnt my lesson. I should step aside and see to my things which I have neglected so, I have to be strong and lonely, not to care for anyone and anything. It hurts me so much when my sister is treating me just like a colleague or a stranger. I'd rather have a stranger who treats me nicely for an interest than a sibling who systematically insults me.

I wonder what can I do to reduce the tension, what method to apply to stop going over there. Okay, that's the outer method, but what should I do in my inner self because I feel like I'm getting cold, and you know why, because I don't have a house and or a family and I need their warmth. That's what I actually beg for when I go there, I visit them because I need their warmth, the warmth of a family, because, if I had a family, I would not be so dependent on her, that's what I like to think, I believe that if I go there often enough, something happens, I get some comfort in my loneliness. But when I go there, I gather I'm a danger to them, but how come haven't I realized that so far, that I was the nuisance. She would have wanted the house to be cleaned up without me being there. In fact, I was the nuisance. After all, that was true, but the child was the one who was telling me to stay and she said the same and I thought she was saying that with all her heart. It never crossed my mind that she was not speaking with all her heart and I was an intruder. It's a normal thing, after all. Maybe it's normal to drive your brother away to stay with your family, but I was doing nothing wrong, I was only rejoicing.

Well, I … it's just been an earthquake and I got really scared. If God gives us a big earthquake, we all die for our sins, and I'm a sinner, and I should learn something from my sister's way of being. Human relationships have grown very cold, in fact it is normal to hate, but hating your brother. I hate her, I have moments when I wish I would never see her again and the farther I get in time, the more I realize that I'm getting colder, and if she insults me again, I shall remind her everything else, how could I forget, how could I forgive, how to be a good person with my sister so I can be a good person with other people who are strangers to me. What can I do to keep close to the good Lord and to my sister, to her home?

Chapter 25

Rafael, being sad, said to himself: "I think I'll go to Dragos at the monastery once again to find some peace of mind. The fast of the Dormition of the Mother of God will soon begin and I will be at peace again, the fast gives me so much tranquillity in my thoughts. Why do I have to follow others so that I couldn't do anything. And he set off for the monastery.

Rafel was now again with Dragos at the monastery. He came unannounced. He just came over because, after the fight with his sister, Rafael was feeling so badly that he needed to run away and cry. His sister's nasty words caused him such a pain, that his entire mind was filled with regrets, stress and troubles, all the pains and all the sufferings he had experienced before, especially due to women, came to his mind, because that was his way of growing bitter and getting motivated, finding excuses. Because of the blows and pains he would receive systematically from women who treated him only as a surrogate of their pleasure, like a sex toy, due to his physical beauty that had brought him just troubles, he was so disgusted and terrified that his was mind now producing only those images of times when he was constantly humiliated and scoffed in his love and his deepest feelings, that made him suffer to dementia. He had to set himself free somehow. He didn't want just sex, he wanted love.

Sex was no use for him. Every such attempt, when love was dragged again into the gutter of cheap passions, was so terrible that it unleashed moods that he felt like blowing his own brains out, and since he could not find another way out of those moods, he felt the urge to break loose and travel by car outside of Bucharest, coming here to his collegemate. He didn't tell Dragos any of those thoughts he had to protect him from such pains. Dragos might have been disturbed by such desires and terrible feelings from time to time and he didn't want to unleash them with his

134

thoughts. He did not confess his heaviest thoughts to Dragos, but he felt such a relief just thinking of the monastery because he's always considered himself a monk in the world the same as Dragos was at the monastery, he also lives like a monk, a teacher and a company clerk. That was the place where he would get filled up with joy, with hope and could pray unhindered and could get away. It was the weekend when he recharged his batteries and could erase from his mind, until the following week, all the reproaches from his sister, who also had a many issues to deal with, her children and her job, and paid no mind to him.

Rafael's thoughts were wandering again. "Poor Dragos, he left for the monastery eventually. He was so disappointed with women that he went into the wide world and he ended up where God wanted. The Lord or the man works in mysterious ways. What was he thinking and feeling when he went to the monastery, who knows? Is he happy? But hey, am I happy? I'm happy in a way, I have two jobs that I like, I have nothing to complain about, I make money and I have this satisfaction that I did something and I have this dissatisfaction that I have not done something else. I want a family, a wife, children to look after them, to be a regular guy, as they say. Yet, all this time, I was like a Dragos, a monk, the difference is that he was in a monastery and I was here, in the world, two very strange paths. Still, Dragos was a nice guy, even though he is heavy drinker, when in college, he used to drink and then went to the bathroom to throw up.

I wonder if everybody does the same after drinking? Or maybe just some who can't take too much alcohol? Others, who can because their body is used to such a habit, do not have immediate reaction to this poison, but they are destroyed for life. Their body is destroyed slowly, they claim that they live as long, regardless of their drinking or no drinking. So much constraint to do things that make you feel bad and you don't even have any regret, but promise that you will do just as bad next time. But Dragos is one of the persons who got saved from all these! I may have played a role in all this stuff when he came after me at the monastery, at Golia, and then when he saw his girlfriend with the married painter. He must have been so disgusted, poor guy. Then, he searched for Corina to tell her that he was in love with her and wanted to marry her, not to go to the monastery but marry him. But, eventually, they both took the vow and poor Dragos has even become a priest.

He is in such a beautiful monastery and it seems to be beneficial to him, he even enjoys it, nothing to say about it. I feel great when I go to this monastery where Dragos is. I call him so, but his monk name is Theodor. When I asked where Father Theodor was, a monastery brother said to me:

-Father Teodoru is at the service now and cannot receive you, but if you want to expect him.

-No problem, I stay and wait for him.

In this expectation, with the short road leading to the monastery, his thoughts were unbounded in their natural stream, in the sleepless mind. He recollected other moments from visits to Dragos, which mingled with the present ones.

Oh, but how happy was the poor guy when he laid eyes on me, he did not even make his prayer. Other times he used to oblige me to do the prayer with him, he was so eager to pray together. When I was a student, I really wanted to have a mate or a friend to pray with and to talk for hours about God, but I did not have that particular friend, now Dragos was the one who lived this joy and eagerness of meditation and prayer that I used to experience at that time. The wheel turns seemingly. But I suspect he was somewhat very disturbed and unsettled since he felt so much the need to pray and make me pray along. He would only calm down these states by struggling to think about God. Now I'm the one troubled, and that's why I'm here, to calm down, and he's the one very composed who can help me heal my soul. Meanwhile, he had gotten in monastery. I see him very calm, at terms with his fate, and I sense no restlessness and trouble in him or I may be wrong. Perhaps he conceals his feelings, even though his face is very bright, very serene, and he also transmits this serenity to me. It is so nice to be blessed by God with such a friend.

It seems like nothing has happened, as if we wanted to be two college mates who are constantly concerned about God's theology and we are constantly discussing about that. And that's exactly our situation. When in college, I wanted so much to have someone to talk to about God but I had no one. I used to talk to those monks from Golia, but I wanted to talk to someone constantly, it would have been great if I had a brother-like colleague and they wouldn't have been all pagans. They all went mad with that sex craze paganism, you wouldn't believe, just some lost children, some of them got saved, others, God knows what to has come out of them and where they settled. One does stupid things when young, but, later on, nothing happens. If your body grows ill after your vice has destroyed it, all you can do is go to hospitals to get treament. This belief in God heals you, gives you strength, cures you of lots of nonsense, if you don't pay attention, you take upon yourself new and bigger nonsense. Everything must be kept under control, without pep talk, without unnecessary exaggerations, because God does not want the impossible from us, but He wants our possible, as we can bear and do.

Dragos looks very nice in monk clothing, being a monk is truly something romantic. Dedicating your life to worship God is quite magnificent, never marry and living in virginity all your life. I still get a bitter taste when I think about marriage.. Very many people get to a certain age, they never marry, they have no children, have no spouse and they regret bitterly, they are constantly sad and are eaten up by this issue, just like me. I wonder why don't I free myself from this desire and this state, why don't I abadon myself to God's will and let Him choose the kind of life to should lead. Because this matter, being married or not, is so important that you'd better do it with much prayer and free your soul from this desire, because you cannot do this by yourself, it is not up to you or you alone. Why so much needless suffering, because I have a passionate soul, this makes me suffer. I keep trying in vain to make a girlfriend, everything falls apart like wax before fire, because that relationship is not from God.

And, instead of enjoying some beauty, I spend my mental time with all sorts of deceptions. Well, I was wrong, but why don't I learn my lesson from that deception and I am messed up most of the times. Instead of being stronger and steadier in my judgments, I am weaker and growingly unable, I suffer more for no reason, while I am quite happy on my own, I am happy because I am free and strong, but especially this freedom that I feel makes me so content and happy that I would not trade this freedom for nothing in the world. I couldn't have this freedom without God's help and gift. Then, why can't I abandon myself to His will? My own will seems to be much better. I am often annoyed and it seems to me like an act of cowardice if I drop this issue, this desire. It seems to me that if I do not cease to suffer, that is, to give up hoping of ever finding the right woman, when I find her, I will no longer be able to love her. But this is a nonsense.

I must first be at this peace given by God in my heart and in this joy, so I can reach happiness.

The way I manage to read and meditate on this world and, especially, my moods of prayer, relaxation and peace that I experience, they give me so much freedom that I don't want to lose ever again. I lead a life so pleasing to God, I really don't know how to appreciate all these and I believe that this life of mine is not devoid of beauty if I'm not married. Well, that is not my path, I must follow a different path and I must stay on the track. My loneliness is so beautiful and pleasing to God that I truly am the happiest man, because my manhood does not consist of the large number of women I've had but of the way I knew how to defend this God-given manhood for something better. I think about Dragos now, he was the greatest sinner during his youth, but he went to the monastery, it's not relevant how and why he got into the arms of God, all that matters is that he is there. I was with God from the very beginning, I did not go to the monastery but I preferred to live like a monk in the world and have a job, to be free and act as I feel and as I think. I'm in a deadlock now, I feel a sort of indifference, fatigue, as if I got bored to pray, I don't know, I have moments when I feel how different I am from God. I don't know what is wrong with me, I have never thought I would get to this state of boredom after that mystical moment from my youth.

Dragos loves God more than I do. In fact, no one knows what the poor guy is going through, is he happy or unhappy, he can't say, although he seems to be truly happy here. As if I'm not, but I see myself such a wuss and I often get rebellious in front of God for everything that I have, instead of thanking Him for the beautiful life I have led. What do I want to do? It would be very easy for me to start doing God-knows what stupid things! But, then, could I go back to whatever I have now so beautiful. And I find in me some sort of restlessness so to say, as if I keep waiting for a miracle to happen to me and I always meet the temptation which is everywhere, all the way. I thought I was struggling with myself to be a good person, but I'm nothing but a great wuss. I thought I was fighting, I was leading a spectacular life, to God's liking, but I'm a fool before Him and I'm not worthy of anything. I'm kind of warmish, there is nothing I can do, and as if I'm doing nothing all day long, and I am truly sitting around all day without doing anything. But, most of all, my mind is not active."

Meanwhile, Rafael, deepened in his thoughts, arrived in the monastery and strolled through the courtyard looking at flowers and trees.

"It is quite serious in this existence, in this world, that we live terribly addicted to others, we cannot be free precisely because we are addicted, we believe that we can receive happiness from the other, but I can get happiness from myself alone and if I am not happy, I won't be happy with others either. Unfortunately, our addiction to others is toxic and, therefore, we must constantly fight with ourselves to keep our freedom. That is why we need to be free so that we can be happy, but it concerns an inner freedom, not just the freedom to do whatever I want. Yes, I can do whatever I want and only what I want but, thus, I will live terribly addicted to others because I no longer trust myself and I need someone to confirm my freedom or my degree of freedom. The moment I invest feelings in someone I expect that person to give me something in return as if in any debt to me. But that person doesn't really owe me anything because he has nothing to give me. I expect him to give me what I can never have because I expect this freedom that I can only have through myself and it depends on my level of understanding of about everything that I am or I want to become. I won't be able to love the other if he loses his inner freedom along with me, he can be the one that I love only if he is uncontraint to do so and wants to do that and, by doing it, he feels fulfilled like a free being. This freedom is very complicated as some people or all people cannot experience it because we believe that freedom can be subjected or the outcome of freedom allows me to subject because I am free to do whatever I please.

Never will I be free if I want to master anyone. I will be truly free when the other has the freedom of choice to act or have as I want him to. That's why people cannot love because love means obedience and addiction and this is the reason why people feel so good in the care of God. They feel free to do whatever God tells them in the soul to do, because God is all loving and lets us be as we feel and how we can be, and He does not constrain us, that is why maybe we should not to be so judgemental about what others do or don't do. He is free to live his life as he believes, in his laws and in his sins or mistakes, everyone has the right to live his own nonsense down to the end. We are so free but all that surrounds us makes us live our lives so constrained. We experience strange addictions to people and things, to our fantasies, but mostly to our illusory desires. They make us lose our inner freedom, petrify our heart and we believe that we have suffered terribly, but the problem is that it's an unnecessary form of suffering that we could have avoided provided we had abandoned ourselves to God's will and we would have let Him decide for us. As He is the supreme freedom we must first let Him choose and offer us and then we must accept and receive this gift as the gift of freedom. But if I do so and take no action, it does not mean that I resign and don't do what I was supposed to. I can have this attitude after having striven with all my will and my strength for that. Had I not striven, this passive position becomes harmful to me and turns into mockery. I lose my dignity before God. Because He knows best what is good or not for the other.

For us as well, because we do not know all the aspects. Oh, I wish I could reach this ultimate understanding of freedom. I often fail to see the meaning. I keep wanting more in those moments of suffering and, thus, I find it hard and I keep calling God to help me and bless me with a meaning so that, post-suffering, I can understand some of that woe. You see, this is the ultimate state, so that, after sufferance, you can become stronger and wiser, tougher with yourself, you can stop focusing on the transient things of this world which are so misleading. Without judging anyone, I believe that each of us must see to himself and we all should follow the natural course of life.

Chapter 26

He leant against the church wall and gazed at the sky, his mind was wandering again. "That's the way it is, we have to move on as we are, with this desire to always learn from our suffering and to behave nicely with ourselves, with what we are or we are not, or we want to become and can not be. That's the problem, we need to learn to be free firstly with ourselves and then with others, because you cannot give the other the supreme freedom unless you are a free person, and this freedom can always be achieved through constant thinking efforts.

I believe it is the daily effort to be free with God, that was what the saints were talking about when they looked at the purity of mind and heart, they spoke about this freedom as obedience to the will of God, the supreme being who knows best what is good or not for me. One can achieve this understanding on daily basis through continuous meditation, because you can have this state now but you might lose it tomorrow and so on. We believe that freedom is a state that we have now and here and we believe that, thus, we have gained freedom and we will have it forever. This is the ultimate mistake because we are wrapping the spiritual concepts in vestment of concrete and we treat eternal things as clothing items or objects, things we cannot get rid of. Things are different and this is the source of suffering, the fact that we confuse things, everything we experience is mixed up, as if nothing was right, but we, with our understanding, we are the ones who don't really know what to do with it. We constantly make these meanings differently, but we do not materialize them into a force that frees us from useless desires, and, thus, to be, to become and to remain free beings, logical beings.

We believe that things are given from the very beginning, that freedom is given to us and we have to take it the same as we take a book in our hand and use it as we like. This is my great frustration, that I cannot be a free being because I am afraid and I do not want to have this permanent exercise of my freedom. I have heard somewhere a title: "The Slice of Freedom," well, not slice of freedom, but slice of effort to be free all the time, this is the great mystery of Christianity.

In a world where everything that is spirit is wrapped in an amorphous and heavy matter just for the sake of giving things a form, and so you can count them, the forms become without foundation because the forms had been tempted to steal the spirit and fool us and lead us into a big mistake. This is the great problem of the current times, that the spirit is to be wrapped in a matter, even mathematical principles must take shape, it doesn't matter, and all we intend to live needs a shape so it can be entered in a database and eventually accounted for a tax. Here is the roughness of these times after two thousand years of Christianity and travels to the moon and through the universe. Something must happen, a new paradigm must be created, the paradigm of the spirit that rebels against its false forms, which only express a great lie, because the spirit with its eternity shall not be subjected to any form but be experienced, felt, loved, the spirit is God's love and this cannot be put into words, it is the expression of supreme freedom. It's the greatest mystery of life. After all, which is the supreme love you could have with someone, either you could give your life for her or, if you love her and she loves somebody else, you would not hate her but you would even be able to love her and let her be, give her this freedom in your soul to be with the one she loves even that person is not you. But such a thing is impossible to do with the soul. That would be the case provided she was fair and honest with you, but there is betrayal most of the times, if not every time, and then what could you do, how could you free yourself from pain and hatred? You have to set her free, especially in your heart, but not just as convenience, that means that you are truly free and you offer the other the supreme freedom. Do must not shut yourself down in a permanent hatred as if nothing can change and you have to kill yourself, to die because that person is not in love with you. This is pure theory, but in reality, when it comes to the suffering inflicted in you by that person, you think differently, because it's a form of betrayal after all, why did she stay with you if she had not loved you, just to use you?

There's no other way of salvation but the path of healing, you move on with God, being serene in life, because that's better, that's how God wants to us, but it is hard with this tendency towards hatred, you have no choice, you have to fight with it because the hatred for the other one is so great and it starts out of the blue and you'll find it difficult to get rid of it, shake it off, mitigate it. That's why you have to act in such a manner that you won't hate anymore and this hatred should be as little as possible or, if it is unstoppable, you must not let it get you, because it will ruin you. You have to fight with it and not be defeated, because hatred is a trap in which we all fall, it is impossible not to hate, but we have to go nicely through this hatred we all feel and experience, to learn something from it and, thus, we shall become free and overcome it to become noble beings, to be God's boyars and not people's".

Rafael was trying to figure out all these because he didn't want to hate people anymore, as he often felt so helpless, he hated deeply some people from his past whom he remembered and could not get rid of this hate. He had to move on, he knew that had he gotten rid of that hatred, he would have healed and would have been a free person again. This is how Christ tells us to be, free beings next to Him, free from any sort of hatred for our neighbor, to give the other supreme freedom and, thus, we will also become free from the daily nonsense that make us ill and bound us. Yet, how difficult was it for Rafael to do that? Now, he was eager to meet Dragos whom he had seen through the window of little church altar, where he was tidying up and cleaning. He didn't come out straight away but chose to stay and finish, because had he done so, he wouldn't have returned and the church altar would have been untidy and messy. He was so happy when he was sweeping and washing the floor, he could just fly. He was looking forward to have a profound discussion about everything that's most beautiful in this world. But Dragos also knew that Rafael was coming to the monastery for a purpose, he came to calm down, he must be troubled by something, but, at the same time, his soul was longing for God.

Chapter 27

After having treated the venereal diseases and after having gone through such a good a period, Maria was ecstatic, taking walks in the park with her child in the stroller, she used to take him to the Cernica Monastery, to St. Calinic, almost every Sunday, then, the child had new problems. Apparently there's a killer who desperately wants this child's life for something ugly, perhaps for hell, since all these evils never end and you get dazzled to find them out, dazzled that such things even exist. It seemed like a malefic and invisible spirit wanted this child's life and it was attacking him with all the evils in the world.

"Lord, do not take my baby. Maria was praying. If he dies, I'll have nothing to live for. Don't You understand, my Lord, that my life is pointless? Why did You want me to come to this world? Why did You want this baby to be born? Can't You see that his life is meaningless. Why should he be born if he still dies? It would have been better not to have been born at all!

-But you wanted him to be born. Didn't you want the baby as much as me?

-Yes, I wanted him. I realize now, in fact, I have realized that for some time, that I was the only one who wanted this baby, Mihai did not want him. Yes, I wanted him to be born, I wanted a baby, but I was the only one, I wanted him too much.

-Yeah, you wanted him too much!

-Oh, I wanted this child so much. This child is my life. Lord, how can I be so alone.

-But you're not alone, you're with God.

-God abandoned me, He doesn't care about me!

-Nonsense, how could He not care!

-I feel like I'm going crazy. Why, why is this happening? It's too much. I'm tired of this life. All I have is this pain in my soul. Oh! The pain in human soul is so strong. You suffer until you go nuts. Yet, ironically, you don't lose your mind. There are few who lose it! They go insane because something cracks inside their brain, not because they carry too much pain in their soul. Nothing of what's inside one's soul can be seen, nothing at all. Everything stays out of sight! Lord, I don't want him to die, why should this child die? I have struggled so much. I want him to live!

-.......

-Yes, but my wish is of no importance to You?!

-............

-Nothing, nothing but my thoughts, only me, me, me, with my pain, this endless pain. I want to vanish at the same time with this kid. I don't want to live anymore! What's my life good for? Why did you sentence me to life! I cannot live anymore! I want to die. I want to disappear as if I had never existed!

-But that's it, you are, you were, you will be.

-I don't care anymore, what's the use, I wish I had never existed, it would have been great if I had not existed!

-If he dies? If Gabriel dies? Gabriel! ... No ... no ... he should not die .. He's been connected like that to life support for a month".

Maria collapsed crying, nearly fainting, on the hospital bed. She felt like screaming but she was exhausted. She couldn't find strength to scream. She always wanted to cry her lungs out but she was ashamed. She was not alone in the hospital. Had she been alone in her house, she would have screamed her brains out. But in this case, she could not scream, because she still had a dose of dignity. She was still lucid.

-I haven't lost my mind yet but I will soon go insane. It won't be long until I get off the edge.

-I cannot accept the death of my child! No, no!

-If he dies, I will kill myself!

-But why kill yourself? Have some hope!

-No, there is no hope. No hope.

-Each person should have hope!

-Should!!!!!

-No, I'm hopeless. There is no more hope in my mind! I've lost everything, I have nothing, I have nothing to live for, I've lost all hope."

Maria was crying again, shaking, sitting on the hospital bed. She was alone in the room, staring at her child who had been connected to life support for a month, without any results. She would have screamed, but couldn't, she feared her baby would get scared. There must be a complete silence in the room, no shock should happen. Her inner shocks had to happen inside her heart, inside her, in her soul and nowhere else. They were not supposed to come out

-Lord, I can't take it anymore. I feel I'm going insane! I wish I could lose my mind all of a sudden, Lord, so that I would not be aware of anything. This very awareness is burning me, suffocating me, these are the torments of hell. I don't want to live this anymore, Lord. Why did you punish me like this? What have I done? Maybe I don't even exist! Maybe You don't even exist, why do I suffer so much! You don't care about people's pains. My suffering does not matter. Why, why is this happening? I want to know that. I want to know and understand. I cannot love You, Lord, in this circumstance! I almost cannot believe in You anymore. Why so much suffering? Who uses it!? Why should I suffer so much? Why am I like this? Why? Why? What have I done? Or should I do nothing?"

Maria let the tears run down her face reaching her neck and down to her chest. Her hospital gown was soaked with tears, everything was wet in front and she was trembling. Her mind seemed to have plunged into darkness. She got a terrible headache all of a sudden and she felt her heart draining, as if the soul was no longer there. The soul had shrinked from so much pain. She wished she had been emotionless. She would see objects, the table, the chair, which were inert, doing nothing. Everything seemed to be so unfamiliar. She felt that she would go insane if she continued with that thought. She desperately wanted to do something to escape. The objects around her seemed to be hollows that opened up to swallow her. She saw her child in that condition. She went to him, kissed him, caressed him. But the child had no reaction. Her hands were cold and child's hands seemed to gotten cold, too. She felt horrible, it seemed that the baby was cold. Her imagination continues to unfold and to add to reality. Suddenly, Gabriel was dead in bed, disconnected from machines, everything in her mind was on a very large, hyperbolised scale. She saw a nurse coming impassibly in front of her and telling her:

-We are sorry, there is nothing more we can do. The meningitis virus has killed the baby. Do not despair, lady. Do not despair. We're sorry. That's all we can do.

While imagining this, Maria took a new look at her child and everything seemed to have frozen in the hospital room. The bed seemed to have been made of snow and she was in a freezer. She stood up slowly as if she feared she would destroy the glacial silence and would crush the air and thought to herself:

-There's a window on the tenth floor which was open half an hour ago. I'll throw myself from there. That's it! It's over. The baby is dead. My life is over! I cannot live anymore. If the window is shut, I will open it. I won't go with the elevator as I could raise suspicions! I'll walk up the stairs. There are seven stairs, not so many. Nobody usually uses the stairs. I won't run into anyone. Even if I run into anyone, they won't suspect a thing.

Maria had two images in her mind which kept repeating obsessively one after another on the screen of imagination. The baby, her little baby dead in the hospital bed and her release, jumping off the tenth floor. She had seen that jumping from a height on TV several times, in movies, in videos. She was mentally prepared for self-destruction thanks to the media which had been working on that for a long time, infesting people's desperate soul. The society has intensely worked on that. Everything seemed so beautiful and liberating all of a sudden. This floating gave her the feeling that she was relieved of pain and she shouting in her inner self:

-Lord, I don't want to commit suicide, but there's no other way out, I don't want to suffer this much, I want everything to come to an end. Anyway, You don't love me. Anyway, nobody loves me in this world. There's no point, I don't want to die, but I all I can do is die. The suffering is too much, I can't take it anymore. It's all over, it's over. I don't want to die but I can't live anymore.

She kept repeating unconsciously in her mind, in an automatism of despair, the prayer of the heart, "Lord Jesus, have mercy on me," but it was all just an automatism, something else was being prepared inside her. She was praying rather unconsciously, like a despair of the spirit, like a flickering of the unconscious, like a force of soul, stronger than her.

The image of the open window was running before her eyes, persisting in her mind like an obsession. She continued:

-Does it have a curtain? Or doesn't it? If it doesn't, I'll see, it's gonna be harder. If it has a curtain, it will cover me. But I'm almost there, two more stairs and that's it, and that's it …

Maria climbs each flight of stairs almost running. Bearing in mind the image of her dead child lying on the hospital bed.

-This is it, I'm over it, I get free from everything, I got rid of everything, I'm over it. Life is no longer important, not even before God. God doesn't love me. He has never loved me or the baby if he wants to kill us. He doesn't care.

And she kept repeating "Lord, Jesus," in her unconscious, she was praying all the time, an automatic praying, because she had been used to repeat "Jesus, Jesus, have mercy on me" when her mind was at rest and was running no more images.

Maria was crying hard-bitten:

-No, He doesn't care about my existence, God is evil if he wants to kill us both. God is evil, He doesn't love me. Had He loved me I would have had a good marriage, I would have had a man beside me who would have loved me instead of living like this, in such loneliness. Why? God is evil, He doesn't love me. He doesn't want us to live. If he doesn't want me to live, He doesn't want my child to live, I won't live! Anyhow, He doesn't care about my life! So, I'm gonna die along with my kid and that's it.

Maria was already tired by the ninth step and went up the stairs at a slower pace gasping for air, she couldn't run anymore. She climbed one step, then another one, and yet another as if she couldn't go up anymore, her legs and hands were shaking. She had a terrible headache, but pulled her strength up to walk, so she kept walking, stepping ahead with determination. She climbed one more step saying to herself:

-God doesn't love me or the child, otherwise He would not let him die. "Lord, Jesus". He doesn't care, "Lord, Jesus," we are his dumb toys, what does He gain by our being alive, nothing, nothing at all. "Lord, Jesus."

She climbed one more step saying:

-It's over, my child's life and my life. "Lord, Jesus", the unconscious answered, as a retort to that thought.

When she set her foot on the third step of the ninth flight of stairs, a thought came to her mined with such force that dazzled her, it was so powerful, like a thunder in the space of mind, which made her collapse trembling so much as if the temperature had been minus twenty degrees.

-But what if he pulls it through??? !!! The thunder of that thought slammed her mind.

Maria was paralyzed by the force of that thought which screamed inside her mind with such power!

-Yes, yes, if he makes it, she repeated. And suddenly she started crying and sobbing like never before. She got soft like a rag, like a handkerchief flying softly down to the grass, pulled out from the clothesline in the yard, at countryside. She leant against the wall and sat down on that step she couldn't climb, the sobbing was so powerful that she couldn't hold back and burst into tears so noisily that the sound invaded the stairway and made the atmosphere unbearable. Yet, nothing happened, no one heard because nobody was using that step, those stairs which were empty. People use only elevator to go up.

-If he pulls it through, if he pulls it through, if he pulls it through??????? That thought was howling in her brain!!!!!!!!

They were repeating obsessively like a wheel, those words, just like the other images that were groaning, images of the dead child and the open window. "If he pulls it through"! She saw that in her imagination, the face of the child raised from the dead. Who's gonna raise the child if she dies. She was shivering, suddering with fear, cold, amazed at what she could have done, could have thought, her teeth clenched and got dizzy, babbling in her mind.

-I must have hope, by all means, He can resurect him, He can do a miracle with me, by all means, this death would be absurd, I have to believe he'll pull it through. What's wrong with me?

She wept even more bitterly, but this time in total silence, she took out all the pain, mutely and ugly like never before.

-If he pulls it through!!

Maria saw the child jumping around her, she saw him in her imagination and smiled when seeing her kid, laughing and alive in her imagination, she fainted at the sight of such image in her mind.

When she came to her senses, she was shivering so much that even the stairs seemed to shake along with her, her sobbing knelt her right there.

Shaking and pulling knees to her chest, she went off again. She fell in a state of unconsciousness that was quite pleasant and restful. She had no control over her body, she leant against the wall, holding her head between her knees and soaking her chest from so many tears dropped for God-knows how long, it seemed an eternity.

A few minutes later he came to her senses, having a terrible headache and feeling tired. She felt like falling into a deep sleep. She could hardly restain herself from lying down on those cold and unaccommodating stairs. But she got up to her feet trembling, leaning against the walls, she went down the three steps of the ninth flight of stairs, crawling to the elevator, leaning against the walls. She got into the elevator and went down to the third floor. She got to the room where her baby was sleeping, in the same condition, without any change, still connected to machines, but she said to herself:

-My baby is asleep, he'll get well, there's no other way, he will wake up, I must get some sleep, to rest, anyway, I'm all wet from my tears. "Lord, Jesus, have mercy on me, Lord, Jesus, have mercy on me" and kept repeating so while climbing into bed.

She collapsed on the blanket and fell into a deep sleep like she hadn't have for months.

Chapter 28

She fell asleep on the bed and the headache was terrible. Tears were flooding her face drying out in the meantime and, keeping her eyes closed, she was reaching out to child's bed, as if ready to hug him, ready to wake up to give him something as fast as she could, to do anything, but her hands were hanging feeble and sleep was invading her body, healing her.

A nurse comes into the room and saw her asleep. She was surprised to see her sleeping, because she rarely would see that woman sleeping and she often wondered how to could she resist sleeplessly for so long. She enjoyed seeing her like that because she would always see her exhausted and kept telling her to get some rest so she could hang in there for her baby. She took her by the hand and tucked her in bed, took a blanket and put it on top of her, covering her so she would not get a cold. This nurse was kind-hearted, she was fond of her and they would often talk about God, and the nurse would tell her when she asked:

-Why are all these happening to me? Why all these happen to people. I can't take it anymore. I can't live like this anymore. I often wish I hadn't existed.

-We are not to know why we go through all these. I am terrified about what I see, as well? We cannot understand the reason of God. Human mind cannot comprehend. Better to leave us in His hands and not want anything more! Let's trust Him.

-But God really wants to kill us??!

-No, He doesn't want that! It's just that we can't understand! I am a nurse and I want to help, to do good to as many people as possible, but I cannot always do that. I am thinking of God, I fast and pray, as well. I'm horrified by people's illnesses, but we must not despair. We have to stay strong.

-...

-And you're strong. You have to be patient, it'll be okay.

-But it's been one month since he'been like that. She would burst into tears.

-We must wait, be patient, miracles happen sometimes. We don't know everything. Medicine does not know everything. But I'm hoping he'll be fine. It can't be otherwise.

-Do you think so?

-I'm positive! Let me pray to God for you! You will see that everything will be fine. He will get well and you will play with him and raise grandchildren from him.

-If I'll be around.

Maria couldn't find the courage to think about grandchildren. This child was her life and nothing else. She would smile, she liked the thought but couldn't imagine further on. Now, after this bitter cry, Maria was sleeping in bed and was having a dream of herself as a ten-year-old who could fly like in fairy tales. Everything was so beautiful. That dream was like a therapy. It was like she was a little girl flying through the botanical garden in Iasi. She remembered the garden and her grandmother. She dreamt of an immense field of roses and lots of bees. She dreamed that she could fly like a bee over vineyards and reached the wooden church beyond the vineyards, across the border, which she could spot on the horizon and never actually reached in reality, but she got to it now, in her dream, in these moments so special to her. When she could get there, she thought, "I finally got here after so much time."

As a bee, she landed on the curch door which was closed. She had a feeling of sadness because she could not get in to kneel down before the icon of the Mother of God and pray. A heartbreaking sadness came over her. Why are churches closed and she can't go in? But suddenly she remembered that she was a bee, so she could enter providing she found a crack between the door and doorcase. Flying around, flapping her wings, she found the right place and flew inside. What a joy, just her, alone, with God in that small village church. The light was dim since the doors were closed and the windows were small and she, as a bee, was flying to windows and looking out. She could see the field streching before her eyes and a sense of freedom invaded her eyes and soul. Then, she took a look inside the church and saw as the light coming through the windows to illuminate everything around. She had an extraordinary urge to go to the icon of the Mother of God, sit on her hand and cry. She saw herself, as a bee, sitting on the hand of the Mother of God, crying and asking for help, crying until she nearly fainted. The dream continued like a liberation, with her standing on the hand of the Mother of God, gazing ar the candle light in front of the icon and an endless joy flooded her soul after all the tears. She felt like she had no more lead on her wings and she could fly. She wondered so much around the church, looking at that light and the special state that made her cool down and feel free, as though she had forgotten about everything, all she could feel was the pleasure of flying before God and the Mother of God. It seemed as if she could feel the power and light of God which are infinite. God, as well, suffered terribly because his son was sacrificed for the salvation of human beings, and the Mother of God suffered dreadfully when her son was crucified. She was feeling so close to God and his suffering, as though she started to grasp something, a meaning which vanished quickly. She felt the need to fly, to rise into the light. She flew back to the door and found that space she had used to get in. When coming out, a strong light flooded her eyes and it seemed that, as a bee, she blended into the light and sky blue. Then, she flew away. She could see a large field of grass and many sheep grazing on that meadow. Yet, it seemed she was alone in that dream, with no people around. Then, she floated, flew up high above the top of trees, as if she had been on a plane. She could see from up there the flocks of sheep, which seemed white dots on that green meadow, and a breathtaking sun, resembling a red fire disk, appeared on the horizon. She could float far away. She wanted to fly up to the red and powerful sun. It seemed like the sheep and the grass turned red at sunrise and she seemed to have been dressed in red, in bright red clothes. Yet, however red was everything around, she could fly and feel good in this space, in this red, so red world. It seemed like she was in a very large room, illuminated by a red light bulb. This dream calmed her down and she saw her face in this child-bee who was a representation of her in the past, as if she saw herself being freed from everything she could no longer live, think and bear. She was freed from the death that had gotten into her spirit.

Chapter 29

Something bad happened to Maria's kid, a drama I might say. There was a reason why the poor thing kept staying in hospital, with so many injections and so many drugs. Now, on top of everything, he's got viral meningitis. How did he get the virus, where from? From vaccines for children brought from overseas. They say Romania is subject to genocide to reduce the population, especially a food genocide. How could vaccines for children be infected with the meningitis virus and how did this happen? We have no idea. There was a big scandal in the media on the subject and what was the use, since this child, after having spent so much time in hospital to get well, caught this disease, just like that, as a gift from the West. The scandal lasted for a month in the Romanian press and what were results? Zero. Each one tries to pull it through on his own and with his own body.

How could all this happen? In fact, we only know the truth from the press. Yet, which is the real truth? Mandatory vaccines had been brought from abroad to protect children up to two years of age against all illnesses they could have had at this age and later and all who were inoculated with those vaccines got meningitis. Since Gabriel had to be vaccinated mandatorily, he got this virus as well.

Those vaccines had been brought already infested from the West. Murder, actionable negligence, diabolical experiment, take those pharmaceutical companies to court and find them. What's the use considering these children will be destroyed for life. These vaccines could be produced in Romania, we have a drug factory as well, but why not buy these vaccines from the West, they were safer and cheaper and somebody got a bonus worth tens of thousands of euros for this transaction or, who knows, rumours say hundreds of thousands of euros or even millions of euros. In fact, the amounts of money allegedly stolen, in frauds with the state, are so big that we cannot even begin to imagine, and I believe we will find out very late about the extent of the loot. An honest person has no unit of measurement here. Just like Romanians have always believed that everything we produce is not good, but has low quality and it's cheap, whereas absolutely everything that comes from abroad has better quality, we are in the same situation here, the good and high-quality, but more expensive Romanian vaccine is dropped, and they buy the allegedly good, cheap and deadly vaccine from overseas. Well, Romania is market for cheap and low-quality drugs, or expensive and poor-quality drugs imported from the West.

Romanians turned to the international drug market as everybody, when ill, would be desperate to get all sorts of drugs, desperate to pay any amounts of money, no matter how expensive they are, just to get them, no matter how much money you spend on them, the main thing is to have them so they can make you healthy again. That's the case now, why not buy Western vaccines for children up to two years old. But the decision was made at ministerial level, because there were some commissions and some big money to be cashed in by someone, a person no one knows about. Everyone will pay for what he does and one who is greedy for money paves his own way to hell and self-destruction, but in the meantime, there were children who died, others will be crippled for life and others will get well with God's help and body's strength.

Children were vaccinated and then, instead of becoming healthy, they got sick and passed away one after another. Subsequent tests revealed that the vaccines were infected with the meningitis virus, but it was too late. Gabriel was in the same situation. The kid was inoculated and got the meningitis virus that sent him into "the loftiest and the most beautiful coma." What are the assumptions of the press and which are the most likely causes that any normal mind would think of and could comprehend? Is there a Mafia of drug makers as we speak? In Western countries or anywhere else? Most of them are privately held and, maybe by mistake or maybe on purpose, some of these vaccines have been infected with this virus. So the company would not lose money, they had to come with a solution. Much money would have been lost provided those vaccines hadn't been sold. Money above all. The drugs could not be retailed on the domestic market because that would have been a bad move and they would have ended up in court. The same as in other civilized country. Since Romania had become a true merchant market paradise for many countries, why not find some fools who, for a bribe of a few thousands euros or dollars or even more, would accept the transaction. These vaccines were to be marketed here and, why not, even a little cheaper. Possibly the one who got them had no idea, no one is doing any tests on them, because who might think that someone could commit murder at this level. The person who bought the vaccines was glad, he took a big commission for that, maybe even the money for a studio, it would have taken him years to save that money and buy it. Romanians are also greedy when it comes to buying things from the West, because those are definetely better, the deal is struck and the children are dead. Who shall be held accountable for this murder?

Who is responsible for such a thing? The company which sold the drugs to the Romanian state and the doctors who gave the vaccines, or rather Romanian doctors who did not run tests on medicines? How could one sue them, that person would have to be o trial for years to come. Could theose children become well again, could anyone bring them back from the dead? It took a while for doctors in Romania to understand that the vaccine was infected and some children got sick and others died. Many opened their eyes to the West and to their benevolent attitude towards us, but it was too late. The love of money and profit is so great that one could resort to murder. Romania is a country located somewhere on Earth, why be bypassed.

This baby was so miserable in the first place and, on top of that, his health condition was additionally harmed by others. The hospital director was swearing like hell and spitting around, but how could that help? He took a stand in the press, a huge scandal was created, but after those outbursts of anger, things calmed down and people continued to hold their children who were sick, dead or scarred for life. The happy ones saw them healed. Yet, how many could say they have been harmed and got away unscarred.

In the first years after the revolution, Romania became a real paradise for foreigners who wanted to get rich overnight and above legal limits, a real tax haven where black labor was something exploitable and violation of elementary labor rules was common behaviour. Things are the same nowadays, we keep boasting that it's the big crisis and we're not getting out of it. Many years of work in Western countries followed that period when people were laid off and could hardly find some kind of work. Romanians would go there to work and get money, so they could build homes here in Romania or make a fortune. Some remained in those foreign countries without ever wanting to return. Yet, following this crisis, people return home tired, hungry, without much money in their pockets and unable to find work anywhere. He who owns a piece of land in the countrysie is blessed, as he works that land to eat and live, in poverty, but, at least, he can survive. This is the living standard for many people, this dire poverty. But, in the countryside, if you are hardworking, you are not poor, you are a farmer. Should there be another vision? Hard days are still to come for some Romanians and even harder for others. Blessed is he who is healthy and rejoices in his own, praising God and wanting to grow up in heart-related issues. Health is the most important asset.

Chapter 30

Rafael reflected much on what he was experiencing, on what he wanted to experience and on the work he wanted but could not do. He thought it was so weird he would not have any spare time. He used to have plenty of spare time when he had been a student but, now, time was used for as much work as possible. He was working around the clock. Work helped him forget about all kinds of problems and questions he was asking, because he had all sorts of anxieties. He worked hard, there was no more room for anxiety. Anxiety was healed while asleep and by sleep, that was all he cared about. But sometimes ... ... he enjoyed making money. He had the feeling that he had escaped from poverty, although he hadn't hated his poverty, but even enjoyed it. But now he was happy with his work, happy for what he managed to do. The job was very relaxing compared to the thousands of concerns he had and the hundreds of questions he could not answer. He was so bored that didn't want to do anything and would often give up things. He enjoyed school as it different than what he was doing on computer, at the firm. He had a car and that helped him. He could travel fast from company to school. But Rafael was rather interested in meditation. Meditation was awesome for him. He loved to meditate, that state of insight and reflexion was beautiful. He was feeling well, relaxed.

It was so nice when he returned home by ten o'clock at night, when he was sitting in the armchair with a cup of tea in his hand and meditating. The armchair seemed to take the shape of his body and warmed up his tea, sipped drop by drop, just like the thoughts that flowed freely through his mind. He would reflect on what had happened to him during that day. He enjoyed meeting people, seeing their reactions. He was terribly fond of reflecting on what they were thinking and, especially, how they could put into words their life experiences in an unseen manner. People's reactions put into words were terrible. He often felt ill-fitting with them. As if he had been in the middle and he had been thrown at relapsing words and images, hitting him like ping-pong balls. He was smiling or struggled with his soul to get rid of these images, blows, attacks, words. Or, perhaps, he felt the urge to decode them, they were like symbols of unknown worlds.

It would have been so nice for him to be far away from innuendos, glances, instigating words. It was amazing what he could understand by the words of those who were throwing them upon him. The "reflection of reality", that was spinning through his mind. "But why am I experiencing such an obsession?", he wondered. Why did he like so much to reflect before himself. He was a loner and chewed his own loneliness, hearing each word dripping inside him a different world, a different reality, other than the one he was living on daily basis. Then, he said to himself:

-"I work too much. But what could I do? I can't do whatever I want if I don't work that hard. This work gets me into a spin and, yet, I would really need to go some place, to go to the seaside. But it's cold now, it's almost winter. Though the sea is great during this period. But the mountain, the mountains. Actually, everybody tells me so, to go to the mountains, to the sea. I would drive to the countryside. It's hard for me to get there. It takes about seven hours of driving. Mountain and sea. Going there to spend my money, how stupid. I'm going to a strange place to feel bad. To be cold, to hate food. I don't know those people. No, no, I must go somewhere where I can enjoy time. I would have felt good at home, until recently, but I begin to feel like a stranger there as well. Before buying my house in the capital, I felt that was my home, the house built by dad and mom, and I used to feel this constant sorrow caused by the fact that I didn't own a house, that I wasn't able to get my own house. But now I have this one and I'm fine, the girls are here with me. They make just as much money as me, or even more, it's good. But why do I feel like a stranger when at home? I don't feel like home there, with my family. I could relax there. But why does that heaven-like house seem so irrelevant now?"

Rafael kept his eyes closed, he had already sipped half of his tea. The inactivity of some people is amazing. Being in a state of relaxation. He was scrutinizing his colleagues. He loved to lay back, relaxed and look around. When writing, he created characters based on some colleagues whose features were exaggerated or turned to an unknown direction, striving to find the ideas, states and demonstrations he wanted to debate and highlight. To that end, he had to meditate and be by himself. He closed his eyes because there were many numbers, the TV set and computer screen in front of him. He needed to stop seeing the fluctuations of light he had taken with him once he had left the office. He felt strange, neither good nor bad. He had a neutral inner state. As if he couldn't care less about anyone and anything. He wouldn't speak about hate, but neither about love. He was feeling so strange, rather neutral, but that state seemed to detour him from a well-known direction.

-Strangely, I sense some sort of separation from people and I've worked hard to achieve that, and I no longer have that emotional addiction to someone, to something, to people, words, states, I'm no longer dependent on all those and, yet, I'm not comfortable at all, being so inactive."

He was distant, no longer committed as if he was missing something, but that gave him inner force, though he was feeling growingly lonely. As though he had nothing else to care for, really care for, and to be constantly concerned about. And he didn't trust people. He was convinced that every man is capable of anything. One must be prepared for this, but not paranoid.

"-Well, now I'm not going to think about what harm could somebody do to me? I don't know, if I needed help, few would come and help me. Provided someone helps me, that will be totally and very uncommon, exceptional and totally accidental, because people, most of them, do good by accident". This state of contemplation experienced by Rafael was some sort of a mind therapy, soul cleaning. This state of the man sitting in the armchair was one of liberation. Rafael was praying. He used to pray while driving his car as well. While at home, he would kneel down or not, that was his prayer, the armchair. With his eyes closed, he would pray to God, that was mind's liberation from all the finderprints of mankind. The trace left behind in his mind, his soul and his brain, by a man sitting beside him or the outside world. The world we live in, what image can it take and what reflections does it determine inside a person's mind or in Rafael's reason? Could we know, could we control, could we understand those states?

Rafael was struggling to understand. "Can I swim contrary to the wave? Can I swim against the current? But what wave? What fight? What life? Why am I so afraid? Why do I live in such an unexplainable fear?

Yet, I'm not a chicken. A state of unexplainable anxiety? Because I am a strong man inside but I admit to myself that I have a state that sometimes depresses me, I don't admit that to others, because it would be pointless and I'm not stupid, all I have to do is take care of my fear. Had I not been afraid of life, of the other, I would not have felt such a great need for God! Terribly! I, we, cannot know what is in the mind of the other, so that we can defend ourselves! But I can imagine, I can discover through what others do! I feel so distant about other people. I wonder how can I be close to them? How can I help them? It is quite difficult to help others! In fact, you should not even have to help them. You help them in exceptional circumstances and only those who really need it. You only help them when they ask for it. But this help I offer others can be straight forward, because I don't know what they could do. I detest people! I wonder why?! Why do I feel and why am I surprised at these thoughts? By pictures? Because I have moments when I'm really afraid of what I'm living, of what I'm thinking? Am I a contradictory human being?"

"How can I get into my mind and understand it. I live in my own mind.

I always live in this state. And now I feel the need to sleep. Sleep is mind's best shower. ust like the body gets dirty by coming into contact with people and the world, so my mind gets dirty by coming into contact with the world. I've got to wash off my mind all that I hear daily, what I see daily and that is why I have to wash my mind like I wash my hands. The best way of washing is this laughter in a state of consciousness and sleep in a state of relaxation. Too much lucidity, but why do I always want to do lucidity exercises. I want to be lucid. But that lucidity hurts me. Being lucid is a very difficult exercise or, when I work hard, it becomes even harder. How to be lucid when I'm looking forward to go to sleep and think of nothing else but maybe dream of flying and being happy? Or maybe this work forces me to lucidity, isn't it too much in this pride to always call for lucidity? But who needs my lucidity? I do! Who else needs my lucidity other than me? It's good to be lucid. Be lucid. To live in a state of lucidity. But if I look at the others, I can see that. Lucidity is an interesting state and especially a very dangerous inner state sometimes. Provided you immediately sit at the feet of Christ, you shall lose everything. I think I should write all this, if I described these thoughts, I would become a great writer. But I should not see me bigger than I actually am. I'm always in search for something! But what I'm looking for. Communicating with another person is more important. But people do not communicate, they expect something to happen to them miraculously or everything to happen inherently. Inactivity gets me into depression me. This work that I do depresses me. What did I get from everything I read? I haven't got anything? I feel such a strong need to wipe off all this darkness I live in.

And this can only be done through constant cognitation. I can move forward by reflecting and, thus, I get rid of everything I want to eliminate, these tensions from everything that is restricting me. I get rid of these mental anxieties only when I can comprehend them all. I get rid of all these inner states only if I manage to identify them, to re-live them and to clear the off. How can I achieve lucidity? How? Through a permanent thinking. I believe that the definition of freedom should be given based on a person's ability to think. Thinking can endorse a person's freedom. I'm a free being because I can think. That's why I'm freer in this armchair because I can now reflect and pray to the one who created me for the great purpose of being in the world. The job can be a state of freedom, what would life be without a job? Living like a plant, like a parasite, do nothing. Oh, what a disaster! If I can do absolutely nothing for others, then life gets closed, limited to myself. How sad!

Lord, I would really love to read, but I have no spare time. If someone had told me when I was a student that I would fall asleep with a book in my hand, I think I would have punched him, now fatigue is taking control. I feel better in my own mind, by myself in my own room. I am under the impression that I don't use all the time passing by! I don't even know what I am going to do, because I usually do nothing. Time passes through my mind and I continue to be alone and I'm still as lonely as yesterday and the day before. Well, I've lived a half my life in loneliness, I'll live the same the other half and that's it, it will all come to an end. I mustn't worry about it, God is the only one that matters in everything I do and everything I live, I find in Him solutions to all my soul conflicts and disasters, that is the solution in this life."

Rafael finished drinking his cup of tea and fell asleep in the armchair. He woke up five minutes later and realized he had been sleeping. He made his bed and tucked in rolling on his ideas until he fell asleep again like a baby.

Chapter 31

He woke up again later on. He had insomnia and could not sleep. "Oh," he said. Once again, sleepless at home after work in the evening. I've worked too hard and can't relax". He kept staring to the ceiling in the dark. Rafael stopped meditating and turned the TV on, switching to the classical French music channel, some violin players who were giving a concert with Vivaldi's music. He was crazy about classical music. Vivaldi was an example and a raw model for him. Vivaldi was the Red Priest, the one who had led his life in exemplary purity and created that music for the glory of God, for His greatness. Vivaldi's music was for Rafael like a keen prayer through which the genius had defeated life and time. He thought: "How could this man compose such music; I once watched a documentary about the life of Vivaldi, the priest monk, how could he have lived in an orphanage and create that music for the students? The scores were played by girls, because girls wouldn't have jobs. Boys were taught crafts to upkeep their families and girls were studying arts. Yes, a true genius, this music is relaxing; it frees me from all the mental pressure accumulated all day."

Rafael got out of bed and poured some tea from the kitchen in the cup sitting on the table where the TV set was on. He looked through the window. It was snowing outside. He was alone. And, somehow, he was feeling good, he was not afraid of loneliness, he was not a coward, but he was struggling with this need, with this tendency. He would often think about hermits, how come those hermits did not fear in that creepy wilderness, why should he be afraid? What sort of a man is the one who has fear?

"Yes, I'm often afraid, I'm not afraid in traffic when driving the car, but I'm afraid when I get home and the house is empty, there's nobody here. Yet, I don't always have that feeling because I always feel free, my need for loneliness is greater than fear." Rafael looked out the window at the snowfall. Suddenly, a joy spread through his entire being. "It's as though I woke up especially to see the snowflakes, that's why I have insomnia." He watched attentively the way snowflakes were falling in the light of the street lamps. The light from blocks' windows reflected the snowflakes falling ruthlessly all over the place, over cars, trees, over house lights. Raphael's eyes were resting, Vivaldi's music seemed to break through the walls of the apartment and fly, along with his soul and mind, to embrace the snowflakes which would not fall on the ground anymore, but they were falling into the sky, as if the snowfall didn't come from the sky, but heading from the ground up high. It seemed that, with this music and Rafael's dream, the Earth was moving to the sky towards an unknown world. The sense of mystery he was experiencing could not be put in words. But his questions, his anxieties, went somewhere far, into a world where only God can perceive this restlessness of the soul.

Rafael swore he would never suffer anymore. He would not suffer due to any woman, nor any man or child, or a job, or an invoice or phone call. It seemed absurd to suffer for all sorts of things. Such unnecessary suffering seemed abnormal. He was afraid for a number of reasons. He said to himself that, had he educated himself not to suffer, he would become stone-like and would never be able to love. He imagined that, if he gets detached from everything that causes his suffering, then he will turn so cold-hearted that he will never be able to love again. In other words, he was afraid that when he finds the right woman and has to love her, he won't be able to and, thus, he will lose her and will also miss the last chance to happiness. But why did he always link his happiness to the presence of a woman in his life when he could be just as happy by himself.

Then, he was telling himself that things were not quite so, that the soul has the strength to love, even if it is secluded in loneliness for a while. Besides, the lack of love is not prerequisite for despair and its disappearance. Even though we live in an absurd world where God is not present, because man lives a reality outside of Him, we can carry this world of love within us and can have the strength to go farther no matter what through this light of eternity.

Rafael kept looking out through the window at snowfall listening to Vivaldi's recital on TV. Then, he thought:

"I wonder if I could ever be happy? Why isn't God giving me a wife and children, to be happy with? Because I have everything I need. I've got money, I have a house, a car. I'm no longer in poverty. My sisters are doing well with their families. The baby sister is married and has two children. The other one will marry as well. I see that their love relationship goes very well. I don't think they will break up, or am I missing anything?! She didn't tell me a thing. It snows so nice outside. She bought a house as well, she might soon have a baby, each of us will have our own place in the world.

Rafael watched ecstaticly the snowflakes falling on the ground.

"The woman, a miracle of my mind. The more I have set apart from girls, the closer I have grown in my mind and my soul to an imaginary lady I don't know. She is a faceless woman, with no resemblance, no shape, an abstract woman to which my desire is bound. I constantly want to find her, to meet her. I've been looking, I've talked to all sorts of girls, women, but I can't find anything to get attached to. I need a certain secrecy, a certain mystery, and that woman must believe in God, because that way she will not leave me and the children as she is afraid of the Lord, not because she loves me since this feeling of love lasts so little. Yet, this is not a criterion either. People are so small when it comes to feelings, but the character of a believer is as tough as a stone. Just like Christ said.

I don't like the body of some women. I have to like their appearance as well. If they are too ugly or their face, her face is not appealing, I can't get near her. Am I a monster? Why can't I find a girl to marry? But a woman who has accomplished something so far. A strong woman, not a woman to support, she should be college graduate, have a proper job. A family-oriented woman! How will I raise my children in case she has my child and leaves him in my care, oh, my God, my good God, and she runs away with another man or cheats on me. They say men are evil. But there are evil women, too. I'm so scared. Is it really so hard for me to have a family? To have my kids? It is impossible for me! Oh, my God, it would be so nice to be able to accomplish this! My soul longs for that, it's vital! There are so many single women, why can't I find a kind-hearted, pure, clean lady, just like me? I only have dreams and fantasies and I am always left. I really wanted to go with some girls all the way forever, until God, but everything stopped at the very first steps we took together and I always returned to the status of single man. Everything would fall apart after one or two weeks and I would be single again. But this illusion that I expect to find someone makes me sick, haunts me, harrows me, deludes me and it makes me suffer terribly.

What actually happens? I meet someone, we talk for a while then, nothing happens. All that woman wants is to get into my bed faster, to experience the pleasure, and it makes me sick when I when I see her so impatient and I see that her eyes are so empty, lacking life and soul, I get trembles, as if she had poured death into me, we cannot be with God. I get so scared that I get black stare and I feel like running away from her, I realize even more the empltiness I live in. These fantasies kill me!

Oh! Lord! I'm so miserable! It would be so nice if, in this apartment, had been two children of mine and my wife who would call me:

-Rafael, come help me!

-Rafael, come and cook polenta.

-Rafael, look after the girl because I'll take a bath.

Rafael also imagined a little boy, like he once was, running through his room in Vivaldi's music. And a sister-like warm and kind woman, full of joy and never quarrelsome, puts her hand on his shoulder and tells him asking:

-What are you doing here? Looking out the window? What are you thinking about? Come on, stop thinking about work? Come help me! Rafael burst into tears and let them dry on his face while gazing at the snow outside that was reflecting so nice on the window.

Vivaldi's music stopped and commercial's brutal noise came on TV. Rafael startled. He looked at the window and saw his face crying, he saw his tears running down. He was disappointed, because he didn't like to see himself like that, although he would often look at himself crying in the mirror and he stopped at that point, as if ashamed before himself and before God.

-And I told myself not to cry anymore. I feel my head will burst unless I let the tears come out! Rafael wept further, until he let it all out. He knew he's get a headache after crying, but that was all he could do. He sat back in the armchair, turned off the TV as he was annoyed by that commercial and played a CD with Vivladi on the cassette player. He stopped crying, poured a cup of tea sweetened with a teaspoon of honey, and laid back on the armchair closing his eyes. He imagined himself and his wife and children, all dancing through the snow, running around, sledding, having snow fight, just like he used to have during his childood with his parents who had been so happy to have him. When he was thinking about the kids he could have had and bout his wife, he could never see their faces, it was like a movie where you could not see actor's faces. But he felt his soul close to those children and that woman from the future, who would be his.

-Well, who knows, maybe someday I'll meet you and I'll have all these and, then, I'll have a good snow fight with you. An immense joy filled his soul to this hope.

Rafael stayed with his eyes closed, he stayed like that and sipped the hot tea. He would always suffer from having no family, suffering horribly, he could not imagine life otherwise. He couldn't get this idea off his head. He wanted to become mature and couldn't give up on that. For him, family was the greatest fortune, a holy thing you should not touch because it is from God. A mystery and a gift from our Creator where the soul is always. When would meet some friend and couldn't find strength to smile, he got small, really small before himself, because that person was having a family and children and he did't. In case that friend criticized his wife, Rafael felt badly hurt, as if he had been hit in his illusion of happiness, in his fantasy and desire for family and love. Rafael tried to talk to his colleague or friend in such a beautiful way about the two that his friend would say:

-But, how can you see all these so well, you're right, how come I've never figured that out. You are a true friend, Rafael. How come you are not married?

-....

-Yeah, you're too good. Never mind, you will have all these one day, you'll see how beautiful that is and I'll ask you then if you still want to speak like that?

Rafael returned to silence without being able to say anything. That's how he was, too good for his time and not enough smart for women. Or, that's why he wasn't so interesting for them. He would rather reject everything that was ugly and, since the good and the beautiful were so scarse in life, he had not met yet anything at this level. That's why he was so lonely, you cannot give your soul to betrayal which turns into prostitution.

The truth was that Rafael grew tired by a woman very quickly. He got sleepy. He accessed the Internet to connect. He would speak to various girls on the net. He dated some of them, but quite rarely, because he found it hard to have a dialogue on the net with a girl who got his interest. When that happened, he was glad and would even meet with her. But he was quite bored with these practices. Yet, he was hoping that someday, when God will allow, the miracle would happen.

Rafael was miserable and he sometimes cried out of despair, but he would never cry in the presence of anyone else. He would always cry only when alone, in his room or in his car and ept saying to himself: "you are really strong only when you are alone and free". This Rafael was so strange.

Chapter 32

Where was that boy when he thinking about himself? Nowhere, apparently. He was afraid to think because he felt horribly lonely at those moments and was going through two moods: he either was embarrassed by his thought or he would say: "I'll go mad if I think about this for two more seconds, because something like that is impossible to happen. Why does this really exist?" And he would avoid the topic. He remembered all sorts of nonsense now and then and he would feel again fear of unnown or fear of ridicule. He often wondered: "Am I mentally ill to have such thoughts? Or, if I have these thoughts, could I ose my mind? Maybe not in the near future, but somewhere, sometime I might end up in a nut house. Or, perhaps these words "nut house" are so ridiculous. Then, everything we do is just a concrete thing that does not mean much to me or to another. What do I do all day? I work, work, work, and, in the evening, when I get home, I have to do something and what do I do? I watch TV. I watch all sorts of stupid things. Even there I find things I am trying to avoid all day, the same 'nut house'. Or am I the one who gets to the nuts house sooner or later. Too much work. All that I do can only take me to hospital and in the best case scenario.

Just like now, when I can't sleep from so much fatigue. Maybe not even doctors will be able to do anything to me if I persist in these thoughts. In fact, I don't really know what's wrong with me, but does anyone know what is with him and what he wants? Because, indeed, I have a number of concrete goals. I want a family, I want kids like any normal man that I am. Or, perhaps, I'm not a normal man because I'm too intellectual and I meditate on daily basis. Yes, I shouldn't have such thoughts anymore. Too much thinking is not benefic. "Rafael lay back on his freshly made and re-done bed, he lay back thinking to turn off the TV he had just turned on. He had expected so much to return home after a day's work. All he wanted was some peace. He has peace now, there's no computer, there are no papers, no people around him, he is alone enjoying the peace of his room. But can he stay like this? He would like to write but apparently he is not in the mood. Tiredness prevents him from doing anything and now he really wants to lie in bed and sleep. But can he have peace? All the images of the entire day are present in his mind and they come to dellude him even more and confuse him by feeding all sorts of desires. The lack of family, wife, children, of the normal life that God has given us to live, puts pressure on him and disturbs him so much that he could cry. He tries to cover this wound by praying, but with partial success.

Though he has a quiet room and sleep, the daytime stress does not let him fall asleep. Why? Because he worked too much on that day and is not even able to get some rest. He can't escape from the images in his mind, he wants something to happen, but it seems that nothing does, as if he wanted a miracle to happen in his mind and all those images would disappear. He walked slowly to the window to watch the snowflakes, to see them in the light of the night. No luck, though. They all got mixed up. A colleague offended him so much at work today and now, instead of sleeping, that image of an evil person who knows nothing but laugh and tread on soul with offending words kept coming to his mind. The words come like a hammer on the display of imagination and he re-lives the shame and stress of the day that cannot escape from and imagine that this day is like any other, it's always the same, but he was caught off-guard this time.

There are days when he can bear this stress, this reproach and stay detached, but he can't do that now, he even relives the reproach on that day to maximum, far-fetched levels.

All he can do is wonder again:

-How can people be so evil, speak so badly. That woman is one of those who are constantly annoyed by anything, who laugh at anyone and at whatever people say, nothing is good, because good is only as they see and do, everything else that comes from others is not good, valuable and should be dumped.

-You have the brain of a sixth-grader!, his colleague shouted in his ears.

-But how can she tell me such things? How can she offend me like this? And what did I do? I didn't say anything and took it all in. But why can't

I stay untroubled and stop repeating all these right now, when I have to sleep. The truth is I'm very stressed now and can't do anything, not even have some rest. I think, I think, I have a firm grip on reality, a reality that subdues me and allows me to do nothing, that makes me feel bad for every word I get out of my mouth, I've come to feel embarrassed about my own thoughts at this point. I need a judge that I'm not afraid of.

I need somebody to communicate with and, yes, in a way, I found this, the prayer, God, and I eventually believe this is the only pleasure I can enjoy and I feel it like a constant attraction for my mind and soul." Exclusively experienced by myself. "This is a spiritual pleasure, which is only in the first person and exceeds any money, any person who could hurt me, who could make me constantly suffer. Yes, I believe everything that people talk about is irrelevant, inconsistent, everything that people speak about is excluded from an eternal order. Not even words have any importance on the screen of my imagination, as if I am no longer aware of what I've done, I'm a stranger to myself.

Why can't I sleep now? The image of the person who is constantly offending me, my boss or anyone else, comes to my mind. We are so narrow. God gave us the luck, the great refuge and others cannot know our thoughts, cannot read our intimacy, in fact, no one in this world can know what I do, what I think and how I feel. Not yet...

This can be a great refuge for me, I have a consciousness that only I can live with, and I am the only one who knows about it and I am the only one who knows what happens to me, whether good or bad. I feel some sort of liberation, a defense, because none of my thoughts can be known, I truly feel free now, this freedom is a great miracle, I'm somehow relaxed, the thought of God saves me."

Rafael was after a heavy fight with his boss at work, actually an underman, too, and he could not get them out of mind. They both are on his back, after having planned this in advance, not just in his case, but with all the employees, as if they were two tyrants. But he had to make efforts to get rid of them inside his mind, because that's his weak point, he's concerned about taking this mood out of his mind and wants to calm down.

He is lying in bed, turns on the TV again and zapping around, watching all sorts of nonsense he no longer cares about. He turns it off. He turns on Radio Cultural and listens to symphonic music.

"-Those people were who created such music were so wonderful, aside from money. Nowadays, it seems to us as if they had never existed, they seem some ghosts, very few feel the music. Then, why should I feel so bad when I'm offended, when I'm not listened to, since people are so lonely and small-spirited."

After all those chaotic thoughts coming to Rafael's mind, he fell asleep on Mozart's music aired by the music radio station. Isn't it nice how he relaxed! That's a good, free-of-charge therapy! He fell asleep in the armchair nearly dropping the cup from his hand and suddenly woke up, put the cup of tea on the TV table, made his bed again as it was messy and fell asleep without thinking of anything, switching music from radio to CD. He fell asleep on Vivaldi's music until the last song was over, the music stopped but didn't notice that. The silence of snowflakes healed his soul until the next day, alongside the beautiful sleep in which he dreamed of flying. He became strong and in command over his problems.

The morning came quickly and Rafael was woken up by the cell phone alarm. He had to go to work. A hard day would follow, six hours at school, because he would not give up his half-time teaching activity. He starts at 7.30 a.m. until 12.00, after which he had to be at the company by 10.00 p.m. Rafael was pleased in a way.

He gets out of the house rushing to the door:

"General discussion about suffering gives it no value, yet suffering in particular cases gets the human value. When we try to understand something, we want to understand the general approach, not the particular case, because that particular case involves us as well and that's upsetting for us. We see our own pain reflected in the other persob and we want to run away from our own pain. By running away from our pain, we run away from the pain of others, we don't want to know anything about it because it enhances our own pain and misery, because suffering is ugly. What can we do then?" Rafael was meditating while heading for the car with the key ring in his hand. "I must set my mind, set my mind so I won't suffer. But, how can I prevent my own suffering? By putting my entire hope and trust in God. With my own comprehension, my own mind? By understanding it, I somehow eliminate suffering or I enhance it by re-living it, eliminating it in the end, there is a hygiene of mind anyway and I should take it into account." Then, he added: "Whatever good Lord wants."

Chapter 33

Rafael's main concern was meditation, he would spend minutes staring into space, reeling thoughts and anxieties that he couldn't tell anyone but God. He was driving to school reeling thoughts. Traffic was crowded, bumper to bumper, honks, screaming, swearing, nervous people. Excellent time for the morning meditation on the world.

"I am afraid to reach the height of heaven, I am afraid for it." God's greatness is too much for my soul's pettiness. The human being is so fallen. We are so helpless. I need something, I need to understand things generally accepted by people because their understanding is good and practical but it is automatically accepted by anyone. On the other hand, it comes in a total contradiction with what I see and how I feel. It's one thing to understand something and it totally different to accept something because you have no choice, because you have no alternative to suffering. Why so much fear where there is no fear, why so much boldness and cheekiness where only a shy thought should reach the length and height of an idea. Too much scattered and recondite beauty in this world which remains hidden to our eyes.

Lord, I can't see Your beauty, even if I live in the midst of this beauty. I want to move on, but to put aside mankind's trifles and people's pettiness. I'm so bored with this world, I don't know what to do to understand. Why is Your beauty concealed from our eyes, from my eyes. You know how I am, Lord! I would like to have the power to see. It's like living blindfold in front of a flower of this world and I can't see it. But I can see the ugliness of the world and I allow it to contaminate me, it's like a virus. Why am I attracted to her? Ugliness fills my mind through her mental pressure and stops it from breathing. And then, then it shakes me. I often think I fight against world's trifles, but, in fact, I'm getting caught up in them. Why so much ugliness? Why so much decrepitude. I'm sad and I'd like to move forward but, aside from this daily ugliness, where should I go, where could I run away from this crowd, from this madness on streets, since I have to go through it every morning. World's ugliness can be a warning to me that things can happen even worse than as they do now?

How can I see Your beauty if the ugliness in my soul interposes between me and You like an impenetrable wall? How can I come before You as a beautiful being if the passion in my body has perverted my mind, strangles me, chokes me, doesn't allow me to think, it takes me away from the beauty from my mind. I can only remember my evil thoughts which dominate me and I experience the frustration of the failure to meet some needs that I fear and I don't really need? I can only see my fleshly needs that I can't live without. But I can't live, Lord, without the needs of my body. Why am I so dependent on my needs. Can't I have other needs? I am a man who carries the soul everywhere, I am tormented, because my soul wants to exist and it's sentenced to non-existence and it is screaming inside me. It's like beauty would be shouting under the stones I step on and my soul would scream along with the beauty covered and hidden by stones and I would only hear my heartbeats at a higher rate. It wouldn't hear my soul. How is it possible for me to be unable to see, God? Whom and why should I detach from? I'm not just a body, Lord! My soul is screaming inside me! My body is calling it, clenching it with its needs, with its necessities, with the insistence of some glands that will only swell and relax! Lord! My soul can no longer bear the pressure of body's instincts and their leading strength. How to be farther away from whatever is driving me in the darkness of a day or night, it's the darkness of an inability to see, which is the deception that leads me to a meaning that is far from me, from my soul that is feeling pain now.

Can I be so miserable? What will happen to my soul after my body breaks down?! Should I be concerned only with those needs of my body which is deteriorating by each breath anyway, a cell loses energy every second and so on, until everything gets weak, stuck, dry, squeezed, crushed. It seems I'm in a forest where trees close in on me because I cannot fly above them. Would it be better if I fly flew with my body? This claim for gradeur fills me with contempt. I want to be farther away from world's ugliness. How can I look for beauty? It's like getting a golden thread from so much earth, so much clay? What is the meaning of the word 'salvation', "salvation of the soul", which is so popular, so frequently uttered that people laugh at these phrases? What's the meaning of these words that millions of people died for so that we stay on green today and drive on red. What's the meaning of these wonderful words that people laught at because they no longer understand the meaning of their lives. Because they have taken distance from something essential in this life. Lord, I can only be alone, but, with You, my loneliness is saved from my soul's destruction. Isn't my soul wrapped in all kinds of desires that I cannot escape from and which some people cannot quench? But why so many? I'm slave of my own desires. Why can't I get rid of them? I'm bored with what I want to get comfort in because whatever I want is hurting me! How can I want something good for myself, so it can be my good and not hurt me? I really don't know how to do this. I find it so hard to move forward. But why do I always want illusory things? Why do I wish all these? Can't I do anything to stop wishing?

I sit in my room or in my car and nothing happens to me. This silence often makes me feel uncomfortable. It seems like a void comes over me and I cannot move on. I'm so sad. How comes those monks of Yours were so cheerful? They left some written testimonies that I could learn from. I often feel I cannot understand my own words. Why? Am I happy or not? Maybe I am sometimes or maybe the happiness of my loneliness scares me. Lord, be good to me and let me not be scared. I need You so much. I want to move on but I don't know how. Your every word seems so unknown, unknown for my life. Why am I a stranger to you?! I am the stranger who always avoids You. I am the stranger of Your creation and I walk in the wrong direction. I'm a loner because I'm a stranger. I am a stranger to my soul. A stranger to me, am I a stranger to this beauty I live in. How can I come closer to one beauty of Yours? How can I bring closer one Your words and live it? I wish only one beauty to heal my mind of ugliness. The ugliness of this life nails me down in one point. It makes me a slave. I am scared of the ugliness that I makes me a loner. They speak about aesthetics of ugliness. It's a things that affects you mentally. Healing is only Your beautiful light. You must have a strong mind. I used to think I was big or unique. Living in the ugliness of my body and my needs that I wanted to get rid of, I used to see myself as unique, but, in fact, I wasn't unique, I was alone, terribly alone. There are hundreds of thousands living alone just like me and who don't know how to solve this loneliness. Being alone, wanting to get rid of loneliness, but bragging about your loneliness, believing you are unique, but hundreds of thousands of other are just like you, yes, that's what I believed. How ridiculous deception that sinks me more. God save me."

Car horns, the suffocating congestion on the street, the difficulty of driving amidst the thousands of cars that crammed into each other were unbearable, you needed nerves of steel. A driver left his car with hazard warning lights on and went to buy a begel from the pastry shop on the side of the road, blocking the entire traffic. It seemed so stupid and senseless to block so many people in the morning, in such a congestion, for a begel. If one lane gets blocked, the bumper-to-bumper traffic becomes horrendous. Such a thing is unbearable. Some people's senselessness and mockery at others is appalling.

His thoughts were reeling again in the tense expectation of driving at a snail's pace. Rafael was rebellious against the world, against human evil, against evil soul that fills the human body subjected to deterioration. He was afraid of death. Body's death gave him chills but he was especially afraid of what could mean the death of the spirit. Spiritual numbness. He could not fight with himself. He couldn't take world's stupidity anymore. He was driving all the time, almost forgetting the days when he was traveling by bus. One day, while waiting on the red light, he saw a beggar pissing in the middle of the road, in front of everyone, also touching his car. The man was paralytic, had a crutch in his hand and seemed to be drunk. When he finished, his hands and feet started shaking again. Rafael said to himself, "Hey, he's pissing, pissing on my car! This makes me sick. Could the man really be so degraded?" Why?

He was outraged by human malignancy, by indifference. He could not accept stupidity. But he could not stand particular stupidity which destroys and kills the human being and doesn't let it develop. Stupidity and hatred go hand in hand, stupidity is no joke. No matter how intelligent a man is, he can accumulate much hatred and stupidity in his soul. Rafael knew something else, he knew it was not enough just to care for someone, just to please your conscience. He was annoyed by the drivers' uncivilized behaviour. When driving, everything seemed chaotic.

The level of civilization of a country, a community is always reflected by children's behaviour and driving. People show a brutality that hurts, harms. Common sense had gone into accelerated degradation.

Rafael knew he had to be stronger, to keep on fighting with understanding and kindness. The mess on streets was driving him mad, making him suffer, suddenly bringing him into a bad mood because he could guess the chaos a country, a community or some people live in judging from the dirt on streets and from places you live in. Some people force others to live in chaos, other people's chaos upset him and he could only feel better after he got rid of the mess and disorder outside and retreated to his cell where he could be alone and happy, as happy as a man who lives alone with himself and God, like a monk among people, can be. People's mess, which could not have been caused just by poverty, but also by indifference and soul pettiness, made Rafael suffer even worse. He was like a recipient for suffering. He couldn't take so much indifference anymore. As if he had been a masochist. He only looked ahead, just ahead, and nowhere else, but all these were clinging on him. He was afraid to drive at high speed because, judging by the way people were driving through the city and how civilized people were, you could run into someone who jumps in front of your car without looking, like in fields, and hit him on the back. He was afraid of people, he was scared, so scared.

He often wondered how could God allow manking with such malignancy, he would always imagine that God's kingdom has much light broken down into thousands of colors and our world is extremely opaque. He always wanted to look at the clouds. He often felt the need to saty and meditate about life in heaven. Everyone seemed to be a stranger, an unknown person, an impossible being, because there was no more love and understanding, there was no respect, neither respect of children to their parents nor respect of people to God. Love, this word had a perverse meaning, one would even be afraid to utter.

He seemed to have wanted to explore more of this alienation of the human being, this feeling of separation which was so painful. After all, that was a state of collective consciousness of a people. Stranger from this reality, stranger to this world, stranger to himself, he was seeking new meanings, searching all the meanings in the words of Jesus, seeking salvation through them and cleansing the inner despair. He perceived this state of alienation from ourselves as the greatest ailment and the most threatening danger to the human species and he felt lonely and abandoned in a deserted world, maybe even stuck in the morning traffic.

He stared at the windshield and saw in his mind the saving images of the monastery, the snow in the mountains, that pure white, which had taken him away from the swamp spreading under the wheels of his car, which was lost among other cars which were honking like being played off against each other by despotic god. There's so much brutality in people's souls, especially so much violence in his soul, forcefully inserted. How could he escape wickedness, how could he get rid of so much ugliness, because God is exceedingly beautiful, then how come we, humans, are so ugly, do so much destruction and are so evil?

Rafael suddenly remembered:

"Maia, a eighty-eight-year-old woman, died. What's the use for the dead person in a coffin carried to the cemetery with or without rant. How stupid! Just the body. This ugly and deformed body thrown in a coffin, in the grave, the body we put so much hope on, the body that tortures me, which makes me shiver, which fills me with pleasure but, mainly, with my need for pleasure, which gets hyperbolic dimensions at spiritual level, and how much despair, as if everything ends in a dead body that means nothing, a rotting body eaten by worms. Or in a coffin, a body, like a coat that you have cared for and worshiped like a god. I know these things, I understand them and they give me the creeps. Otherwise, absolutely nothing. Where am I? I can't adapt, I can't calm down. But I can't analyze my mind, my thoughts, my obsessions, I'm scared of what I feel, what I think! As if I see nothing, I can do nothing. I'm in a constant chase after my body, which is asking for food because otherwise it dies, dies and dies again. I almost hate this body. Well, I don't hate it, but many bad things come from my body. In fact, from the mind that cripples and abuses the body. How weird we are! It would all be absurd if we didn't have soul."

Rafael started crying again, speaking in his mind, stepping on pedals so he could drive one more meter through the crowd of jammed cars. This morning, traffic was infernal due to the first melted snow. Things are better when it isn't raining. "God has given us the strength to use our body that we can see, but our soul remains a mystery hidden forever so that we don't know, just as God stays hidden from us, being the greatest mystery.

With the body, living at the level of its perception, all we do is limit our existence, we narrow it and, then, wishing to do God knows what terrible things, we overuse it, ending by destroying it, causing its death before time. That's the reason why, in our times, the human being wants and calls for healthy living, but how can one lead a healthy life unless one leads a spiritual life. My thoughts stir the passions of my body. So much pornography everywhere and naked women are on all TV channels. I'm sick with so much pornography. I will stop watching foor good, I won't even turn it on. It's true that I get home tired and I feel the need to relax and watch TV. I watch a movie or I see some news but I also watch the pornography that runs before my eyes. I'd better watch a movie on the Internet and I've solved the problem. These money-making mirages are amazing. But how much money can one get from pornography? Why not? Our pornographic industry. A great industry to do bad. But I can't calm down my soul. I have two jobs. School children are very aggressive. Children's aggressiveness is high because the aggression in their family is high and since children are always fed with aggression, people are cold and indifferent to each other, and I experience one disappointment after another. On daily basis!"

Rafael finally stepped on school's stairs and ran into classroom because he was a quarter-hour late and had a lesson to teach. He expected the headmaster to shout at him but got away that time. The headmaster was in a similar situation as him and there was no one to shout, he hadn't arrived yet.

Chapter 34

Maria was crying and praying in the hospital, squatting in bed, looking at Gabriel. It was very early in the morning and she had to go to work. She would come back in the evening. She would spend all day with bated breath until the evening when she would come see him again and watch over him:

"God, how can I make this life of mine be other than so helpless, dry, unimportant to me, I want to do something with my ideas, my thoughts, my way of being, of living. It seems as if I were somewhere so far away from what I really am. I don't know, everything is so empty. If I could get closer to me, to You, and keep away from this world which is measured only by this loneliness constantly injected in me by the world I live in. I wonder what it would be like? How can I get rid of this loneliness, Lord, and how can I change this life which is a total failure. Why should I be this way, because I'm the one who doesn't know where she's going to and I believe I've lost everything. Why must I lose everything, Lord, and what can I gain so that I could move forward in this life which is burning me. What can I do to raise above this reality, to be as far away from this world as possible. How can I coordinate my actions because I really feel so helpless and vapid as a person. I want much more because I really don't know what to do.

I feel strange and I don't know why, I'm too pressed in myself and too inward-looking. All I see is my own pain that I don't know how to get over it, I seem to lose my mind. God, I didn't want all these to happen, yet, they have. I see myself from outside, I see myself from inside, and everything I do is so unappreciated, as if all this life is disappointing me and I'm so helpless, small, busy only with what is now and here in the immediate reality. God, how I wish I could be different, I could turn into that being that I am not afraid of, but I fear of the future. I don't want to be afraid, as though I wouldn't have thoughts anymore. I analyze myself and I cannot control my pain, the more I control my mood, the more intense it gets. Oh, God, I wish I could get over all my troubles."

She had a good sleep last night, after all she'd been up to all day, and she didn't see the snowflakes falling in the night. Rafael had seen them. She braced herself, got dressed and went to work. The freezing temperatures of a true and sudden winter hit her and she ran through the melted snow to her car parked behind the hospital.

Rafael was meditating while driving home. "I wonder what drives a person towards aggressiveness, what is making him evil? How can I be aware of human wickedness. Is it admissible for two people to share a house but be separated, without communicating with each other, without talking, without knowing each other. How is this alienation happening? What happens in a person's soul when things are like that? What happens to him? Why are we so alone? What should we do? Where could we go? How to find our path? What is happening in our souls since we are so secretive, so unknown to each other and especially to ourselves. How can we master the evil, the wickedness that erupts from us. God punishes us for our sins. The bodily torments go very deep."

Rafael thought while driving his car and said:

-I shouldn't meditate so much so I won't run into somebody. Moreover, those drivers are cutting my way without even caring and I must think of the worst case scenario in traffic. It would be great if I would move on with my soul without any problem. But I can't separate from all these! I'll pay attention to traffic."

Rafael needed to get some rest. The fatigue filled his body, but he could fight the sensation so he could stay awake behind the wheel. He was not allowed to be distracted, he was not allowed to get carried away by thoughts. Yet, the funniest images, the weirdest ideas, the most unbearable reflections were coming to his mind at that very moment. He was afraid he could kill someone, he could just hit someone out of the blue, or be hit. He had to be very careful. The fear of death overwhelmed him. He couldn't grasp how killing, murder was possible? Someone who wants his or somebody else's death. All sorts of thoughts, all sorts of ideas gave him the fear, a state of irritability he couldn't get rid of.

Rafael was driving and absolutely hated the very busy traffic. He encountered several "traffic jams"–as he had heard someone making fun at traffic jams from Bucharest streets. He was watching attentively how the gas gauge was moving, because that meant a very high fuel consumption, much higher than usual. He would have liked a much cleaner and more beautiful city, with better people, better dressed and more civilized, with more optimistic people, and no longer hearing swearing on the street. Well, there was nothing he could do, he couldn't want that because it was already night, it was very cold and people were packed in bus stops, tram stations. Rafael said to himself again: "Lord, thank You very much for having my own car and I don't have to freeze in bus stops. Poor people, poor schoolchildren! What a nonsense, the cars stay on green light and go on the red light.

Not normal, but this happens all the time in congested traffic. A Police officer is in the middle of the road, out in the cold, to coordinate traffic. It gets colder. I can't stand cold. This freezing temperature troubles me, annoys me, makes me hysterical. I think loneliness is good somehow because nobody's nagging you, but I often want that, someone to nag me. I can't explain the tendency to violence of this world, this society. To attack everything that is the holiest and most beautiful and has been preserved so far?! Violence and brutality towards moral values, values that others had sacrificed their lives for. We live in a sexual age, a morally dark age, the print of this scourge, decadence and self-destruction is everywhere, like a shadow of a demon who sees everything and stands above. How do I imagine that? Like cartoons. The monster, flying all above all, it's huge, it hovers over the city and its shadow grows and can be seen everywhere, on houses, on giant blocks, on people. He turns off the light. People cross this city, this very small universe without being able to understand who is the shadow or who has caused that shadow."

All of a sudden, Rafael put a strong brake on. He was driving in the third gear because he had just passed the red light, he was driving as close as possible to the car in front of him but a taxi driver sped up and cut his way. He put a brake, but the taxi driver ran into the car in front of him.

He said to himself:

-"Oh! Lord, what a reckless man! He wanted to go faster through this crowd. What a man! Now, Police is coming, a bunch of people gather around to see what he's doing and what he's done. He bent his car's metal as he didn't even touch the other car, which was a very expensive and crash-proof car. He's got a Dacia. What a reckless man! But he cares less! Is that his car? It's company's car. He doesn't give a damn! If he smashes it, they have insurance. Oh … I haven't made insurance for my car! Rafael startled. I'll get one from an insurance company. I hope I don't need such policy! But, hey, if you get run into from the back and that person leaves you with the broken car all you'll be able to do is sit and cry. What would you do? Pay with your own money. I'll pass by them, it's their business! Thank God I was careful. Thank you, God, for having protected me!"

Rafael got home tired of driving, he jumped in bed and lay down for a few minutes, then he took the remote control and turned on the TV. It opened to "Realitatea TV" and, then, he headed for the kitchen. He started to warm up food; it was Lent and he was fasting. His fasting was benefic and he was feeling great when fasting and praying to God. He felt calm and secluded from many other things. He was inner-oriented during this time and said, "it would be so great if I could be self-contained all the time. This seclusion is very good, but in mind, not just superficial. It's some sort of self-defence".

Rafael was so happy when writing; he would identify himself with the characters and feel wonderful, as if living even more in the world he had created for himself, he was happy and didn't know how to express this happiness and offer it to others. But why are we so scared of what we feel, what we want to experience or not. Things that assault us from all sides and we cannot back up, as if we want to be somewhere against our experiences and to wipe out everything that makes us suffer and live only beautiful things. That's what Rafael wanted: to experience only what was beautiful for him and for our inner being. Writing was a true joy for him, a state of total relaxation, but, at the same time, a state of tension that made him extremely miserable. He was going through contradictory moods, which he lived one at a time. When he could not put down on the paper his feelings and thoughts about himself and his life, he got sad. He could not understand this world and tried to find its drives, he liked people as they were, and he got angry just because he wanted everything to go out perfectly, as he had always wanted, flawless, but he could not understand existing things and things he didn't want to remember, and carried further his inner tension. He was a man of contrasts.

Had people followed the good feelings, wouldn't they be more relaxed? Why is this instinct of self-destruction is so powerful inside us, in some people working really intense. Why do we allow to be misled by our feelings and thoughts. But do we have a reason? How do we find that our thoughts are good or bad, as we often think nonsense and we don't know where to begin to make a good start in our daily work. I wonder if we stayed longer with ourselves and meditated, wouldn't our life become more beautiful? We often get enough of ourselves and we don't know what clsc to do because we are constantly with ourselves and that is why we are afraid of what we live or what we could live and have not lived yet. Why do our desires subject us so violently and we can't really fight them and ourselves. The events we live daily are facts with unknown aftermaths, which influence us later and turn us into different persons. What prevents us from being strong beings? What prevents us from being ourselves? What prevents us from loving ourselves and we let the instinct of self-destruction work inside us? What attitude should we take in life so we can do something? Where do we find inner strength that turns us into different persons, where do we find the strength to live and think? Where do we find the our strength to act and work?

Rafael finished his dinner and, since he was so tired after the previous night's insomnia, he switched all lights off and fell asleep soundly until the next morning. When he woke up, he looked out the window, there was a bright light outside, the day was about to be a warm late autumn day. He raised his arms up and said: "If it's so warm, I'll go to the park after work to look at trees and stroll in open air, I need it so badly. How nice! Good morning, Lord. I'm so happy, thank You."

He prepared, ate his breakfast and left for work. He did not go to school that day, just to his job.

Chapter 35

Yes, she met Rafael on that devastating evening for her. He has the name of an artist and saint, but this guy is truly victorious from all points of view. He is thirty-five and, to this age, he has made his own life, he works in a large company in Bucharest, a computer firm where he is a shareholder, he owns a house and an expensive car, which is hard to achieve for any man who lives like a monk among people. He has preserved his body's purity to this age, he is a virgin man who can't imagine betraying God and he is a very honest, just man, he behaves firmly with his other colleagues and does not accept compromises. He wanted to go to the monastery after college graduation, but he chose to live among people because that how he thought he could do good to other people. Rafael studied Computer Science-Mathematics and, together with his two sisters, who graduated Accounting, managed to get on their own feet, each one in their own way, his two sisters are married, he was the only one who showed no sign, he would always say that if God sends him a wife, he will get married, if not, he will live his entire life like this because he doesn't want to lose the moral and spiritual freedom he has reached. But who would want to know and put into practice Rafael's struggle and life in a society haunted by the plague of sexuality and corruption, deviated from the level of Christian morality and common sense morality? Maybe we will go into his house sometime and see how it looks inside and we will find out what he's eating, what he reads, what he writes and what he thinks. But, have some patience.

Rafael used to come in the evening, after work, and stroll through the Municipal Hospital Park, to look at kids, to walk with his two nephews. He used to take them out to play and take care of them, so that his sisters could have, thus, some spare time and he could feel like a child or a father. In case the children were too tired or didn't want to go out for a walk, although they were extatic when he came by, then, he used to walk alone and look at the children who were screaming, fighting, spitting and having fun. Though he was very funny and childish, they were having fun romping through the park, but not too much, because he didn't allow his nephews to do stupid things, he would always teach them to play nicely and showed them mathematical games, making them draw with chopsticks in the sand all sorts of geometric figures.

Tonight, he came alone in the park and sat on an empty bench, as if waiting for him. He stayed later than usual, because he liked to pray to God standing on a bench in the park, in open air. He had been to St. Dumitru at the Mitropoly and confessed there, and now he was for some fresh air because, the following day, he would have board meeting at the firm and had to sign some very important contracts. He wanted to be clear-headed and could only clear his mind here in the park with children playing, or by strolling around the water, which had a purifying effect on him. He would often say to himself:

-" Didn't Christ say we should be like children? Well, maybe that's what I'm trying to do now."

Rafael was a good person and he didn' t get tangled in small things. That saved him from any trouble. He had to fight a new battle against himself, he didn't want to live in his fantasy and in his erroneous opinion about himself. He wanted to be a very active being, but one who doesn't live in the idea of doing something, but in the reality of the things done here and now.

He stayed longer than necessary that night and it got dark, children had left and he saw someone sitting in a strange position, neither on the bench nor down, at some distance from his bench. That woman or that man seemed to sleep or not, seemed to have fallen into that position. As Rafael was very curious and used to always help someone, he went to investigate and, when he arrived at that bench, he saw a very elegant woman sitting there, with a pale white face, in a visibly negligent position and she seemed to have passed out. He touched her hand, but the woman did not react. He saw she was holding a purse, a rather elegant and expensive purse, it was quite obvious. He insisted to see what was wrong with her, he shook her, but nothing, the woman did not wake up. He took her pulse and it was quite weak. He reached in her purse to see if he could find some paper, besides her identity card, he found her car keys, an expensive brand.

"-God, this woman has passed out here. Her name is Maria Lazar. I'll take her to the hospital since it's across the road and I'll tell them she's my sister. He took her in his arms and immediately carried her to the emergency room, where the doctor admitted her right away. He injected her with calcium and magnesium, but she still didn't recover completely, she felt dizzy. They put her in intensive care, in i.v., running medical tests He immediately went and bought her the necessary medication with a credit card because they didn't have the drugs in the hospital as much as she would need and the girl finally regained her senses. But she was still semi-conscious because she couldn't remember anything, and she was given a sleeping pill.

Rafael got home well past midnight and had a hard time falling asleep until next morning. His mood has changed completely. He suddenly became a different person. As if he didn't recognize himself. As soon as he woke up, he left for the hospital to see how Maria was doing, he gave some money to the doctor, bought more drugs, he bought a big flower basket, of course, and put it in her room because he requested that she should be accomodated in a separate room, they didn't see each other, they didn't meet because the girl was asleep, and he left because he had some big problems to solve at the company. He was supposed to be there at nine o'clock in the morning.

And that's where it all begins. Maria and Rafael get from each other what they have been longing for so long in such a natural and normal way like the most precious gift received from the Good God. They both had so much peace and quiet in their hearts that they seemed to have known each other since forever, and the entire time spent before they met had been like passing through a world's black hole. They seemed to live the eternal life together before God. This is where the eternity begins.

And the other travelers in the infernal traffic, who collided with them and had caused accidents, had to be forgotten for good. Time, here on earth, always being so limited, should be spent only with happiness.

Chapter 36

Since the moment when he met Maria last night in the park and carried her in his strong arms to the hospital, Rafael seemed to have entered another dimension. He thought Maria was the most beautiful woman he'd ever seen on earth and wanted to go see her. He had no idea who she was, what she did. He was restless. He could hardly wait for the work day to finish and go to the hospital to see how she was doing. He had ordered from a florist another big flower basket to be taken her to her room. He imagined how happy she was when she saw the fresh flowers in the room. Money was not important, all that mattered was to bring endless joy to that woman. Surely she was single, had she had a husband, she wouldn't have been alone in the park, that man would have hurried to see her, to help her, he would have sent someone to help her, she would be called him to save her, she wouldn't have been in that state of complete abandonment as he found her, a human being belonging to no one. Such a thing has never happened to him before and it could only happen to single persons who suffer much, and that woman was definitely suffering terribly and he had to be her rescuer.

He had been worried all day long. He would have made a phone call but what could he have asked and, especially, who could he have phoned because, amid that panic, he hadn't gotten any information. He stopped by the hospital in the morning to see if she was okay and the doctors didn't allow him to go in, telling him that she was under strict observation and he should come back later in the evening, they assured him that she was okay. All he could remember was her name, Maria, nothing else. He left half an hour earlier from work and traveled through infernal crowd across Bucharest to get to the University Hospital, where so many people were facing their destiny.

He knew the room number and the floor so he went straight there but he didn't find her. He suddenly felt desperate, as if he had lost some treasure, and rushed to ask a nurse what room she had been transferred to, who she was, where, on what floor how she was doing, he gave a box of candies to the nurse, he had come prepared. She took him straight to her. A bright light hit him in the face when he laid his eyes on her and he seemed paralyzed. Maria was so transplucid as if she had no body, only soul. She was in the room, near the cot of the baby, who was feeling fine. She was smiling. She also smiled at him when she saw him, and Rafael spotted the flower basket. Maria looked at him and said to him with a low voice, crying:

-It's you...

-Yes...it's me... and he swallowed his words.

Maria reached out to him and they stood hand in hand for some time, then they sat down on the bed in the same state, staying close to each other in silence, without saying a thing. Maria couldn't utter a word and neither could he, as if his mind had emptied of all the words he knew. Maria was floating as if living in a dream. Since he was silent holding her hand in his, she started looking at him. She analyzed each feature of his face in profile. She said to herself, such a childish, pure thought, as if she was looking at her brother, although she had no siblings, she was the only child of her parents: "What a handsome boy, if I had a brother, I would have wanted him to be like this guy".

She looked at him as if she wanted to count each strand of hair on his head, each wrinkle barely visible on his forehead and around his eyes. They stood next to each other holding hands tight. Maria didn't even notice that her hand had been in his hand for so long. Rafael looked at the child, who was playing with some toys in his cot, and was fascinated by him, by the way he looked, by the way he was playing or how he was turning around. He was speachless, he was in expectation and time seemed to have stopped. Maria looked at his bag where she could spot an Orthodox Bible and broke the silence:

-Do you believe in God?

-Yes, I do, Rafael nodded.

Maria took the courage, opened the bag, pulled out his Bible and opened it at random. She read the text about the life of Jacob, who wrestled with the angel, he sees Rachel from a distance: "When Jacob saw Rachel, daughter of his uncle Laban, ... Interestingly, it wasn't Rachel that cried but Jacob ... Jacob came to find himself a wife." Maria startled and quickly shut the book. Something pierced her straight into heart, she felt sick and afraid, a shiver shook her from head to toe.

Poor Rafael couldn't find the courage to look at her, he was looking at the child and was dreaming. He was fascinated by the light coming from the window to the baby and, since he was curious to see where the light was traveling across the room, the light led him to Maria. He was secretly staring at her; she was looking down shuddering at what she had just read in the Bible. He saw her so frowning and opened his mouth for the first time. Maria could hear his voice at last.

He said softly, like a prayer, but very firm and determined in his speech:

-Why did you shut it? It's the most beautiful book.

-I know... I've read something that scared me...

-It scares me, too, I take it with me and, when I have time, I read it. I bought it from Sibiu, from the Metropolitan Cathedral last year when I was traveling with some friends.

-It's from Sibiu, said Maria, gaining courage.

-Yeah.

-I've never been there.

-Well, we'll go ... and stopped embarassed.

The child started crying out of the blue and Maria, shivering, seeming controlled by an invisible force, shaking hard, rushed to the cot. She picked up the baby, who was screaming so loud, she didn't know what to do first, to put him down or run and call the nurse. She pressed the buzzer in a state close to dementia, with trembling hands as if run down by electricity. Rafael went to her, hugged her and her baby and took the child out of her uncontrollably shaking hands.

-I have two nephews, my niece is three years old, let me hold him. Maria let the baby in his arms and headed for the door, to call the doctor or a nurse, she was already in fibrillation, her legs were shaking, her entire body was shaking, as if bitten by frost, cold, passion, helplessness. She could only think of death at each whimper of the child.

Rafael took the baby in his strong arms and Gabriel cuddled with him, lay his little head on Rafael's shirt, made of expensive, white, soft and freshly ironed silk, so warm, scented and velvety, that he whimpered a few more times then he cuddled in the strong arms of the friend who had saved his mother and, after a few more whimpers, he went silent. Rafael's hug made them father and son forever. Gabriel needed to sleep on his father's chest or gain strength and grow up strong into the light. Maria came and brought the nurse. When she saw them she said to Maria:

-Ah, your brother.

Maria took a long look at Rafael, with her big eyes, then nodded. Rafael didn't say anything, he hardly heard that, he was paying attention to the child. Some sort of father-to-son warmth and energy exchange set in between them. Rafael was no longer a single father. The nurse looked at the child and said nothing, she smiled and left the room. Maria sat down on the bed feeling tired and still shaking and Rafael was holding the baby in his arms and the child had fallen asleep in the meantime, resting his small and warm frail body on Rafael. Maria could not believe her eyes. They stood close to each other taking peeks, without making eye-to-eye contact, as if being afraid not to discover each other, not to know, not to meet soul to soul, even though their souls were already embraced. Maria got up and put her ear on Gabriel's body to see if he was breathing, she sat down on the bed again and, a few minutes later and she put her ear on baby's body again as if she had lost her mind of fear. It's hard being a mother.

-He's breathing, he's breathing, whispered Rafael.

-What beautiful flowers, Maria whispered.

-I'll send more, said Rafael, who was couldn't decide whether to be familiar or formal.

The baby was sound asleep, but Rafael kept holding him out in his arms. He looked at Maria and understood everything without any words or explanations. Rafael fell in love with her at first sight and knew very well what to do, even if he was afraid of this love. Maria felt dizzy, she had a headache and felt drowsy, and slowly lay down on the bed, on the pillow, and fell asleep. But, in her heart she fell asleep right in the arms of Rafael, just like her child. All three of them were asleep embraced. Rafael sat down on a chair beside her, head to head, heart to heart, holding baby in his arms. He looked at both of them being asleep, but he was not sleeping, he felt neither hungry, nor cold. He felt so good with that little and warm baby in his arms, as if they merged into one face and one body. He stood in that position for more than an hour, watching the sleep of the two. He had come to help, to protect, to care for them. He was feeling happy, strong, smart, head over heels at first sight, like a teenager. After a while he looked at the sleeping Maria and let the tears of loneliness drop on his cheek and he thought full of fear, shivering just like Maria when she was reading about Jacob's tears when he saw Rachel, and kissed her: 'this is the wife I've been waiting for so much, this is my baby" and he shuddered, letting tears go down until he let it all out. The more he looked at her, the more he recognized her as his fantasy woman.

When she got up, Maria found him holding Gabriel in his arms and told him:

-Haven't you got numb?

He shook his head.

-Let me get him.

He shook his head again.

They stayed so, looking at each other. For the first time, Maria, after such a long time, looked at him and smiled. She looked desperately straight into his eyes and, when she could no longer look, she let tears fall in the deepest silence. She felt so much peace, silence, so much beauty, innocence coming over her that she felt like hugging Rafael, but she stood back so she wouldn't embarass herself and she cuddled at his chest solely in the privacy of her heart. Rafael tried hard not to cry, not to embarass himself, he was so intimidated that he didn' t know what to say, he was just experiencing so intense feelings which cannot be expressed. Now, his soul was speaking for him and it was saying everything. They stayed in silence, taking in each other's peace and calm indefinetely apparently and sipping from an invisible glass of love, after which Maria said to him:

-You have to go to work tomorrow, you mustn't be tired, you should get some rest, to be strong.

-Yes, I'll have to go to bed, to get some rest, I'll have a hard day tomorrow, I have a meeting, in the board, another meeting and signing important contracts for some payments. I'd like to exchange business cards.

Rafael gave Maria the baby who was sound asleep, he hugged them and gave a brotherly kissed to both of them, he whispered 'good night' and left. It was midnight.

Rafael got to his car but didn't leave right away, he stood there for a while, until the storm inside him calmed down, then he started the car gently and left. Maria was watching him from the window, without him being aware. She could see everything in the street from up there where she was staying as that was on the top floor, an excellent place to see the city's skyline.

He got home and went straight to bed without saying a word. He was peaceful like never before. He was convinced that something had happened. Maria felt the same peace and serenity and she slept until 10.00 o'clock in the next morning. When she woke up, the child was playing quietly on the bed by himself, without crying, without whimpering. She saw Gabi smiling for the first time and that smile filled with light her inner world and all the unbearable torment she'd have so far. He was contaminated with father's energy.

Chapter 37

Rafael couldn't sleep all night, thinking of Maria and her child. He fell asleep late, woke up in the morning and left for work. He couldn't wait to leave beacuse he had decided to visit Maria and her baby boy every night at the hospital and take care of them. The time came when the work hours were over and left again half an hour earlier. Of course, traffic was terribly crowded, he lost his patience to keep stepping on the brake and come to standstill. Traffic is terribly crowded in Bucharest in evenings and in mornings, you'd better avoid these hours. He always avoids them as much as possible, but, then, he had no choice, he had to be contaminated by others who were honking, cursing, fed up with spending time behind the wheel and stepping on pedals, brake, first gear, second gear and first gear again and so on. He eventually got there, but had a time finding a parking space. Though there were so many parking spaces for the hospital, they were all taken. Parking spaces were the biggest problem in Bucharest and in other developed cities of Romania after the revolution. He found a cramped space where he could barely park the car without scratching it and hurried up by elevator to the top floor where Maria was with the baby. To his great disappointment, Maria wasn't there, but her mother was replacing her. He said desperately:

-Where's Maria?

Her mother stared at him so long as she had no idea who he was and a trace of a smile played in the corner of her mouth.

-She hasn't arrived from work yet.

He left without saying a word. "That boy is weird", mom thought, "but he's really desperate for not seeing her, that could be a good thing. When a man is so upset because he doesn't meet the woman he's looking for, that's a sign of lovesick, maybe Maria's got some luck, who knows ".

Rafael was so sad and wouldn't dare come closer to the room where

Maria's mother and the baby were staying because he was afraid he might disturb and they would get upset with him, let alone that nothing seemed familiar. As he was so tense, all of a sudden he missed her so much as if they had known each other forever, even though there had been just three days. Glimpses of their first meeting came to his mind while he was heading with the admirable melancholy of a young man in love, across the street, to the park in the front of the hospital, where he had found Maria passed out on the bench. He was taking rare steps towards that place. He was looking at trees, at children, at people, at the leaves covering the ground. Although it was autumn and warm, leaves had fallen on the ground after the first snow, just like a tormented soul, trampled under feet. Yet, he didn't have the same feeling as on other occassions, he was quite eager to lead a different life. The cool evening air enveiled him and gave him such a state of well-being and pure breath that made him fly.

He was amazed to see Maria sitting on the same bench. He ran and sat down next to her, without saying a word, with a big smile on his face. Maria gave him a distant look, as if she was living in a nightmare she wanted to escape, staring at him with big, big eyes, she was on the verge of tears, but kept it all in so she wouldn't get into an embarassing situation, but, eventually, she let go all the pain she had accumulated for so long. Rafael looked at her and, as she was crying silently without saying a word, he took her hand and stayed so indefinitely seeming detached from eternity and reality. That silence was healing them both, they couldn't utter a word because the whole reality of life was locked in soul's muteness.

Rafael was looking at Maria, whose tears were falling uncontrollably, but she wasn't shaking anymore. While she was bringing to surface all the virulence and pain gathered inside her for such a long time, a peace of mind and soul took hold of her, a a state of calm, sanity, balance, strength, due to Rafael's simple, speechless presence. She was absorbing strength and energy in a new form, unknown to her so far.

It seemed that, by holding hands, some sort of a strange exhange of energy of omnitude was made, like a transfer of light from one to another. Maria took from Rafael his strength and power that she had lost, and he took from her warmth and suavity he had never had. They were like two siblings now rejoined after many years of separation. He couldn't touch or hug her, he felt numb, besides the fact that those feelings were totally unknown and unfamiliar to him. He could just sit by her without saying a word. They would have spent an eternity like that. Those quiet moments spent together were the most numerous and the most mastered words they could say to each other. None of them could speak. The soul needed a rather long time until it could open to another soul. That silence superceded, like an eternal union, the thousands of words that could not be spoken.

Maria felt such comfort beside him on that bench that she ran empty of any thought, any tense feelings, any toxic state, she had never experienced such silence and peace near anyone. Rafael had such a gentle look and behaviour that she fell in love with him in the deepest sense of the soul.

Rafael thought he was dreaming, he looked at Maria and couldn't touch her, she seemed to be made of light, he would have wanted to look at her even more, but he was afraid of something unknown. Silence. Suddenly, that silence of dusk in the park was interrupted by the cell ringtone. Maria flinched, took the phone out of her bag and picked up:

-Yes, mom, we're on our way. Relax, I'm fine. Yes, yes, yes...

Rafael didn't hear those words anymore ... he was in a dream, in a sweet state of imagination.

-Shall we, said Maria?

-Yeah, he approved nodding. Holding hands and veiled by their secret love, they headed for the hospital, to the child who began to recover.

Rafael, by his simple presence and attitude, changed the life of the two one hundred and eighty degrees, switching it from death and despair, from pain and torment, to hope, joy and vivaciousness.

All four of them spent time chitchatting about work for a long time and, when it got late, Rafael said:

-I'll give your mother a ride home.

-Yes, Rafael, thank you, said Maria.

All of a sudden, Rafael became another person on the way home. He got cheerful, chatty, funny, he told mother all sorts of jokes, stories from his job, they had a good laugh and fun all the way. When they got to destination, her mother was still laughing.

-See you tomorrow night, madam, kisses.

Her mother got off the car laughing, she told him 'good night' and thought: "What a crazy boy, you'd say he's never had any pain, super funny, I'll tell Maria all the stuff he told me".

Chapter 38

Rafael was going to Maria at the hospital every evening, they would walk the baby out, tell all sorts of jokes. Maria used to telling him:

-My mom was right to tell me you were very funny and chatty, I was beginning to think you were really mute because you had barely said a word.

The child was recovering, Maria came one night and told her:

-They discharge us tomorrow, if I promise everything will be ok, I'll continue the treatment and eliminate all negative emotions, the baby will grow up healthy and will be strong and full of life.

-Hurray!!! shouted Rafael and hugged her. It was the first time he had done that almost instantly and without giving it too much thought, as the most natural gesture possible. It had been only two weeks since they had known each other, how nice. Maria surrendered in his arms. She hadn't felt tenderness and love since her breakup with Mihai. Love was now giving her a big smile, cuddling her again in its strong and secure arms. Rafael took her hand and said:

-Hadn't we been in the hospital courtyard, I would have taken you and spinned like kids do in the green grass, that's how I used to play with my sisters when I was a little boy.

-Yeah, how nice, you two are like two siblings.

-We are the best brothers, we have always been the best brothers and so we will be. That sounded like a declaration of love to Rafael.

-Of course, we will stay that way, said Maria overhelmed and a little confused because she expected him to say something else, she didn't need a brother, but love, yet, she didn't know Rafael's way of being and that, in his opinion, that was love. She got a little sad.

-We will never break up, added Rafael, hugging her for the second time.

-I feel the same, never.

They looked into each other's eyes, soul to soul, then looked up to the stars, to the moon, to trees. The child was reaching out to Maria. Rafael went to him and touched his little and thin hands, took him in his arms, rocked him, walked him around. Maria looked into Rafael's eyes and saw "that" spark ... and full of emotion ... she instantly got over sadness.

-It's over, young man, we go home.

Maria started laughing.

-When will they fill the discharge form?

-Tomorrow at lunch.

-Well, then, I'll request a leave of absence from work and I'll come to help you, to pick you up.

-I'd be delighted, though my mom is with me.

-And what shall we do? Will we go with two cars.

-Why not, I will follow you.

-Excellent, I will have you on my tracks like in American movies.

All four of them left the hospital the following day. They seemed to have been like that since always. Maria had the feeling that she would never return there ever again, as long as she would live. She was hoping from her heart that the nightmare had ended once and for all.

Maria and Rafael became inseparable. Their friendship was natural, but not as some young people nowadays understand the friendship between a man and a woman, everything goes down to sex like in the primitive commune. Today, mankind is still in this Age of Slavery as far as relationship between a man and a woman is concerned, they still treat each other as servants, therefore the divorce rate is so high. Divorce is now in fashion, not love, like God allowed for two people to love each other. The moral degradation gives you the creeps.

Rafael didn't want to experience such things with Maria. There was just love in their case. He had no idea what was that about anyway, and Maria wouldn't even dream about having sexual intercourse with Rafael. She felt sick, disgusted, just to think about it after the trauma lived with Mihai.

If she had any thought about sexual satisfaction, she would instantly see Mihai in her mind welcoming her with that brutality of an animal she couldn't escape and would resume her fight with the ghosts of the past. She would start shaking, being sick, nauseous. A new series of reprisals was coming to her mind and she didn't have any idea how she could get away. Mihai was linked to any issue related to sex, not to mention that, when he left, Mihai had given her venereal disease, caught from his whores, and she had had a hard time getting healed. She had had nodules on her body, weird states, itching, stinging and pains and had to get a gynecological exam. She thought he had taken some fungus from somewhere, when, in fact, one of the worst sexually transmitted diseases was spreading inside her. Who could have gotten her sick if not Mihai. That made her stop thinking about him. The rest was just disgust, outrage, loathing, hatred and misery. When thinking about Mihai, she would start shaking and suddenly become hysterical.

She once spotted Mihai from a distance and started shaking so hard as if she had seen the devil itself. She felt the urge to run away, to hide and never lay eyes again on such ugliness, such a man-like monster. Why are those people like that? She remembered that, in Balasa paintings, some monsters were painted as having the sweetest human appearance, those are the evil people who only know how to turn into ugliness and misery everything that is beautiful in their soul, in their life and other people's lives.

She considered Rafael as an oasis of light, as something pure and didn't see any sexual instinct or lust in him. That was the reason why she felt so close to him and safe in his presence. They would always discuss only about the Bible, about God, about saints. Had he made any hint about sex, she would have kicked his butt and would have ceased any kind of relationship with him and would have broken up with him for good.

In a split second, he would have turned into Mihai, ruiner of her life.

They used to comment whole fragments of ancient theologians, used to have never ending discussions about Christ the Savior, about holiness and the purity of life. Rafael laid accent on virginity, happiness, purity, and on the fact that a real man must be virgin when getting married, not dirty and loose, the same as a woman. After getting tired of all the pleasures and after having tainted his body and soul with all that he had randomly encountered how could he get married and pass the heavy sins to his wife as well and the burden of his sins would come over his offsprings. The same would be for the woman. She must enter the church as a virgin and be a virgin bride, like his grandmother would always tell him:

-When you get married in the church, the priest sings to you "rejoice, bride, ever-virgin" and you must be worthy of such words."

As for Maria, she had no reason to fear these words, because she had entered the church that way when she had married Mihai. She used to tell the same to Mihai, her future husband, even if he hadn't quite agreed, there was nothing he could have done, he had to obey. Maria said to Rafael:

-Now that I think of it, I guess Mihai was going out, fooling around and cheated me even before our wedding, as he couldn't hold it together and stay clean beside me. He was clearly lying to me since we've ended in such an ugly break-up, as if I've lived in Eugen Barbu's Pit. I could never know the truth.

Yet, Maria was guessing wrong about Mihai, he had been faithful because he didn't have to wait too long for their wedding, they had married relatively quickly, so he had been enjoying everything that was to become his. Maria was wrong, why should she say things like that? She had had a happy marriage until those problems occurred and he left them both, her and the kid. Maria had no idea and misjudged him. Mihai didn't have any woman after they had met again and decided to get married. He had changed radically. But Maria had no way of knowing that for certain. She had been convinced back then that it was just the two of them, now everything was falling apart. When she heard Rafael talking to her like she once had talked to Mihai in college, her would heart suddenly fill with something new, an immense joy, as if she was going back in time and then, in the past, she wasn't talking to Mihai but to Rafael and she and Rafael were talking then as they do now.

This boy seemed to heal all her past and to overlap it with his kindness. There was something strange in her mind. She felt as if something mysterious was bringing them together and God was the most important for them, as though they were living in some magical triangle in which Christ was somewhere high above but still quite close to them and they were at the base. When she was listening to Rafael commenting on Father Staniloae everything that meant cosmogony, happiness, creation, communion, her mind seemed to be cleared from all scars of fear, fright, darkness, pain, and something miraculous was happening in her mind. She could have been listening to Rafael for hours on end without falling asleep, as if he had been a teacher who had passed to her all the secrets of philosophy and life, as if he were the greatest interpreter and scholar.

-You know, Maria, all I have done so far was to work, read and go to church. I've read so many books, that I get bored now when I open one because I already know what's inside, it may still be a surprise in terms of the story, but very rarely.

-How nice, Maria replied, it's so nice that you can say that, you have been safeguarded from human horridness, this sin that burns the human being and turns it into ashes, just like it happened to me. If you knew how much I wanted to have these conversations with Mihai and I never had because he would make fun of me. I've read books as well, but not as many as you did, but I've always lived with this failure that I couldn't read more, I couldn't think more, I couldnt 'pray more.

-It's ok, I've read books but you've had a baby to enjoy and take care of. So, it's not really a big loss because it's not that important how much you read but what you create and how much you manage to think on your own, just like I do now. I feel the urge to think about certain issues, to read about those states that are inside me and in my thoughts. I have to think and express myself in my original form.

-Do you write? said Maria, asking him as if she had a revelation.

-Sometimes, yes, Rafael replied, and said that hiding the fact that he might be discovered.

-You should write down all these, you'd become the most famous writer because it's very different from everything that is written and published nowadays.

-Yeah, that's right, this alienation from God upsets me. However, the farther are others from Him, the closer to Him I want to get, nothing more. Yet, I want a certain reconstruction of the philosophical mind oriented towards the highest ideals of mankind, of man since always. I believe that every historical age deals with these alienations from the human being, and the general spirituality belongs to people who only want to follow the group. Only the strongest is not the same as the others, gets rebellious and keeps close to everything that alienates him from the last judge and such a spirit, like Sisyphus, tries and manages to roll world's boulder back to the height, then this boulder rolls back down again, and, so, the purpose of every scholar of the world is to be like Sisyphus, to roll the boulder of the spiritual life from the base of world's decay to the height of the spirit so it can heal the world, so that mankind can be closer to the heart and light of the heavenly heights, and not to decay's darkness at the bottom.

-So, you're like Sisyphus.

-Yeah, that's how I feel.

-It means that God has made you strong and you have tried to maintain this strength and this height.

-Well, I thought that whatever you write, whatever you read must mould you in the first place, that is to say, it must make me become a strong person so that no one and nothing could divert me from my attitude to keep the right path, namely, the way of God. Whoever is with God is a strong person and must learn to be hard as a rock, not have heart of stone, but be hard as a rock, just like the Savior told Peter: "upon this rock I will build My church".

-Write that down! I have often compared this God-related soul strength with the power of a rock standing firm before storms and life, and it resembles him, who hasn't strayed even though he rolled in pain, he stood by Christ until the end of his life, when he was crucified in Rome.

That was the first time when Rafael felt like someone understood him, understood his ideas, facts, thoughts, meditations. That was the first time when Maria felt that the man in front of her didn't see her beautiful body like a statue of Michelangelo, didn't treat her as a sexual object, as an expensive possession, as a trophy, just because she is beautiful, but, for the first time, a man could see her intelligence and her mind force to penetrate the most mysterious things of this world. Rafael found in her that conversation partner he had never have. He felt that her faith would never be able to break him away from Christ but, on the contrary, she would keep his soul anchored in that beauty of faith that is love of absolute. Rafael saw in her his work he was struggling to write, to construct as the highest philosophical picture, a new system, a new edifice. She was seeing in him the man from her mind, the man of her intelligence with whom she could continue her meditation she had long abandoned since she had been single and student in Iasi or since those moments when she felt alone beside Mihai, whom she had been expecting to come home and she was sometimes, rarely, writing some poems but kept them away so she wouldn't make a fool of herself because Mihai would always laugh at her. Had he found out she was writing poems, he would have been laughing for months and would have told all friends and acquaintances, she would have become their joke, an object of amusement.

She couldn't talk about God with Mihai, she used to go to church on Sundays, but without telling him. He used to wake up when she came back from the church service and pretended he had no idea about it. There was a silent agreement between him and her that he would keep out and, at her quick return home, she warmed up food and put on the table, they were eating and laughing together. After that little time syncope, everything returned to normal and they continued to be happy, enjoying each other.

Mihai thought that Maria's going to church on Sundays was a real waste of time, while Rafael considered that was essential to do for one's mental health, spiritual evolution and steadfastness in life through God and Christian faith.

Chapter 39

Had Maria seen in Rafael the slightest attempt to sexualize the relationship, she would have left him, she would have yelled at him and kicked him out within twenty-four hours, but his behavior was so virginal that Maria didn't even dare ask him things, what he was thinking about, waiting to discover that along the way and from him, if he would bring it up. Did he or did he not have any woman or was there any woman in his life?

"Maybe he had some as a man, but he suffered much and now he does not want to think about it. Just like I don't even want to think about it, I leave things come naturally, without forcing anything. If he tries to come on me, I'll kick him out, that means he's only trying to cool down his hormones, he would make me sick and would only deserve to leave him immediately. I'm not interested in such things. Such men are weak. I've been trying to avoid such turpitude all my life. I'm determined to never marry again and spend my life as I do now, like a nun in a monastery, to live like a White Friar, like monks live alone in monasteries, I could live so as well. I don't need another man all my life as long as I live". Yet, the man was standing right beside her trembling with fear, from the depths of his soul.

-How about Rafael?

-Well, Rafael is different, we are connected by God, by Christ. I see him as a brother, I don't think of anything, this guy is too good to suspect him of anything, he hasn't made me doubt so far that he wouldn't treat me like a sexual object.

As for Rafael, he was on top of the world, any conversation with Maria was an opportunity to write. He could create one novel per week or continue his philosophical and divine novel because he wanted to write a philosophical system, similar to a path from man to God. He used to say that that theology explains God's path to man, and my work must be like a unique journey from this alienated man to God, to Him, the great truth, the greatest truth, to Him, the Christ, who shows us the way, He is the prince of this world, of this existence and of this beauty.

Oh, he had so much strength, he hadn't told Maria about his calling to write and think, but the gate of the word kingdom seemed to have opened up for him and he was sipping the deepest meanings of life. Maria had become his guardian angel for several weeks, his poetry, his work, he felt the urge to lay all his thoughts down to her feet, he felt that he could pray with her, hand-in-hand, with the greatest joy before Virgin Mary's icon just like he used to pray alone when in Iasi, his beloved city of Iasi, place of the holy Saint Paraskeva. He wanted to take her, Maria, to Chernica and then, after all things experienced together, to send their prayers to Saint Callinicus, to intercede with God for their love, and to write down with his most delicate thoughts about human holiness, about purity, about all beautiful things, this thought of seclusion from the worldliness that devours us. He wanted that all three of them, she, him and that wonderful child, would pray together for the health and recovery of that kid, would pray to Saint Callinicus to intercede with God that he, Gabriel, would never fall ill again, would become strong and healthy.

He was also scared, he felt like he was plunging uncontrollably into this abyss, but hoped that God wouldn't send him something as deceitful as in the past, but exactly what he had been waiting for all his life. His previous experiences had gone wrong, but, now, he was experiencing the joy of prayer, he had the feeling that nothing could go wrong between them as long as Christ binds them, he felt that the connection was indestructible, he had the urge to tell Maria he wanted to marry her, but was afraid it was too soon and she would think he was crazy. He was counting the hours until they would meet, so long hours. She was his spiritual world that he had accidentally encountered, his place of joy allowed them to meet, everything around him seemed like an ivory palace where he was living and would never leave. He felt that whatever was happening between him and Maria was like that from the very beginning and he imagined that was love, that constant prayer, and, therefore, he couldn't be afraid anymore, healing little by little. It seemed that he was living just to write and meet with Maria, to meet with her and then write again.

He had never experienced anything so beautiful and divine. He thought that wasn't a deception like in the past because all he was living was real, and Maria was the smartest human being he had seen on the face of the Earth and she was so beautiful, he had never seen such a special person, she seemed to be from the cover of a magazine. That's what a girl of his poems and secret writings about beauty was supposed to look like, as this Maria that God had put in his way so he could save her, see her, heal her and bring her to life, to joy and hope, her and her child, so small and ill, who, by God's power, was showing his strength. They both represented health and life for each other.

Everything was like a miracle in his life and he kept silent. He was completely mute. He didn't tell anyone but God about what had happened to him lately. Nobody knew his experiences, absolutely no one, except for his notebooks. The same thing happened to Maria, but at least it all made sense in her case. She was afraid to think that this could happen to her. She couldn't even dare ask God to give her such love again. She was too scared and, when she thought about Rafael like a trace of love, she felt the urge to run away and started shaking from head to toe. But each meeting slowly healed her.

That's how great loves are lived, like true suffering, a suffering that gives you strength and love heals you, and all these in prayer and the deepest silence, because love and pain are human being's most incomprehensible mysteries and undiscovered secrets here on Earth. Love is healing, is liberating, it puts you on track and you want to live in a world that accomodates you to exist in the greatest light and in God's endlessness which lies beneath the foundation of its creation.

Chapter 40

Maria was alone and she imagined everything she wanted to say to Rafael, things that she would definitely say she they meet face to face:

-My dear, the world I'm living in is completely new and I'm afraid to imagine how it might be, and, all that, in your company. It's as if I have experienced for the first time in my life something totally exquisite, for one time only. If you knew the depth of this love I feel inside, its presence, but this love is hardly what I have imagine for years it would be. No, it's a state I've never experienced. This power I feel inside is amazingly great and you are at its core.

It seems that I see your face for the first time in a light and image I could have only had in my dream sometimes. Back then, I believed that what I was living could only be my new deception about the world and my need for love, but now I realize that those states did not express my despair and my need for love but something else, namely the eternity and normality of love inside me, because love is God's eternity in which we must live from now on, from this very moment. That was my need to experience something absolutely wonderful, that was exactly what I am living by you right now. I had no idea that you could be so wonderful to me. I didn't know that you, with this inner facet of your love, could have such a beautiful soul which would fit perfectly into my inner world and be in harmony with me and my way of being and, thus, heal me.

Your face, its presence in my inner world, seems to represent everything to me. You bring beauty inside me and I need no touch, no word, just your presence can be magnificent in my soul, a perfect healing of everything. I seem to notice now, for the first time in my life, that I have a soul that can be happy. It's as if I have gone through fire and now I am alive, having something wonderful inside me and with a body strength that is beyond me. I am me because you are you, because you are in me. I haven't understood why God said that this love, as we live now, is everything to our lives. I couldn't gather. But, now, meeting you, I seem to have become something wonderful and I have acquired this perception over the world and life".

It is amazing how Rafael was a presence for Maria even in his absence. Isn't that what God is telling us? To love him as the last and first presence in our love and our lives. That is the reason why any love, whatever it may be, includes the infinite in its strength, because each state leading to love can be but a drop of God's eternity. What are we looking for in this world if not the love of God and His magnificent eternity, if not this is our only way worth living for and Maria was truly living this. She would have wanted so much to thank God for this love, but she couldn't. She gave so much thought to God for this unimaginable mood of reflection and indescribable joy.

-My dear, I am no longer afraid now. I used to fear in the past but not anymore, I'm no longer afraid of anything bad that, in my opinion, could happened to me, Iused to fear that I could have lost all things that I deemed to be unparalleled. Oh, Lord, Thou art so great and wonderful. If You allow us mortals to live these eternity-like states. Yet, why did I have to go through such pain and suffering so I can feel such a happiness now? Why? Had I not suffered so much, I couldn't have treasured love and life now. Than You, Lord, for I have suffered so much and now I am a human being resurrected from the dead."

Maria was day dreaming again. She imagined Rafael coming to her and flying together somewhere away from this world, together with their son who now seemed to have a different name, a different body, away from words, stars, clouds, skies, as if all three of them were no longer on Earth, but somewhere in an abstract world, where happiness was the only option, a never-fading happiness. That's how heaven must be like. Could we, humans, ever have the strength to experience such happiness, such an intense happiness?

Every gesture of Rafael seemed to bring new meanings for Maria, new forms of happiness. She remembered every word she had told him and he had told her, and she felt a growing desire to see him, to feel his presence, to be close, but no matter how close or far Rafael was, he was present in her inner world. That was the most fascinating thing and the most beautiful feeling she had lived so far.

Love is wonderful but its frustrations are even greater and we must run away from them as fast as possible all our lives and, if we cannot be happy together with someone, we'd better educate us to be happy by ourselves before God. The cruel reality is preferable instead of a long dream because it's better to be realistic than live in a fantasy.

Chapter 41

Rafael couldn't hold back anymore one moth later. They would meet every evening, he often spoke about his ideas about his theological thoughts, they went together to Cernica and St. Dumitru, bowed the child before icons. Rafael was the one who was taing him everywhere carrying him in his arms, as if he were his child and they were acting as if they were a family. They grew inseparable. Maria had her heart in her mouth not daring to put her hope in that happiness, just waiting for it to come. She allowed him to take her everywhere, praying to God to do somehow and spare her of a new suffering as she couldn't bear another one. She used to lie in bed with her eyes closed before going to sleep.

All of a sudden, she winced when she realized they were of the same age and, for a second, she saw herself in him and viceversa. She felt a blow to the top of her head and warmth spread throughout her body, similar to fainting. She suddenly was filled with such a great love for him like never before. It was a unique feeling that she didn't even know it could exist. Harmony in two, as if they were two in one. "And the two shall become one flesh" sprang to Maria's mind. She was amazed, scared by this unique feeling experienced by her soul with such a purity and she got baffled, closing her eyes and nearly crying from so much beauty. She let herself go, carried away and overcome by this heavenly feeling that she couldn't resist because it was whatever she had become through this feeling. She fell asleep. When she woke up, she resumed the flow of thoughts. If possible, Lord, don't let Rafael cheat on her, but be a good, nice man.

One Sunday, after Vespers at Saint Calinic, in Cernica, he prayed with all his heart to the Saint to help them and watch over Maria, to make her accept to be his wife, because she is the one he is in love with and he can let her go. He had never ever fallen in love with deep with a girl, a woman, he had no idea. While sitting on the lake shore and watching the fish jumping in the sunset of the late autumn, Rafael, unable to keep for himself, almost unconscious of love, said:

-Will you marry me?

Maria winced, got scared, her lower lip started trembling, being unable to make a sound, going mute. The child was sitting in the pushchair, next to them, looking at each of them with lingering eyes. Maria looked at Rafael and couldn't believe that he was the one who uttered those words, the fear choking her. She didn't know what to say, all she knew was that she wanted it from the bottom of her heart. Rafael looked desperately at her, mad, almost crazy, choked by expectation, by suffering, just like her. Maria looked into his eyes and stuttered:

-Christ is between us.

She started crying. Rafael looked at her with tears coming out of his eyes uncontrollably and couldn't believe that he was crying in front of somebody for the first time. He had dreamed about that a number of times in his unconscious and innocent dreams. His knees were shaking and he couldn't hide his emotions, he got cold sweat and let his tears fall, revealing his anger and contempt, his loneliness accumulated for so many years, in his eyes, in his soul and the entire inner fever of a man who thinks, rushed outside, in front of this woman who was crying in front of him and looked at him how he was crying.

He was speechless while crying, looking at her with a face expression that touched Maria much that she got dizzy and felt the need to lean against someone and, since she had nothing else around, the trees were at some distance, she took his hand and cuddled to him just like her baby had cuddled to his chest and calmed down in the past without being able to put him down from his warm and strong arms. So was she now, beside him, warm, cool, sweaty by the chill of emotion and fear, of scare about a new suffering like a cataclysm, because all they could share was the fear of a new pain and loneliness, started all over again, without any ending in sight.

Maria looked at him, close to his chest and among his tears dropping over her, she nodded and said:

-Yes.

Rafael replied quickly, forcibly, hurriedly, looking down, then to the church where St. Calinic was, stuttering:

-Still, there is a problem, I must tell you something essential about me so you can know that from the very beginning.

A confused smile appeared on Maria's face.

-I've never had a woman, in that way ... you know.

-It's natural to be so, Maria replied with a clear expression that she didn't understand what Rafael meant, she didn't understand words' meaning. She thought he meant to say that he hadn't wasted his life with loose women.

-It's not that. I decided to keep my virginity until marriage and live like a monk in the world. Had I never married, I decided to be so for Christ.

Maria stared at him in perplexity as if she had met someone from another world, an alien, as if Rafael had no body. She was speechless, didn't know what to say. She perceived him differently, as if she couldn't touch him, as if he were made of crystal or diamond, one of Michelangelo's marble statues. It was like she was having a figurine totally made of light before her. For a moment, she turned back the time and saw herself years before walking pure to the altar and marrying Mihai. For several seconds, Mihai seemed to be Rafael, and any previous events seemed to have been a farce. She said as if she couldn't find her words:

-I should have been like you, as well ... but I was ... so... when ...
-

Rafael stopped talking and all the tension between them suddenly vanished. Their faces started to glow and smile. Maria told him:

-You haven't lost anything, you have gained everything, because you have chosen to live with God and lead your life by His words. You are a happy man because you have been protected from many troubles, you have avoided many evils and you have always endeavored to be a strong person who dominates himself and who wants to have Christ in his heart. You have been happy in your strength. You have avoided many things, this is the royal path of life, this is the highest form of existence for a man and for a woman. You're the same as Kant. That is not easy, but it's the glory of life, because you have sought to live in the glory of God. Maybe... not maybe, this is definitely the miracle done by God with those who suffer and those who trust in Him and don't grow apart from Him for a moment, namely us.

Rafael shrugged and continued, hugging Maria even harder, with Gabriel looking at them as witness of their love. He was babbling happily.

-I've had this ambition since the beginning: if I never marry, I will live like a monk among people, as pure as saints, even though I had to struggle with myself. My body can torment me as much as it wants, I won't give up. It hasn't been easy, but neither hard, I've pulled it through.

-You must keep doing so from now on, as well, said Maria laughing, looking at him relieved from everything and for good. As you can see, others don't pull it through even though they are married, let alone if not married... hahahaha ...

They were laughing their heads off. Laughter helped them release the stress and tension accumulated between them.

-Poor souls, they live in hell and similar to hell. They don't know what freedom is, said Maria appalled.

-Yeah, it's the hell of your own decadence, it's the hell of your inability to love and respect your feelings.

-What's they got to do with us? We have our lives to live.

-Shall we go? asked Rafael.

They both had the feeling that they had left all bad things behind, they were together, the two of them, their child and God, who had joined their destinies forever to eternity. Taking Rafael's hand, Maria said:

-I want us to make a secret wedding, so that no one knows, we'll have the marriage officiated at the City Hall, just the two of us, then we will have the religious ceremony on the same day here, in Cernica, or at the Mitropoly. It could be any day of the week, not necessarily Saturday. We'll find someone to be our Godparents.

-No, said Rafael, we'll go to the monastery, at Dragos.

-What monastery, how nice, but who's Dragos?

-The future Patriarch of Romania, well, yes, I'm kidding. I have a college friend there, a friar, and he knows about you, about me, he knows about us and has someone there who could be our Godfather, a very wise countryside priest who participates in our theological dialogues. He's very witty, has two children who left abroad. That is if you agree with all these.

-You have considered all aspects.

-Sure I have. God first and then the rest.

-How nice, I'm speechless. Don't bother about the rest, everything goes into the normality of existence. God has given us a perfect body, full of miracles, it's important to rely on its signals and joy comes naturally, the same as love. God is Great, for our perfection, we must be with Him.

-That's right, I thought so myself. God's wonders simply happen, all you have to do is live them properly and in line with their eternity.

They headed slowly towards the car which was waiting to take them home.

Chapter 42

Rafael found photos of Maria and Mihai in a book. Maria found his manuscripts and started to read them secretly and she was typing them up at work. He discovered this, namely one of his manuscripts, printed, in Maria's purse, was amazed and couldn't believe it.

He talked to Maria and she convinced him that he had to do something with so many books he had written, to go publish some of them. The book she started to read was amazing and she offered to type it on the computer, proofread it and go to publishing houses and as if they would publish it.

-You would be my cultural manager then?

Why not, isn't that my job, why wouldn't I do this for you, too? I'm good at sponsorships, I do accounting for so many companies and, anyway, we don't need sponsorship. We have enough money to publish all the books that have you written and especially those you are going to write.

-Oh, yes, Maria, but this would be an uphill battle, transcribing each page on the computer and, moreover, they need to be proofread, it makes me sick.

-Well, you will have to read the final version, but, until then, I will go through your texts and I have two secretaries who will do that because this is exactly why they get paid. Aren't you my child's savior and I am the savior of your work.

-Oh, I love you so much, you are the true gift of God for my work.

-You are the true messenger of these times, you are the messenger of the spirit.

-Oh, it would be so nice if it were so! Everything I've read so far in your books exudes a scent of holiness, as if you have sprinkled those words and moods with the flavour of prayers, of flowers growing in church courtyards, and the smell of chrism that embalms the soul and fills it with the purity of eyes.

-You put it so nice, you're right, I've tried to impregnate in my writing the true virginity of the soul which follows Christ, I've always said this prayer: "Lord, Jesus Christ, Son of God, the complete mind all of those who are pure in virginity".

-Yes, it's true. You are the long awaited writer for this depraved millennium, but you write mainly for those to come.

-Don't say that, you scare me. I write and think due to this urge to be as close to God as possible and I believe that the contemporary art, just like art, in general, must be the expression of our need for God and be embodied in the sublimity of this search.

-Well, art has always been so, but it has derailed since the times of Michelangelo to present days. He reached the highest peak of religiosity and perfection, and those who followed him went off the rails, things developing to the current decadence, which is outrageous. Just like Nero is to Christians, so are some of today's writers and artists are to the citadel of spirit, we could speak of a betrayal of some to the spirit.

-I'll write that down in the book, Maria, and I'll mention it's your idea and your expression, not mine. You're brilliant in speech, wittier than me. You're smarter than me, why don't you write poems?

-I'll write poems thanks to you. What do you say, will you allow me?

-Sure, just let me read them to marvel.

On the other hand, talking about contrasts and Mihai's world, there's so much vulgarity we all we are or attend, in many of the places we visit or in the people we meet or try to love but we can't because they don't love themselves and they constantly harm themselves as if their only purpose in life is self-destruction. There's so much repulsive peace in the stupidity of mankind?!

But Rafael and Maria are parallel with this world. It was very interesting how people dressed. Maria took greedy look at people on the street as if she had just returned from a deserted island and had seen for the first time young people running. She admired the way girls dressed, the tight t-shirts on their bodies and the low-waist pants showing a fairly large part of the body beneath her belly button. She thought it was slightly exaggerated, but she enjoyed looking at them, while the boys were wearing shirts or t-shirts tight to their bodies revealing how well the body had been worked out. Youngsters' way of dressing was very provocative, but Maria liked that. The cars running on streets were embarrassingly luxurious and elegant for the passer-by who would have just been sitting around to watch people.

Maria is so happy now, as if she has been away, in a deserted place, where she has struggled hard for survival and, now she is ecstatic about her victory. Rafael was very close to her, as if he were the prince of her dreams and she didn't know how to tell him her secret because all she wanted was to enhance happiness and emotion. Maria forgot about any pain and sorrow ever since they married and since the success of Gabriel's surgery. It seemed that she was just beginning to live and that she needed so much peace. She was amused by each honking and each swearword received from drivers who told her to stay in the kitchen and called her stupid, she found it funny and she even laughed out loud. She was driving her car with so much joy, as though she had never had so much fun and she told Rafael:

-Darling, I will cook something delicious for you today just like we used to do long ago and I will bake a good cake but I won't give you the car.

-I don't want to take it, I lose my ability to drive when I'm with you, I suddenly get intimidated when I see you, don't I, Gabriel?

-I like when mom is driving, but I also like when she makes cookies. Gabriel was three years old and he was speaking with a lisp, he was so cute.

Seeing a trolleybus while driving the car, Maria realized that she missed going through the city by subway and by tram and look at people. She loved people and felt a joy and a need to see their faces and enjoy their presence. Maria was happy and while waiting at a stop, she said to Gabriel:

-Gabitu, do you know that you will have a little sister or brother in a short while? We'll see what God wants!

Hearing those words, Rafael shouted for joy and his face got brighter from an unmatched happiness.

-Are you sure?

-Positive!

-Thank you, Lord, I will have two children, I am so happy!!!

Chapter 43

Mihai had a nightmare all night long and he couldn't get rid of that feeling. He couldn't sleep all night because of that dream which was still affecting him. Trying to relax, he got up early in the morning, got himself into his luxury car and drove alone around Bucharest. He even thought he could drive for fun and go to Poiana Brasov. He could have something to eat at a restaurant, possibly some fries with barbecue, and, then, return home much calmer in the evening. He could even take the chairlift or the cable car, all by himself.

First, he got to a restaurant near a Monastery and, since it was too early in the morning, he could to hear priests' service, he thought:

-What's wrong with those monks who wake up so early on Sunday morning to deliver the service? Why don't they get more sleep, what's with all these prayers? I go to my own company, that makes sense, I can understand that, I make money, but what do they do? Getting up so early in the morning to deliver service, to say so many prayers, it's all useless. As if God listened to some idiots who, by the way, have no idea what they say, so early in the morning.

He put on a smirk on his face and continued his thoughts:

-With sleepy eyes, I would like to become a monk and to pray. I used to believe some time ago that if I pray to God, I don't know what wold happen to me. Still, nothing good happened. God gave me a crippled child and took away the woman I thought I loved, plus, I got a disease that left me nearly impotent with no chance of recovery in sight. All I have to do is make money from this day forward. It's been three years since I haven't got my woman but I'm climbing the ranking of the richest people, I keep climbing, I put my entire time into my business. Hadn't that child been so sick, I wouldn't have lost my family. Anyway, now I'm not even sure that he is my offspring. Actually, I think he could be. What's the use of thinking about these monks who are just some people living in solitude, in poverty. I hate poverty, although, on second thought, I reckon they live just as well, without worrying too much. Yeah, I used to believe that it makes sense to pray so God can help you. Now, all these prayers are useless. Maria raises that child with prayers, ha, ha, ha, a child who let's say that could be mine.

What was wrong with me that I dreamt of him all night long? I must admit that I really miss that child. I wish I could see him at least once. I like him now, I saw him from afar and he looked just like me. I don't have the courage to go near him, as if something is burning me. Actually, I saw him several times while my mother-in-law was walking him in the pushchair. I watched him. I'm afraid of him, especially when he's with Maria. I haven't seen him for a year and that makes me feel so bad. I miss him. I feel my soul burning inside.

This guilt of mine is just terrible. Not to mention that I thought he was going to die. I had a nightmare last night, I'd really want to see him. I know I can't get close to him, but, at least, I want to see him from a distance, it would be so nice. And comforting. I wouldn't suffer so much in my dream, I would be more relaxed.

Mihai had a tormenting dream all night. There was much pain in his heart. He desperately wanted to hold Gabriel in his arms but couldn't. That pain got to him, choking him to tears. Though in his arms, the child was missing, as if he had held an illusion, a picture, and that sensation gave him cold sweat. In the dream, as he had dreamt about Gabriel all night long, he struggled with the pain which subjected him, made him blind and squeezed his heart. When we are young and passionate, we often fall in love with someone who doesn't share our love. Then, we have all sorts of dreams in which we travel with that person, we are always in her company, but she is not real in the dream. If we want to hold that person, we realize that she doesn't exist, we hold some sort of vanishing, imaginary ghost. We have a dream of love, but, even in our dream, we realize that our ojcet of love is nothing but an image, a ghost and, in reality, it doesn't exist, it's just in our imagination.

We are deeply suffering in our dream because of it, dreams go on for many days, dominate us and make our desire grow and, even if the loved one is not present, we continue to love her and on, and on until we see that we cannot live anymore and suffocate. We try to clarify our feelings, but those feelings don't leave us alone. They are so intense that we need a long time to calm down, so we can continue with our lives. We set free from that love spell and, when we fall in love again, we suffer once more. Maybe the state is not just as intense, but it's always the same and we always make the same mistake, we lose our precious mental time with these illusory issues.

Mihai had the desire to see his child but his heart was so hard that he had no qualms of conscience. All he had done got him to live this abandonment. He just said there was no point in doing anything for the child, he had to take him out of his mind because it was a failure eventually and that failure couldn't be his.

He calmed down in a way and he there was nothing more he could do. He could make corrections on himself, but how? And what was the point? He had come to deny child's existence, lying to himself that the kid was his and Maria had cheated on him. In a way, he had calmed down, relaxed. He was no longer trying to deny him. He was fighting with himself to deny absolutely all his feelings. He had an unbearable pain and all he could do was to behave so violently with himself to forget. It was forcible oblivion, but he succeeded eventually. When he remembered about that child of his who was healed, hatred was spreading all over his body and he would go mad. He was acting as a wild beast at work and, in order to compose himself, he would go mute and nobody could approach him.

He often snooped around to see him from afar and, if the baby was walked in the pushchair by someone, his mother or his grandma, that meant he was alive, not dead, and it gave him a great joy and things were going well for several days. He had specifically ordered a tinted-window car so that he could not be recognized on the street or be seen. Thus, he could look at his child as long as he pleased. He wouldn't act so too often, just two or three times in half a year, when he missed his child dearly, otherwise he would see to his business with a calm and relaxed consciousness.

One night, out of the blue, when he least expected, something weird, tormenting happened. He missed his child so much that he was going insane. His heart was burning inside. His consciousness had come to life. He would hold his kid so tight in his dream that his hands ached, his arms ached, his head ached and his entire body got feverish. The pain was even greater when he realized that he was actually holding himself, that the child didn't exist and was running away little by little. Farther and farther, deceiving him with his illusory presence. He took him in his arms again and tried to keep him, but child's image grew inconsistent. He wanted so badly to feel kid's warm body in his arms that he felt such a pain inside his heart and started to tremble. That lack of warmth in the imaginary kid's body woke him up suddenly, he was trembling and choking. He began to cry with hiccups like a child. He needed to hold his baby in his arms and couldn't.

He was feeling bad and was unable to sleep. He felt frustrated, insignificant. How could he feel and be so weak inside? He was very tough with people around him and most of the time he was unrelenting. He had educated himself to be invincible. Now, he was the helpless child from the past, he was the very child connected to the life-support machines that he had been looking at and couldn't help. Now, he was feeling so helpless that he wanted to hold the baby in his arms and couldn't.

He nearly burst into tears but he wasn't allowed to do so because he was the strong one. The absence of that child was terribly painful. He couldn't continue living without seeing his kid. That was his child and he was his father. He knew that him and his mother had been saved, but he wanted to watch him from a distance, at least, if he couldn't hug him. The longing was so painful. That's why he could not sleep, he could imagine the child running around in the house. It seemed he could hear him moving, walking, laughing, running and, suddenly, he felt he lost his mind. He imagined the child calling him "daddy, daddy, daddy." He wanted so much to hear this word now, but it seemed lost forever.

He dreamt that his kid was running around in the house shouting: "daddy, daddy." That image woke him up suddenly and he couldn't control his words or actions anymore. A sudden heartache made him huddle in the bed groaning. He brought his knees to his chest, trembling, bursting into tears that he couldn't hold back. The tears were burning him like fire, as if burning in the flames of his inability to love. He felt so lonely, a loneliness close to insanity. He felt his bed was burning and couldn't lie on it anymore. He wanted to leave and get away from that house, that villa where he had brought and where he had fun with pathetic women. He was leading a different life now. His life was hurting him.

He felt unhappy, but a terribly painful unhappiness, a misery that made him suffer so much as if he had been suffering from an illness without cure, he was a straggler in his meaningless life. He had imagined himself to be invincible and never had thought of death, but now, for the first time in his life, he was thinking very seriously about that aspect, namely that we are mortal and we have no idea when we are going to die.

-That's why drunkenness is good, because, in that state, you no longer think, your thoughts are not so pressing in your mind and you're thinking about nothing.

Mihai didn't know what was going on with him, why he was feeling that way, all he could do was to think of his child as if he had been dead for him. It seemed like a slow death that he didn't realize. Now, he realized for the first time in his life that something had died inside him and life didn't make any sense anymore. He had the money he had always wanted to possess, he had even more money he was bored with. He was single even though he could have the women he wanted, but he often got sick of them. He had money, but no woman spent much time around him because he was the one who couldn't spend more time with them.

They would obviously leave or find someone else. His relationships were as if you would start something and you'd always be stuck at the beginning. You would never be able to complete anything that you could be proud of, to feel good that you have carried out something, that you have invested and it's yours.

Everything that Mihai was initiating dissipated around from the very beginning. That was him. His entire life was passing so insignificantly, it made no sense to do anything for someone else, because he had ceased to do essential things for himself. He had become bored with his own business, although he had to admit that he couldn't survive without it. He had invested his feelings and soul and all his life in his business. He had everything he could have ever desired or sought to attain, but he was empty and meaningless in his soul. Why and what for all these? He seemed to experience this state of helplessness, despair for the first time in his life, he felt humiliated, crushed, destroyed by something unseen, uncomprehensible, an unknown inner force eating him inside which didn't allow him to think about his business. There was a generalized disappointment, nothing could be like before. The state of order and harmony, those concepts had never existed for him.

He wanted to run away from that house where he had lived that nightmare. He was tired of it and wanted to be somewhere, as far away as possible from everything he lived, but couldn't run anywhere. Therefore, his only escape was to get in the car and drive far away from this crowded and restless Bucharest.

Nothing seemed to be more important than this portion of space, so concentrated, that the entire mankind and everyone was living in. Concurrently, there was a pace you had to keep because the most important things were gravitating around this criticized and loved city by everyone at the same time. All the people in this country have gathered here to do I don't know what, to get rich, to make a fortune and to have a better life than elsewhere.

That child he missed seemed to be him, Mihai, he identified with his child who is in torment and lives the terrible state of soul distress. He's a man who doesn't accept spiritual aspects, a man who's rather flesh. Intellectual and soul connections of those related to the inability to love. Mihai is growingly turning into the child he had abandoned and he is now living the greatest pain in this runaway and this expectation for something to happen, but what, other than a greater gap between him and his wife and child, those persons from the past. He kept waiting for something to happen, but that anticipation was only inflicting a bigger pain. That is the condition of the soulless and heartless person, who lives down in the bottom level and doesn't live through his soul. I believe that the one who comes out of this soul order so that he would no longer suffer is pleased to live in the oblivion which swallows him up. An abstract state in which Mihai is the exponent of those who do not bear God in mind and forget about the finality of our lives. The question comes up:

-But what if that child passed away? Suddenly, he was the child, if he had died, what would have happened, and why did I leave him? Why have I lived in that abandonment, why do I persist in this state of total indifference to everything people say is good and why didn't I believe the good was in myself? Why is there such difference in me, why do I go through such things? I'm not an idiot. Why do I keep making these choices?

Mihai wanted to run as far away as possible from these torturing feelings, which should have been so important to him and went beyond him in terms of living and meaning. That child he missed seemed to be himself. Now, for the first time in his life, he realized that he had lost his childhood so quickly and would never meet with that period ever again. The child, his image, so many days of loneliness for him, hurt him so much. Nothing else mattered now but that obsession of pain and loneliness be solved and the inner need to be told just what to do. He was such a lonely father. He was so miserable that he nearly burst into tears. He could barely hold back his tears so he would not cry all the time, especially, while driving the car on his way to Brasov.

When he got to the courtyard of the monastery, because he had that urge to leave from the pub and go to the monastery, such a deep sadness and despair came over him that he couldn't stay too long there and decided it was best to go on that morning straight to Poiana, at Stana Regala. He could either walk or drive there, but he didn't feel like walking so far. He would relax there.

He got to Poiana Brasov. He walked around on foot. It had been a while since he had done so much physical exercise. At noon, he stopped at a restaurant he liked as he had known it for a long time. He had a good meal and got his good mood back, then he got sleepy. He went to his car, reclined the back of the seat and fell asleep. When he woke up, he went to the cable car, the cablechair and all the other facilities. He felt like a child who felt the need to play and enjoy himself. Gabriel's absence was now making him a delayed child who needed to live that childhood. He was living the childhood of the kid he had abandoned with such indifference.

He resembled a tree which had no branches and roots, it was a kind of crippled tree that could only bear fruits and leaf out on a single branch, a crooked one. He was so miserable. For the first time in his life, he realized how miserable he is and how miserable he could become. He stood there melancholically for several hours. That mountain air made him feel better and the fact that he was alone allowed him to think more about himself and his actions and, afterwards, he felt he could breathe. He even cried, alone and quite embarrassed, he was primarily ashamed to cry. He felt more liberated and better with respect to everything he had experienced and decided to stop thinking so much about the past and his child, because that was his life anyway and things couldn't be changed anymore.

He had to make up with her, there was no other way. It would be best for him not to think anymore. It would be best for him to harden his heart and stop lying to himself, just focus on his business and plans for the following day. Even though it was Sunday and he managed to get out of the daily stress and look deep down in his soul, he should better see to his business, where all goes well and should leave those problems as they will find solutions in the future.

He will find solutions, he will see what he's gonna do when the child is older. When he grows up, he will go to him and will give him some money and they will come to terms. He will explain that he didn't really want to leave him, but that was in the past, when he and his mother couldn't get along and, since they were fighting all the time, he couldn't take it anymore and left because he couldn't be with her.

It is much better if they separate and each of them lives his own life rather than stay together and quarrel or spit each other every day, to reproach all sorts of stuff. When he grows up, he will understand, he will be able to buy him, he will give him money as inheritance and all he does belongs to him, his child. Now, he had no doubt that he was his offspring. He watched the kid from time to time and saw him grow, how he looked and the older he got, the more beautiful he became, taking after him.

In a way, that journey took a weight off his shoulders, but hardened his heart because he was running away from suffering and it is better to avoid the suffering than face it with all sorts of thoughts so that you can overcome it.

In the evening, when he returned to Bucharest, he wanted to drive around their neighbourhood, maybe he could see him from afar and liked that thought. He hoped he would see both of them, her and the baby, going to the park to play. He hadn't seen them for almost a year, he hadn't been her for a few years, but he didn't realize the passage of time. He wanted more to see the baby from a distance. When he reached the park, stopped at the traffic light and when he looked at pedestrians he froze: it was her, Maria, who was crossing along with Gabriel, his child, accompanied by another man and a small child in a pushchair on the crosswalk. Mihai didn't know were to look first: at Gabriel who was jumping around holding on to the little kid's pushchair or at the man who had come from nowhere and was near his former wife or at Maria who was now, in his eyes, such a beautiful woman. He looked in awe and wished they wouldn't go so fast, in a hurry, on the crosswalk, he wished green light hadn't come so fast for him. They didn't see him because his car had tinted windows, but he could see them and analyze each one of them.

Mihai started crying instantly and instead of pressing gently on the throttle to pull over, stop the car, go talk to them, he nervously hit the gas and crossed the red light before they could even reach the other side of the road and get into the park. They and the kid got scared of that fast and runaway noise, but they quickly got over it. Maria's life with Mihai was similar to that infernal noise which did not last so long and it didn't last an eternity either. She had a different life now, a happy, good life, that she could enjoy with the little girl she had with Rafael whom she loved and who was the true father for both her fatherless child and the new baby who came into the world as a miracle of God.

Mihai drove like a madman and cried while driving. He cried until his shirt got all wet but couldn't help it. This life is so tough that some things, the most important ones, are given to us just once and, if you can't take them when they come to you, you will lose them for good. He cried until he got home and threw himself in bed, had a bottle of wiskey and fell asleep drunk like a skunk.

The following morning he left with a hangover and sooner than usual for the company to harass the employees again.

Chapter 44

Mihai was disgusted, he didn't expect to see Maria with someone else so soon. He would have wanted her to be neither with him nor with another one, just be as alone as he is. That was nagging him. He was despising her, he didn't expect such a blow, such as twist in such a short time. He felt betrayed and, furthermore, seeing her with another child in the pushchair was beyond his power to accept. He still saw himself as Maria's rightful and only master and couldn't admit what she was doing. He spat with disgust and lit a cigarette. Though time was measureless to him, he thought it had been a short while since he had left Maria. That was in his perception, but, in reality, there had passed several years and she managed to achieve many things during all that time, especially to marry Rafael and bring a child to the world. That was a blessing of God and one of His miracles.

For Mihai, all aspects about Maria seemed to have frozen in time, they were history and he had no way of knowing the evolution of his former wife. When he saw that kid from a distance, he hardly recognized him because he had seen him when he was little, innocent and helpless, when he was expecting him to die and that was the reason why he had left him. How did he grow up so quickly all of a sudden and how come he wasn't in the pushchair anymore? When did he grow up so much?

Now, when he was so big and healthy, he felt betrayed and confused because something like that had happened contrary to his expectations. The child was suddenly was so big, how could he walk on his own feet? That cute child was no longer his offspring, he saw him as a stranger. He was disappointed with what he saw, he wouldn't expect that. He believed that things were the way he sees and how he feels them, and that was why he could do nothing but despise Maria, he felt hatred for that God-given happiness which he threw to the trash bin. You have to be a moral person to live at maximum intensity what God gives you and I believe that it's the hardest thing in this world to be that way.

He was miserable because all her suffering had not been in vain, she had a victory over him, she was smarter than him once again and he was really spiteful. He started to shiver and felt the urge to smoke again. An employee knocked on the door, he wanted something from the boss, but he kicked him out shouting and swearing, saying he didn't want to be disturbed by anyone, that he had a lot of work to do and needed to be alone. That man apologized terrified and amazed, saying to himself: «Good Lord, he's as mad as a March hare!»

He was so disappointed that he planned to never follow them or watch them from a distance ever again. The most important thing for him was to forget about those individuals who destroyed all that he had, who had the courage to be happy without his consent and to interfere with his happiness and his way of seeing the world and things and, on top of that, to be happier than him. He would never forgive Maria for that, for having what he doesn't have, for living what he has never lived, a family, two children. They would be inexistent for him from that moment on.

He locked the door of his office and began to cry so loudly that everything seemed to turn into a soul-killing silence and a terrible inability to love, to hold in his arms that child whose absence grew more and more soul-killing. How could that happen? He couldn't allow that, he would have to take them out of his mind forever.

Those individuals had the courage to be happy without his approval. He had sentenced Maria once and for all to suffering and isolation and now she dared to be happy, unlike him, on top of that, to be happy with someone else. That was far beyond what he could ever admit. Jealousy darkened his mind. Those individuals should disappear from the face of the earth. So much disrespect.

Mihai was almost insane, just like a syphilis patient for a long time. He had to forget those persons once and for all. He felt uncomfortable and he was despising himself because he had tried to peek at them from a distance like a coward, like a thief. Yet, all he was doing was to make sure everything was fine and everything was just great if they hadn't died yet, everything was as expected, that is, well. He was lying to himself to ease his conscience. That state of disgust was also caused by the night dream he was trying to forget so he would hear nothing and no one. Oh, Lord, he missed the child so much! He was happy if he got to that absolution and wanted to put out of his mind those traitors who had been attacking what was his and they had the courage to be happy without his consent. He deemed he was master over their destinies. Yes, he still considered that Maria belonged to him even if he had left her, even if he had not been near her in the most difficult and painful moments and abandoned her, he thought that woman belonged to him and he was the only one who had the right to control her happiness and, now, when that guy had invaded his territory, he was experiencing frustration and a rampant jealousy, close to madness. He was hysterical and felt like breaking and tearing down everything around him, he could hardly control himself. He still thinks he is not crazy.

His resentfulness was extremely deep and didn't know what to do, he felt betrayed, frustrated and lied to. In fact, he had opposite feelings than the feelings felt by one who always betrays. He had betrayed and cheated and, now, he was living in the reverse manner all that he should have been aware of when he had caused such pain to another person. Still, the abandoned person somehow pulls through, due to God's miracle. That person does so well, even if her sufferings are so great and unbearable. It's so strange that our soul doesn't allow us to live but with the feelings we have caused to others, as a punishment. It's strange that the one who cannot repent lives those things with a fantastic hatred which crushes him so hard and unbearably on the inside. That's why I believe that our greatest effort is to free ourselves from hatred and feelings that no longer mean anything to us and to our soul other than a disease of the body and depression of the soul.

Beyond that hatred and contempt, he immediately felt relieved, as if the concern was no longer his. The focus was on Rafael, the man who had gotten his foot in his life and had taken everything from him, his woman and his baby. He couldn't comprehend that he was the one who had abandoned them, but felt like they had abandoned him. Depite disgust and contempt, he felt liberated now, as if he had gotten rid of a heavy burden, way too heavy for him and his soul. That man had taken over all his worries. He did nothing to ease things for Maria and the kid, but he acted superior as if it would have been important to watch them from a distance like a thief in search of prey. He was lying to himself first of all. He was free from the burden of thinking about the two. It was really hard for him to think about them, not help them one way or the other, because he was aware that there was nothing he could do, they didn't need his help. They had money as Maria earned enough so they wouldn't complain about money.

When he got home from the office in the evening, he felt lonely, but careless and he felt like dancing alone in the room and he even danced without thinking about anything. He felt he was the loneliest man on Earth and that gave him a sense of well-being. He was free, so he could continue with his business which was getting better and better. He had gotten rid of the big burden from his past, someone else had taken over his role and he felt comfortable, yet with some rumpled feathers, but pleased. That was the most important, even if he lived a delusional happiness in his madness. Who says you cannot be pleased with yourself when, without being stupid, you lead a bad life but you don't feel that in your consciousness.

Chapter 45

Rafael published his first book, the one Maria had typed, and made his way among Romanian writers. He called press, television at the big launch event, he was invited to televisions several times like a cultural celebrity of the moment. He felt great, but everything was ephemeral and insubstantial. Shortly after, he was no longer in the public eye, no one called him anymore after that event. Most of the press was focused on scandals, not culture, which had its place somewhere in the underground of the consumer society. Yet, he was pleased for the start. He could break through, could speak up, could write articles in newspapers, but didn't like to waste time with such things. He was only interested in the real things about his work. The rest, all sorts of contradictory things, comments from others or trifles, the literary groups of interests were tiring and unappealing. He had time for creation, not for fun. It was like in college, he felt the need to stand back for a while, to write and think about his work, about his next book and so on, he worked on his philosophical system.

He truly wanted was to see the actual literary world, the cultural phenomenon in Romania, just as he was. He wanted to know how people write, what they think, what their word is, where it has its origins, what are the big issues, why people suffer. He wanted to meet as many painters, writers, young artists as possible. That would clear for him the overview on the cultural phenomenon in Romania, which was completely unknown to him and impossible to investigate. The appearance of a book in the bookstore could be good or not. It wouldn't be illustrative. The man behind that book and his heart, his thoughts were more significant to him. He wanted to meet the members of writers' union, the ones of the visual artists' union, and so on. He wanted to have elevated conversations with them, to go to their meetings, to shows, international and national literature festivals, launch events, varnishings, conferences. He felt the need to go out and meet those gods, to do something in this respect, still not all of a sudden, but some day, as he had no intention to waste time with that for the moment. It would have been humiliating. He had to write, write, write. That plan was for later. As for promotion, it was a matter of cultural marketing, he knew how it worked, he would do it. The most important thing for him was to be acknowledged overseas. A matter of international marketing.

He went out with the kids to a little park one evening and Maria stayed at home to cook some cakes for them all. Rafael knew how to cook all sorts of dishes, but not cakes, he had never baked cakes, nor had he enjoyed it, he didn't know how to make them, so he let Maria cook, she was a cake expert. They didn't really like to buy cakes for kids, it was much healthier to make them at home.

He was walking in the park and kept thinking about the new book he wanted to write and put it together in his mind. All of a sudden, a gentleman of his age, maybe one year or two younger, approached them. He was well-dressed, wearing designer clothes and some Mercedes-car keys in his hand, nervously rolling them between thumb and index finger, making noise as a Christmas bell. Rafael flinched, he recognized the person from Maria's pictures hidden inside a book that he had secretly seen, without his wife's knowledge, and had long studied. That person was Mihai. Rafael pretended he knew and understood nothing.

Mihai started talking with them, asked what time it was, about the location of some building, he said nice things about kids.

-You have such beautiful children, especially the boy, he's gorgeous. Is he yours?

-Yes ... mine, replied Rafael quickly, embarassed, looking down.

-Thank you very much for the information, said Mihai and left. He walked around and came back saying:

-I'm expecting someone. Can I take a seat and watch the kids playing?

-Yes, of course, please do. And Rafael rushed to Gabriel who wanted to go straight into a puddle to splash water as he liked, getting his feet wet and getting a cold, considering it was spring, not summer. He said some lie and the toddler followed him. They started running around, playing together, laughing and cheering, but he would not lose sight of Mihai who was looking at the child like crazy. Mihai kept tossing the keys from one hand to the other nervously and fudgy. Since Gabitu was running and jumping around, Rafael could not stay near Mihai so they could start a conversation.

Suddenly, Mihai got up and left without saying a word. Rafael was relieved, he was afraid Mihai would make a scene and scare the kids but it was not the case.

Rafael didn't mention anything to Maria. He kept the secret in his mind and soul to avoid hurting her. Whenever she heard about him, she got the chills, started shivering, had no appetite and turned pale. He just asked:

-Have you ever met with Mihai since he changed the door to the villa and didn't let you in?

-No, he didn't even come to the divorce, he sent his lawyers. He has never seen his child ever since.

-I think he saw the kid beause mom said she spotted him several times sitting in a car with tinted windows and watching them. Yes, he snoops around here, but that's all he does. On the other hand, I can't really trust mom because you know that her desire is often so great that she can turn it into reality. She could have imagined so from too much suffering.

-Yes, you're right, but you can never know. If you saw him.

-Oh, no, no, I prayed to God to do such a manner that I'd never lay eyes on him again in my life. If I see him, I could pass out or smash his head. His mere memory gets me into fibrillation, I shiver as if I'm sick. He is among top 100 businessmen from Romania. It's an achievement to get here. He worked hard, that's all he does: money. Good for him but ... I don't want to see him anymore. When he left that company, he took along more than half of the clients of the former company, as well as some of its employees, and left them in the middle of a crisis, so he had means to develop. He's working with foreign companies only. I have no idea what he does, I don't care how much money he makes because I earn enough money. I'd rather have time to spend my own money.

-Speaking about spending money, how about going on a trip to Greece by our car, without children, or to Italy by plane ?

-Yeah ... .hurray!!!!!! I want Italy.

-I'd like to get to see Michelangelo.

-Yes, I agree, I was there, I saw that, before the flood.

-Well, let's go, why not. We leave the kids with your mom and go. A few days in Florence and Rome will not cost a fortune.

-Yeah, yeah ... I'm glad!!!

-Come on, let's go, maybe it'll help me with the new book, it's a poem in the long story.

They took off the following week. Words cannot describe what Rafael saw there, maybe I could just invite you to go and see, as nothing compares to the actual experience. Why ruin the beauty by telling you about those places. Go and see them. It's not expensive.

It was Maria's turn to make cakes again, as those already made had been eaten during the trip. Whenever they felt the urge to travel, they looked at the map and said:

-Where do we go this month?

-Here.

They would buy airplane and hotel tickets and, that was it, they would leave. They arranged things to be comfortable and not too expensive for them. Rafael went out to walk the kids again in the park. Mihai appeared again. He said nothing this time, he stood on the bench beside Rafael, who was holding the girl in his arms and Gabi on his knees. He sat down on the bench and said:

-I'd like to tell you something.

-I know, said Rafael.

-Do you know who I am?

-Yeah, from photos.

-I saw you on TV.

-.......

-I read your book on the net, it's the first book I've read since college. I made some comments but you didn't answer.

-Thank you.

-I liked the way you spoke on TV, you're already a great writer.

-Well, let's not exaggerate.

-You should get in the public eye.

-In time, not all of a sudden, I have to be careful about what I'm writing for the moment, I have to put together my work.

-That's nice. Maria is so lucky, she's always been lucky, just like when she won the scholarship and I failed. That must be thanks to God, who cares about her and doesn't care about me.

-Yes, she is, but she must be pay attention to those who cut into her luck or take it away completely.

-Hmmm, you're referring to me.

-Well...

-Some things are so complicated. All I could see was business, business and I could never bear a failure.

-Maria typed my book and published it, she pushed me forward as a writer, I owe her this public image of mine, as a thinker.

-Yes, but you are the one who thinks.

-Ohh, you have no idea.

-I've given thoughts to many issues since I heard you on TV, that show took an hour. What each of us should do with his own path. I'm glad Maria has such a man, a true husband like I've never been and will never become.

-There's no telling about that!

-Yes, there is, I know so.

-Yeah, thanks, said Rafael.

-I'd like to ask you something.

-Yeah.

-Could you allow me to hold the kid in my arms. I've never held him. I was angry with him for being such a creature and that he couldn't be my baby. But, now...

-Well, he takes after you.

-Yes, you're right. I was a so stupid, I've lost so much.

-What can we do? Everybody loses something, we make the choices that we deem right in life and, once made, we cannot change them, we cannot go back to that moment in the past, to that crucial moment. This concrete and trembling fact is the foundation of Kierkegard's metaphysics, the Danish philosopher. But ... That's why God is important, we never lose with Him, even if we are defeated sometimes in life, this is an appearance, and, in the short term, you could be wrong because we reason everything within our limitation, your child is proof of that. This is a good lesson I've learned and it's the foundation of my books.

-You must have suffered much yourself, it sure wasn't easy for you.

-Sometimes yes, but Christ is the strength of sufferers. He is the model of victory.

-I would like to ask you something. Is Maria still sick? Did she say anything to you? I got her sick of a serious venereal disease. Did she mention that to you, is she cured?...

-Yes, she and the kid are completely healed.

-What do you mean the kid?

-He got the disease as well.

-I was on the brink of death because of that.

-The wages of sin is death, said Rafael instinctively, going to take Gabi, who was running away from that man, the stranger who had scared him.

-Gabriel, said Rafael, come here for a moment, this gentleman wants to see you.

Rafael took the kid in his arms and, when he wanted to pass him to Mihai, the toddler, with his strong and pettish body, began agitated and started screaming as if he was throwing him into a firepit.

-Calm down, I won't hurt you, said Mihai. I just want to take you in my arms.

But the child was trying to break loose, screaming. When Mihai wanted to take him a bit forcefully, he began shouting really hard and had crying spasms.

-Leave him alone, he doesn't want it and all we do is scare him. Let him play in the sand, with his toy pail and shovels, you'll see him like that.

-Yeah, I'll look at him from a distance. I've known you for a long time, I keep following you.

-I figured you were doing that.

-Really ? Did Maria see me?

-No, she didn't, her mother did.

-Who would have thought I would get to follow my own child.

-Why do you follow him?

-To make sure everything is fine, that you're nice to Maria... But, that is...

-That is... what? snapped Rafael.

-If you don't treat her right and make her suffer...

-Come on, mister, forget it, you of all people, stop being absurd, snapped Rafael. Are you jealous of her happiness or what ?

-Your point exactly.

-Come on, mister, mind your own business, that beats all!

Mihai ate his words. Rafael didn't look at him anymore, but watched the kids, paying atention so Gabi wouldn't fall and rocking the little girl in the stroller.

Mihai sat down on the bench. He sighed.

-That's how things stand, you have everything. I appreciate you, thank you for letting me approach the baby. At least, I touched him.

-That's the way we should be, merciful, I believe in God, don't I? Each of us has a second chance, especially since we are so limited and we don't comprehend the meaning of life, until it's too late to act in any way, that is if we do understand then. He's your child, after all. Your coming here would be good for him. The relationship between a father and his child is holy, similar to the relationship between man and God.

-Yes, you are a Christian, congratulations, I've tried it, too, but I failed.

-Come on, you failed ... that's absurd ... and Rafael went silent.

There was a moment of silence. Then, Mihai continued:

-What do you know ... about the pain of a lonely person, who has no one in his life ...

-If he loved God, everything would be different ... he would have an extraordinary strength, just this child of yours is strong because he has a father, it would be the same for you.

-You are deeply in love with Maria, aren't you?

-.....

Mihai nodded and looked elsewhere.

-Such a pity, I've lost everything, due to one stupid thing.

-A number of stupid things, I'd say.

-That's a man's life.

-No, that's the life we're making and if we fail, we blame others.

-Thank you, I have to go and promise won't bother you again. Maria doesn't want to see me, does she?

Rafael looked at him in silence. A few moments later, he added:

-I don't want either.

Mihai nodded.

-I wish you to be well and happy like I will never be and I couldn't have been when I had the chance.

Rafael shrugged and said:

-God willing, may God help and bless you.

Mihai left. Rafael walked through the park in the cool evening for a while until he saw Maria coming towards them and all his gloom vanished. He didn't say a word about the «big» meeting. He asked her laughing:

-Have you finished the cakes?

-Yes, my king.

-I'm looking forward to have some.

-They are for your highness, Sire, I'm your humble servant. Maria made a bow and Rafael was laughing out loud. They held hands, Rafael took the girl in his arms, Maria took Gabi by his hand, and they all took a walk in the cool evening alongside the fountains in the park. When they crossed the street, Mihai's tinted-window car was still there, in the parking lot, close to them. Rafael gave him a quick glance, but didn't pay any more attention and soon totally forgot about him, because he was expected to be surrounded by joy with Maria, the children, cakes, and why not, another chapter of his book he was supposed to write at night. Wasn't he prospective greatest writer or what!

About the Author

Victorita Dutu is a graduate of Faculty of Mathematics, 1995, and Faculty of Philosophy, 1999, of «Al. Ioan Cuza « University in Iasi. She is a tenured Mathematics teacher at the Traian High School in Bucharest. She won poetry awards and had painting exhibitions all over the country and abroad. In Mathematics, she is passionate about Infinite-Dimensional Spaces. *Ambassador of Peace, within the International Peace Organization since January 8, 2011. *Honorary Member of Maison Naaman pour la Culture-Lebanon, as well as of several poetry societies from various countries. She exhibited at New York Artexpo Pier 94, one of the world's largest art fairs, in 2015, at the Oxford International Art Fair 2015, at the Brick Lane Gallery in London, in Vienna, Austria, at Time Gallery, in 2014, at Chouzy-sur-Cisse, in the heart of France, at the «Matra» musée and the «Jacques-Thyraud» Library, in 2014. She also exhibited in Sanremo, Italy, during the Festival, at the «La Bonbonnire» Gallery, in 2013, in Poland and Switzerland, in 2007.

www.victoriadutu.com

Printed in the United States
By Bookmasters